# NOT AN

## easy

# TRUCE

*A HEARTHSTONE NOVEL*

# SARAH KADES

STA R K
PUBLISHING

**Stark Publishing**
**Waterloo, ON**
**www.starkpublishing.ca**

Publisher's Note: This is a work of fiction. Names, characters, places, and incidents are a product of the author's imagination. Real locales and names may sometimes be used for atmospheric purposes. Any resemblance to actual people, living or dead, or to businesses, companies, events, institutions, or locales is either completely coincidental or is used in a completely fictional manner.

*We acknowledge the support of the Calgary Arts Development and The City of Calgary*

**Not an Easy Truce / Sarah Kades** – 1st ed.

Trade Paperback ISBN: 978-1-989351-73-4
eBook ISBN: 978-1-989351-74-1

# Dedication

*To Adrienne.*

# Table of Contents

# Prologue

Tanner Stone replayed the voicemail again. His sister seemed nice.

He ran a hand through his hair and blew out a breath he had been holding. He hoped Colt made it. His brother. That was still weird to say. He didn't know the guy, wasn't even sure he wanted to.

But they mattered to him.

His laptop beeped, a welcome distraction. He pulled up the encrypted email from his boss. His kill at Bruce Tanner's wedding had been verified. Tanner had been given a shoot-to-kill order by his bosses. The man he had taken out was wanted in seven countries. Gabe wasn't the only agent in the family.

Tanner was still putting the pieces together on who had tried to murder Gabe. From what he knew, there was no way Gabe would have knowingly corroborated with his father and compromised a mission. Bruce Tanner setting up his son to be ambushed and murdered? That was completely feasible.

His biological father was as dirty as they come. Tanner knew it. He just had to prove it.

# Chapter One

B ecca should have turned around a kilometer ago.
She was riding Pixie, her large mare, alone and the fall evening brought dark and cold fast. The sun set early this time of year at this latitude, and the higher elevation always gave the cold more teeth.

She wished she'd worn thicker gloves, but she hadn't expected to be out this late. A familiar anxiousness crept back in, and she wondered for the hundredth time if she had made a mistake.

"Come on Pixie." Becca urged her mount into a lope. Pixie's hoof beats felt like the earth's heartbeat.

Stars started to appear even as the last glow of sunset hovered along the horizon. The tall peaks were dusted with early season snow. There was no pass here, no snaking river to follow, no valley leading through the wild unkempt Rocky Mountains. Just a tall, shear face so formidable most would take one look at it and turn around.

Becca let Pixie have her rein; her horse knew this land as well as she did. They were closing the distance to the rock face. She promised herself they would turn around and head home when they got there, not take the back path out further. She smiled as she noticed the hardy late-season wildflowers dotting the subalpine meadow.

Maybe tomorrow she would come back and snap a few photos in daylight.

A gun shot exploded in the silence, its echo reverberating off the rock face.

Becca gave a start and Pixie answered in kind—in a heartbeat her horse gave a quarter turn and bolted. Becca's brief hesitation gave her mare the chance to breakaway. Pixie was now at a dead run and Becca could only hold on. When she had the horse's rhythm, she felt her body moving in sync with the animal, giving her a chance to pull up. She finally slowed the scared mare back to a lope. Several beats later, she pulled her horse back to a jog.

Adrenaline coursed through her system.

Becca was breathing as hard as her mare as she scanned the horizon. She would have enjoyed the unexpected wild ride if her nerves weren't buzzing on high alert.

Hunting season had opened but poachers were active in every season. Not to mention she was a woman riding alone in a remote area. Someday women would be able to go about their business without fear of being molested, but Becca knew that day hadn't come yet.

She scanned the crown land she was on. The public land abutted her property—the new property that she co-owned with her estranged father.

For half a second, she wondered if he could have something to do with this. She wouldn't put it past him to give her a scare. She scanned the horizon again. The rock wall was now three kilometers at her back and the subalpine meadow had given way to coulees. Those steep, ice-age drainages gave plenty of places for cover. Or hiding.

A low grumble sounded, and two ATVs crested the coulee to her left. Each driver had long range rifles and was in camouflage, not blaze orange. That was a quick way to get shot this time of year. Her unease turned to full blown panic when she saw they both were carrying handguns. Canadians were culturally suspicious of guns in general and handguns in particular. All firearms were tightly restricted and handguns did not make the accepted list. Which meant the two men—and she was sure by their build they were men—were either unmarked law enforcement or criminals. Becca did not wait to confirm their identify or their right to carry. She urged her mare over the steep side of the coulee and disappeared.

# Chapter Two

Officer Jason Chasseur ignored the cold. He was stretched out prone on the freezing ground. Dead grasses tall enough to conceal him rustled in the breeze around him.

He was hunting.

His weapon of choice was a camera on a short tripod with a live satellite feed to the office. His Royal Canadian Mounted Police-issued sidearm remained holstered at his hip.

He snapped off more images of the Fischer brothers, tracking them as they quadded up a double track and over a coulee. They had gotten a shot off, though at what he hadn't been able to see. As far as he knew, Christopher and Austin were the only remaining Fischer brothers still alive, and they didn't use. The other three brothers had been killed by overdoses or drug violence.

The Fischer empire was reputed to be small on the global scale but unusually profitable. Their reputation eerily efficient and violent. Greed wasn't an Achilles heel for them. Most of their counterparts got dead or convicted when greed led the way. The Fischer brothers kept the family business moving forward while exerting about as much face time as a ghost. They were known more by reputation than acquaintance. Jason had been tracking them a long time. No one had been able to convict them, though they were suspected in scores of gruesome drug-related homicides.

Jason took the moment to shift slightly, just enough to let blood recirculate through his cold limbs. He needed to remain hidden yet not numb and unable to get up if necessary. Surveillance in the high country sure as hell beat the office, but the ground was as cold, hard, and unyielding as his boss.

He could still hear their engines rumble, though it sounded like they were idling just out of view. Jason was curious why they had been making rounds in the foothills. The Fischers ran drugs and guns and at first law enforcement had suspected a stash, or even a rendezvous point in the foothills. Surveillance hadn't identified either. Poaching was unlikely; intel suggested the two brothers were more likely to kill poachers, rather than poach. It may be as simple as the guys liked to quad in the mountains. Even violent criminal types had to have down time.

Jason resettled and peered back through the camera scope.

He blinked.

His nemesis Becca Tanner—and he was sure it was her—was guiding her big red mare down a precariously steep coulee wall. It was the same coulee he had just seen the Fischer brothers going over, but instead of taking the double track down that the Fischers had taken up, she was taking a side erosion channel. It put her further from the Fischers but the channel was stomach-dropping steep and had nearly non-existent footing. The animal was athletic and her rider more than adept. Becca was hands-down the best female rider he had ever seen.

But a bullet wouldn't care.

Every protective instinct within him was screaming to keep her safe. She had no doubt just stumbled upon two of the most violent men in the country. He couldn't outrun her horse, or a bullet aimed at her, but he could have her back as she retreated.

He unholstered his gun and moved.

# Chapter Three

Becca guided her mare down the steep erosion channel. The broken ground was better left to tumbling water than a fourteen-hundred-pound animal and rider. She pushed her horse as fast as she dared, hoping she wouldn't find out what a bullet felt like.

She had no idea who those men were, only that they scared the shit out of her. They felt dangerous, predatory.

Her horse stumbled and Becca caught herself before she took a header over Pixie's flattened ears. Four strides later she had cleared the coulee.

But where to now?

She was in a small valley between the coulee and a treed slope that rose to a ridge. It was darker here. The setting sun still touched the tops of the coulee and ridge.

A glimmer of light flickered. Someone was up there. She had no idea why she trusted that brief beacon of light as much as she distrusted the two men on quads. Her brothers always told her she made no sense. With no-where to go but gone, she urged her tired horse towards the wooded area and picked up a game trail. The trail wound through a large poplar grove, too narrow for a quad to fit through and the tree trunks were too large for a quad to run over. Perfect.

A chipmunk darted, nearly unseating her. The woods here were nearly dark, the setting sun did not reach the trees and valley floor. She forced herself to breath. It wouldn't matter if she made it to safety if she broke her neck on the way there. The trail angled up and her horse started to climb the gentle switchback. Pixie's breathing was steady, and Becca tried to follow suit without luck. She could still hear the hum of their four-stroke engines and it terrified her.

They had almost made it to the top of the ridge when a soft whistle whispered on the breeze. At first Becca thought she had imagined it, like a spectral of the deepest most secret part of her imagination. There was only one person on the planet she knew to make that call—and he hated her.

It sounded again.

*"Jason?"*

She felt silly whispering his name. Officer Jason Chasseur, her childhood crush and adult bane, was about as likely to help her as those two goons she just fled from. She called out again, a little louder this time. No one answered. Instead, Becca heard the low drone of a helicopter engine. It was coming in fast and low. Its vibrations re-testing Pixie's already-taunt nerves. The large mare began to sidestep in agitation. Becca tightened the reins and sat back in her seat, correcting Pixie's response. Whispering to her horse as much to herself, Becca pleaded, *"I promise we can lose our shit later, baby, right now I need you. We need to stay solid. That's my girl."* Pixie stopped sidestepping but her body was still coiled beneath Becca. They were on the narrow game trail, nearly at the top of the ridge and surrounded by overhanging branches. There was no room for Pixie to spook here. Becca looked around; she couldn't imagine how this day could get any worse.

A hand appeared on her knee, and she nearly screamed.

"*Quiet,*" the man admonished.

It was Jason. She thought she felt him give her knee the barest of squeezes before he was running a calming hand over her horse's quivering body, a flow of soothing words cascading from his mouth. His voice was hypnotic and reassuring.

"What is that helicopter doing?" Becca whispered. It was circling the coulee she had just fled.

"Working," he answered cryptically.

Becca waited for him to elaborate but the only sound was the helicopter, and from the looks of it, was now flushing the pair of quads out the other side, away from them. She looked down at Jason. "You're working, too."

He nodded once.

"What just happened?" Becca was trying not to be scared. Jason was here. He would know what to do. Police officers had to help everyone, even old crushes they hated. "What are you doing?" She noticed gear on the ground nearby.

Jason was packing his kit with clipped, efficient movements. He didn't look at her when he answered, "Packing."

"Why?"

He gave her a sideways glance before zipping a small duffle bag closed. "You were just out for a jaunt with the Fischer brothers."

"I was not. And who the hell are the Fischer brothers? They sound like a country band."

Jason looked up at her, again, curious. "Why'd you bolt like that if you didn't know who they were?"

It was Becca's turn to give Jason a sideways look. "Every woman on the planet knows the answer to that question. And they had handguns."

Jason resumed packing his gear. His voice was low when he said, "I know we're not friendly, but you see them coming, you go the other way. I'm not kidding Becca, stay clear of them. They're dangerous."

Becca was suddenly having trouble breathing. "Am I in danger?"

"Have you ever seen them before?"

"No."

"Any reason to believe they recognized you?"

"From what? I have no idea who they are."

"Why were you out?"

"My eco-inn opens in a couple weeks, and I needed more click bait."

"Come again?"

"You know, for social media advertising. A photo that people will click on."

Jason shrugged. "Whatever. The Fischers have been seen quadding in this area. Nothing criminal has been observed, but like I said, stay clear of them." He shouldered his pack and started to walk away.

"Wait, where are you going?"

He called over his shoulder, "The detachment, I've got paperwork to fill out."

Becca urged her horse to follow him. "But there were just bad guys."

"Hence the paperwork." He kept walking.

"You're just going to leave me out here?"

He stopped and turned around. "What do you want Becca?"

"For a Mountie, you miss the obvious." Fear had made her waspish.

"Then spell it out for me."

Becca wanted to yell at him. Instead, her whisper was more of a hiss. "Listen, Sherlock, I'm scared. The guy that shot Gabe in the head when he worked for CSIS turns up dead at our dad's wedding, and Colt was kidnapped last month by a rogue international spy. Those are bad guys with guns, and you're a frickin' police officer. I know you hate me, but please, can you just see me home?"

Gabe was the oldest of the Tanner siblings. He had been recruited by CSIS out of university. Several years later a bullet had changed the trajectory of his life. None of the Tanner siblings would have guessed that it would be Colt who would be kidnapped by an international spy.

"I remember your brothers," Jason said quietly.

"Please, Jason, just see me home." She hated admitting she felt safer with him.

Jason muttered, *"I'm going to regret this."* But he came forward and held her horse's reins. "Give me a stirrup."

"Huh?"

"I walked. You want an escort. Give me a stirrup."

Becca kicked out of her left stirrup, trying not to read too much into it. Jason toed into it and hefted himself up behind her on her mare. She pressed as far forward as she could, but all she could feel was his strong, large body behind hers. They rode in silence. It was a recurring theme between them. Silence.

And fighting. They seemed to have two gears, fighting or ignoring each other.

The ridge gave way to rolling foothills. The dark of the valley was behind them, and the setting sun lit the aspen trees. They were surrounded by the full golden glory of autumn. If Becca hadn't just been scared out of her mind by two dangerous criminals on ATVs, and if the man pressed against her hadn't hated her guts since high school, the ride home could have been almost pleasurable. This was the closest thing to a date she'd had in a long time. She banished the thought.

"You're cold. How long were you waiting out there for them?"

"Long enough."

"For what?"

"Why are you talking?" His breath tickled her left ear.

She let herself turn her head a fraction closer to him. "It's what normal people do."

He answered by sitting back. "We are many things, but normal isn't one of them."

Becca grew exasperated. "Why do you hate me so much?"

"You stole my family's land from me."

"I bought it, there's a difference. As a cop, you should probably know the difference."

"Your rich daddy bought it, Becca, *that's* the difference."

God, she wanted to elbow him. "Go to hell."

"Honey, I live there."

They rode in silence after that. Anger had replaced much of Becca's fear. It wasn't an improvement. The ride home was long and cold. The man cradled so close behind her was as hard and unyielding as the mountains she loved so much. As they approached her ranch yard, she noticed him looking around. The inn was a sweeping, two story log building. Too big to be called a cabin, but with a central A-frame and two wings that stretched on either side.

She cringed as she noticed her front gardens needed tending before the snow set in. But Jason's gaze was on her driveway. She swallowed at the lumpy mess. Seven large semi trailers had come in last week to pick up cattle and she hadn't called to get her driveway regraded, yet.

His gaze moved, and he eyed the large solar panels on the inn's roof. Each of the outbuildings and the main barn also sported them. He glanced at her tanks.

She pointed. "It's a gray water system."

He gave a noncommittal sound and she wanted to elbow him just to get some sort of reaction. She had poured her heart and soul into this place, and all he could manage was barely a grunt?

She didn't know what to say or do. Jason's arms still cradled her. "Give those guys a wide berth. I mean it. If you see them on your *property*, call it in but do not engage."

"That's not comforting."

"It's not supposed to be, it's supposed to scare the shit out of you. There are bad guys and then there are the Fischers." Jason dismounted.

Now that he wasn't so close, she wanted to explain. "Jason, I swear I didn't know about your offer for the land."

"That's what you keep telling me."

He held Pixie as she dismounted. She didn't know how many more times she could apologize for something she didn't know in the first place. She opened the large barn doors before grabbing her horse's reins out of his hands. "I'm going to take care of Pixie and then I can give you a ride back to your truck." Jason lifted a hand in protest, but she ignored it. "It's nearly full dark and do you really want to tie up another officer when I'm right here offering you a ride?"

It would likely be a long wait and they both knew it. Mounties had to cover a lot of ground. She felt more than saw him give in and decided to throw him a bone. "You can get a hot coffee in the barn office. I'll be quick."

He shook his head. "You never used to be this bossy."

"There're a lot of things I didn't used to be. I grew up."

They stared at each other.

"Live and learn?" Jason asked.

"Something like that."

Becca left him standing outside. She would be in her truck alone with him in less than twenty minutes. She was giving herself that long to learn how to forget the feel of his arms around her.

# Chapter Four

Jason didn't want anything from Becca Tanner. But a cup of hot coffee would go a long way thawing the icicles that had replaced his legs.

The ground had been as cold as Becca. And she was right, he did hate her. But he hadn't expected her hair to feel so soft or her body so strong. Riding behind her on her big horse had been awful. She felt human. He had felt the adrenaline that had been burning through her body just like he felt when she started to come down as they rode on.

He didn't want to think of Becca as flesh and blood. He didn't want to think of her at all.

He found a Keurig machine in the office and paused when he saw the refillable pods. In high school Becca had loudly advocated for the environment. Her crusading had amused or annoyed more people than it had inspired. She had been up against a stacked deck. In those days Alberta was oil country, period. Now the dark solar panels he had noticed on the ranch house and barn roofs were starting to be the norm. Alberta boasted oil, but sunny days and howling winds made it a renewable energy sweet spot.

He made a dark roast coffee and after hesitating a moment, pulled down another mug and started making Becca one, too. The phone on the barn office desk rang and an old school answering machine clicked on. *"Becca, it's your father. You're being unreasonable. I'm not changing the terms of the loan."*

Becca flew into the office and dove for the phone. She turned her back and spoke too quiet for Jason to make out what she was saying. When she hung up, she didn't meet his eyes. He handed her the cup of coffee. She looked surprised and maybe a little suspicious.

"I didn't poison it." Jason took a large swig of his.

"Why not? Too much paperwork to cover your crime?"

"Something like that. Would you feel better if we traded?" He held out his cup. It was as close to teasing as they got.

She sipped her own in answer.

"Old school answering machine."

She relaxed a little. "It was in Clint's barn. I scooped it when he was getting rid of it."

"A bit of nostalgia, I get it. Clint's a good guy. Kind of like everyone's surrogate uncle around here. So, was that call about my land?"

Becca straightened. "Thanks for the coffee. I'll go finish up with Pixie."

Jason followed her out of the office and into the barn. "Take your time, your mare worked hard today."

Becca set her mug on the wall ledge and picked up a curry comb. "You missed her bolt."

"What do you mean?" Jason took the comb from her and started to brush her horse with wide sweeping strokes.

"What are you doing?"

"Isn't it obvious?" He might not be a Tanner, but he knew his way around a horse.

"No."

"Easy Tanner, I'm just giving you a hand. Normal people would say thank you."

People let their guard down when they focused on chores, and he hoped Becca might do the same. He wanted to know if she knew anything about the Fischers or had run into them before.

He waited for her to object. Instead, she busied herself with the hose and started to fill the water trough. "The gun shot spooked Pixie; I was still registering what had happened when she broke away. We were near the base of that limestone face when she turned and ran."

"That's got to be at least a couple kilometers from that coulee."

"Three, actually."

Jason ran an appreciative hand over the big red horse. "A sprint like that, taking on the coulee and accepting a second rider? You have one hell of a horse."

Becca smiled as she turned off the hose. "I know."'

"What did you see with the Fischers?" He continued combing Becca's horse.

"Nothing much, Pixie and I heard the shot, I had just gotten her slowed to a lope when the quads came over the coulee. I took one look at them and got the hell out of there."

"Because they were men?" Jason had taken enough female victim statements to understand the warranted caution.

She stopped. "When they crested that coulee—I just felt scared. And hunters don't carry handguns. I guess unless they're the kind that hunt people. What will you do now?"

"It's an active investigation, we—"

"Investigate?"

"Something like that." Jason exchanged the comb he had been using for a hoof pick he found on the shelf on the wall.

Becca called over from the oat bin, "Her back left fetlock is ticklish."

Jason went to work and appreciated the heads-up. He was ready for it when the large animal got squirmy. Becca finished prepping the stall and Jason led Pixie in. He closed the stall door.

Becca was standing close when he said, "I can't believe you trusted me with your horse."

"My horse is fine in your hands, it's me I don't trust you with."

They stared at each other a long moment. Time hadn't cooled either of them. If anything, the tension between them had built. Becca looked away first. She pulled a set of keys from a nail on the wall. "I'll drop you at your truck."

"Probably a good idea," he answered.

In the fading light, the front seat of Becca's three-quarter-ton felt alarmingly intimate. With Herculean focus, he stared out the windshield and tried to ignore the scent of her shampoo still tickling his senses. If she was as affected, he couldn't tell; she simply drove and ignored him.

When they got to where he had parked the RCMP truck they saw that the tires were slashed.

# Chapter Five

Becca watched Jason survey the vehicle. His face remained impassive as he took pictures of the damage and wrote in his notebook. He had a tendency to scowl whenever she was around, so it was a welcome, if disconcerting change. He called in the vandalism, but it would be at least an hour before another RCMP officer could make it over, assuming no other calls came in. She leaned against her own truck, patient as Jason worked. The stars were starting to come out overhead while the western horizon held a pale ban of light behind the silhouette of the mountains. It was an image Becca had seen a thousand times. She loved it out here.

"You don't have to wait." Jason didn't look up from the notes he was making.

"I know." Becca enjoyed the peace of the night even in the shadow of their uneasy truce. With him here she wasn't scared like she had been. Nor did she mind the mini reprieve. She had been pushing so hard for so many months to get her business ready, moments left watching the stars come out and the last drops of sunset fade had been rare. She must have been working too hard. Standing in the dark with a man who hated her and whose vehicle had just been vandalized should not be giving her respite. Yet it was. She felt more peaceful than she had for weeks.

"I imagine whoever did this is long gone."

Becca just shrugged in the darkness.

Jason's phone rang. A couple terse words were exchanged before he hung up. "Looks like it'll be closer to two hours."

Becca pushed off her truck. "Right then, let's go."

Jason didn't move. He was silhouetted in the truck's headlights, jotting in his notebook.

"Do you need to stay with the vehicle or something?"

"No."

And just like that, the peace she had been feeling crumbled. "Then what's wrong? I'm trying to help you. It's cold and late and we've both had a crappy day. For the love of god, I can give you a lift."

"I haven't checked the back yet." She thought he smiled but the moment was too fleeting to be sure.

Becca flicked the flashlight setting on her phone on and swept it over the tail gate of the RCMP truck and winced. The harsh beam from her phone lit a dark message crudely etched into the truck paint.

Jason came around the back of the truck and Becca stepped in front of the nasty slur, flicking off her phone. Jason slung his own flashlight beam high and asked, "What is it?"

She didn't move.

"Becca, come on, I have to finish."

She relented. "It's not pretty." Becca stepped towards him. She stood by his side as he read the message. She reached for his flashlight and held it as he finished. Without a word he simply clicked off a few photos and took notes.

"You okay?"

"This isn't the first time someone has felt compelled to share their dislike of me being Métis and a police officer." He actually tapped her nose. "You call me not so nice words."

"I'll call you a jerk to your face but that," she crooked her thumb towards the tail gate, "is something else entirely."

He looked like he was going to say something but remained quiet.

"You know I wouldn't say something like that," she pressed.

"Do I?" He flicked closed his notebook and tucked it in a pocket.

Becca's jaw dropped. "Are you serious?" He had been the one to dismiss her all those years ago, not the other way around.

"Nothing, forget I said anything. I'm cold and tired. You still giving me a ride?"

"Let's go." The day was taking a toll. She just wanted to crawl into bed and forget Jason, again.

Instead, she drove in silence as he worked on his phone. The glow from the screen threw his features in stark relief. Finally, he thumbed off the screen and put it back in his pocket.

With her eyes on the road, she broached the latest thorn in their prickly relationship. "My dad wasn't speaking to me when he bought that land. At first I assumed my new stepmom, Meredith put him up to it. I'd guess she even gave him the money to buy it; it bothers her how much we dislike her. I'm guessing there's either a pipeline royalty or coal seam he wants to exploit."

Jason made a startled sound. "I thought the eastern slopes were protected from coal development?"

"Yeah, and Albertans have to remind the province of that." Becca paused. "For what it's worth, I swear I had no idea you had put an offer in, too. I've had my head down trying to make my opening weekend. My dad and I...we have a challenging relationship."

It had been made more strained by the recent intel from her MI6-connected sister-in-law that Bruce Tanner was involved in Gabe getting shot five years ago.

Silence met her declaration. She glanced over. "Please say something."

"What do you want me to say?"

"That you believe me."

Jason shrugged. "But I don't know if I should believe you."

"Where does that leave us?"

"Becca, there is no us."

That stung. She kept her eyes on the road. Light flooded her rear-view mirror and she adjusted its angle. A set of headlights was coming up fast. Her heart started pounding and the space between her shoulder blades tingled.

"You're upset, what's wrong?"

Becca flashed Jason a look. "That you notice?" How could he notice that subtle change in her body, but not know that she was telling him the truth about his offer to buy the land?

The headlights got closer. It was a large pickup truck and looked to be pulling a trailer. She turned on her left blinker. There was a township road ahead.

Jason eyed his side mirror. "Where are you going?"

"Humor me." She followed rural etiquette and pulled into the empty oncoming lane before the turn. She turned her head as the large truck thundered past, but it was moving too fast to recognize the driver. There were quads on the trailer. It was probably a coincidence. Everyone and their brother went out here quadding.

She made the turn and the large truck kept going. When she didn't see brake lights she took in a full breath.

Jason swore.

Now it was Becca's turn to ask, "What?"

"That was the Fischer brothers."

# Chapter Six

José Martinez sat on his veranda; the waters of the Mediterranean sparkled far below. A peregrine falcon was riding a current along the cliffs. Suddenly it dropped from view. Moments later, the throttled cry of an unlucky shorebird could be heard.

José looked down at the gun in his hand. His brother had given it to him. He turned the Glock over in his hands. The weight of it reminded him of his brother's choices. Cold. Heavy. Final. He had buried Fernando a month ago. Knowing the day would inevitably come sooner, rather than later, hadn't made the pain less sharp.

Fernando had been larger than life, until he wasn't. A foolish and reckless man-child, untamed in the worst way possible. Disgust ignited. His little brother had been caught as a double-agent. That had been unconscionable. When he broke out of prison to exact vengeance on the woman who put him there only to die trying, that disgrace was simply too much.

Action needed to be taken.

José turned the gun over again. When Fernando had mocked him with the gift, the disrespect had been clear. How do you get back at someone who was beyond the grave while also righting the wrong that had clearly been committed?

It fell on him. José would have the last laugh.

# Chapter Seven

The cab of Christopher Fischer's oversized pickup truck was bathed in the eerie light from Austin's handheld data unit. His brother's features were in stark relief, and he looked only a little bit insane.

Austin interrupted his thoughts. "Pretty sure the woman on the horse today was Becca Tanner."

"How could you possibly know that?"

Christopher had recognized Becca Tanner as soon as they crested that coulee, but it pissed him off that his little brother always seemed to jump to an accurate conclusion. After all, he had been the one to go to her door asking questions about her cop brother. He had made up some phony shit about being old classmates. She had managed not to roll her eyes at him, but it had been clear she wasn't keen on playing secretary for her brother, nor had she pretended to go down memory lane with him. Point blank she had said she didn't remember him or the fake name he had given her. Most women just smiled and nodded, eager to please instead of admit they didn't know what you were talking about.

Austin shrugged. "I checked her out when we first flagged her as someone who could reroute or shut down the pipeline. I saw a photo of her and that horse on her website. She's opening an inn next month." Austin snorted. "She needs a sommelier."

"Why is that funny?"

Austin smirked. "Dude, that's like your dream job. You should go for it. Finish what mom started."

Christopher gripped the steering wheel tighter. "It is a dream job. And you could use a bit of civility."

"I'm sure the last guy you gutted appreciated your refined taste in hardware."

"That was one time and that fucking monster deserved much worse. Our reputation is eighty percent fiction, but that carve job cemented it. All I'm saying is a little more culture wouldn't kill you." The remaining Fischers were only as violent as they had to be.

"Of course it could, you and I both know it doesn't take much to get dead."

Silence fell between them. They had seen a lot of death.

"Think that Becca woman will be a problem?" Austin asked.

"No idea. She bolted pretty fast. I'd run, too."

"I told you her brother is a police detective in town but they've never been able to pin anything on us. Oh shit."

"What?"

Austin read from his screen. "Her oldest brother was with CSIS until he got shot in the head five years ago. And – holy fuck! Her sister-in-law was a courier for MI6."

Christopher did not like the math this woman came with. "That would have been useful information to have."

"She might vacation in North Korea but how the hell would I know unless I know to look for it or she leaves a trail?"

"What magical piece of information did you find in the last twelve hours to find all that?"

Austin didn't look up when he answered, "The sweatshirt she was wearing."

Christopher replayed the woman's abrupt exit. "An acronym, wasn't it?"

"Yeah. JCSIC—Jordemorden Central Security and Intelligence Center."

"How the fuck did you know that?"

"I didn't. It was a toehold."

Christopher blew out a breath. His little brother constantly amazed him. A subtle flicker from the back seat caught his attention, though when he turned his head, nothing was there. "Do you smell vanilla?"

"What? No. Weirdo."

Christopher sniffed. His nose never lied, and he could smell faint hints of vanilla. "Are you wearing vanilla?"

Austin exhaled loudly. "Seriously? I'm a dude. And mom always smelled like vanilla; I haven't been able stomach it since."

Christopher shifted in his seat, uncomfortable. He missed their mom, too. "We did shoot off a round. Think that spooked her?"

Austin looked up. "The woman grew up surrounded by rednecks. The sound of a gun shot, especially during hunting season, should not phase her."

"When you say shit like that I can't tell if you're hot for her or not."

"I'm not."

Christopher slowed his speed. They had caught up to the only other vehicle on the rural highway. The truck in front of them turned on its left signal and moved into the empty oncoming lane. Christopher gunned the engine and the large truck thundered past the other vehicle. Out of habit he glanced in the direction of the other truck and swore.

"What?" Austin tried to catch a look.

"Chasseur was in the passenger seat."

"The RCMP dick-wad?"

"How many do you know? Yes, that one."

"Who was driving?"

"Couldn't tell."

"The guy's been running limited surveillance on us. He hasn't gotten anywhere near the test plots though, so we're fine. For now."

"Care to explain the police helicopter that flushed us out?"

"Give me a second." Austin keyed in several commands to his handheld. "Looks like an environmental survey crew reported suspicious activity just north of our plots. They rerouted a Mountie bird up on another call to loop around and that's when they toyed with us. The diversion notes don't mention our site. We're good."

Austin was more optimistic than Christopher. Their test plots were on crown land. So far the only threat had come from grazing leases. Bovine hooves would trample their payday if they weren't careful. Keeping the frames and tarps secure required diligent rounds. They had posted signs for one of the local universities in an effort to make their setup look legit to anyone who happened to stumble across it, even adding a phone number for inquiries. Austin went so far as to paint rocks and arrange them to spell out the school's geography department's acronym, visible from the air. It also reminded Christopher that Austin would never experience those carefree college days.

"Shit." Austin looked up. "A Heritage Resources Permit was just issued for the pipeline right-of-way."

"In English, man."

"Archaeologists are going to be surveying the crown land our test plots are on. Those guys look for shit smaller than your dick."

"Fucking uncivilized ass. I can't believe I put up with you. Can you cancel the permit?"

"Not without raising suspicions. The file we pinched that the Spanish prick wanted shows the heritage flags that the British woman and Becca Tanner's bull-riding brother collected about the pipeline project. We knew there would be archaeology crews, brother. Don't shit yourself."

Christopher's mind pinged with scenarios. They couldn't afford to have a field crew familiar with university research methods stumble across their test plots labeled to look legit.

He gripped the wheel tighter. "We have to stop that pipeline."

It was time to put a little pressure on the Tanner woman.

# Chapter Eight

Frost crunched under Becca's boots as she walked to the barn. The soft sound added to the hush of the morning. The frost hadn't been heavy enough to rime the aspen and spruce that ringed her yard. The trees were tall enough to be useful against the relentless wind, while still saving the mountains views. Limestone and shale peaks glowed in the early morning light, their pink and golden color a soft reminder of a peace and beauty that she was not feeling. Even the fresh frost on the ground that now glittered with an otherworldly quality reminded her that such magic was fleeting. In the full light of day her yard would lose such shimmer and simply be cold and dead, while the mountains would be a bleak reminder that life could be as unforgiving as those jagged peaks.

Last night had shaken her.

For months she had been working long hours, mostly alone, to build her business and be ready to launch her eco-inn on opening weekend. Finding out she had dangerous criminals cavorting in her backyard put her in a difficult position. She needed to open on time. Unlike her father, Becca was not made of money. She couldn't carry her business mortgage without paying guests.

Becca opened the barn door. The smell of horse, hay and leather filled her nostrils, grounding her. This was her sanctuary. It wouldn't make up for the sleepless night, but the familiar comfort propelled her forward. She greeted her herd and started her morning chores. Though even with Pixie's antics, her sober mood never quite lifted. She flinched every time a vehicle drove past, or she heard a sound she couldn't immediately place.

*"Get a grip,"* she scolded herself.As far as pep talks went, it was lacking.

Last night she had looked online for information on the Fischer brothers. Knowledge had always made her feel prepared and they couldn't possibly be as bad as Jason had suggested.

Turns out they were worse.

The allegations against them were shocking, though the brothers had never been convicted. Charged yes. Numerous times. But nothing had ever stuck. There was even a true crime book penned by their aunt about their alleged exploits.

That hadn't made sleep come any easier. Smart criminals somehow seemed more dangerous than stupid ones.

Becca managed to get her horses watered and fed and had just started mucking out stalls when she heard a truck pull up. She nearly lost her breakfast.

With a stealth she didn't feel, she propped the pitchfork she had been using against the wall and crossed the barn floor. She slipped back into Pixie's stall and hoisted herself up to peek out the high window. A shiny black truck she didn't recognize was parked in the yard. No one stepped out of it.

Her cell phone rang and she swore when she saw who it was. "Now's not a good time, mom."

"You kids are always saying that."

No one was getting out of the truck.

"Honestly Becca, how are you going to get a husband if you don't even listen to your mother. Men need to feel like you're listening to them—"

"Mom, a truck just pulled up, I need to go see who it is."

"If you had a husband, he would do that for you," Samantha answered in a sing song voice.

Becca gripped her phone and stared out the window. Finally her mother asked, "Are you okay, dear?"

"I have to go, mom."

There was a brief pause. "Let me know if you need me." Samantha disconnected the call.

Becca stared at the phone. Her mom had never been particularly maternal and any resilience she had in life came with the play book to cut first. After the turbulent divorce five years ago with Becca's father, her mom had been in a haze of her own pain. Samantha's tenuous relationships with her adult children had fractured, seemingly beyond repair. Bitter divorce tended to make all relationships involved brittle.

She didn't have time for an emotional breakthrough right now. The truck was still parked in her drive, and no one had gotten out yet. The windows were tinted enough Becca couldn't get a good view of the driver. Should she call the police? And say what? A truck was in her yard, and she was still scared from last night? They'd laugh her off the phone.

Becca slid the hoof pick Jason had used the night before into her back pocket and grabbed a crop she wouldn't have dreamed of using on a horse. Thus armed, she headed out the side door and circled around to get a better look at the cab of the truck.

What she saw made her want to scream.

She stalked over and pounded on the driver's side window.

Her brother Tucker looked up, surprised. He smiled and held his index finger up for her to wait. She had been terrified and he was busy texting, oblivious. Shaking, she made a beeline back into the barn. Tears had gathered in the corners of her eyes, and she swiped them away.

Becca was still shaking when Tucker found her inside the barn a few moments later. "What's wrong?"

She rounded on her brother. "What the hell were you doing skulking around?"

Tucker looked at her like she had grown a second head. "I wasn't skulking, I was sending a text." He brightened. "And I came by to show you my new truck. I thought you'd like it, it's an electric...and why are you mad at me?"

"Sorry. I'm not mad at you. I shouldn't have snapped." She told her brother the events of the previous evening. It sounded surreal, like she had read it somewhere instead of experiencing it. She wrapped her arms around herself. If she asked her brother for a hug she'd break, and she couldn't afford to break right now.

Another vehicle crunched on the gravel drive and Tucker asked, "You expecting anyone?"

She shook her head.

Tucker headed to one of the barn windows. Becca followed him and frowned. "Where's your gun?"

"At home, locked up where it belongs. I'm off duty."

Becca had never thought much about guns. When you're not under attack a gun sounds ridiculous, base even. Becca was not feeling average, she was feeling hunted.

Tucker looked out the barn window and visibly relaxed. "It's RCMP, probably Jason checking in on you. Or someone stole the truck," he kidded.

Becca slapped him on the shoulder. "Not funny, bro."

"Ow. You should have told me what happened last night, last night. I would have come over and you wouldn't be feeling so violent this morning," Tucker chided, rubbing his shoulder. "Good thing you're not armed. Wasn't it you who asked me not to wear my gun here?"

She slapped him again. "That was different. Jason had come by that one time to drop off Lillian's niece. He completely ignored me, I've never wanted to shoot someone before that."

Tucker cocked his head. "That's why?" He actually smiled, still rubbing his shoulder. "Interesting."

Becca sputtered, "That's called a red flag, it is not interesting."

"If you say so." Her brother called out, "Hey, Chasseur."

She turned. Jason Chasseur in his RCMP police uniform stood silhouetted in the large double doors at the end of the barn. Bright morning sun flared around him like a body-sized halo. He nodded to both of them. "Becca, Tucker, morning."

"Hey, Becca was just talking about you." Tucker deftly ducked before Becca could land a punch.

Jason shed his sunglasses and hooked them on his coat. He stared at Becca; his clinical gaze didn't miss an inch of her. His face gave away nothing. He could have been assessing shoe polish instead of a flesh and blood woman in front of him.

"How are you doing this morning?" His voice bounced inside her head, resonating a bit too well.

"I'm fine."

Tucker frowned, watching both of them. "She's a wreck. What the hell happened?"

Becca glared at her brother. "I'm right here."

"Yeah, and exhibiting classic signs of trauma. You're jumping at shadows. Your hands haven't stopped shaking since I got here. You clearly didn't sleep worth a shit last night and you're snapping. You only snap when mom or dad are around."

Becca didn't correct her brother. She snapped at Officer Chasseur, too.

"You did a good job, Becca. It takes a while to process. I just wanted to check in on you." He turned to Tucker and recounted what had happened.

"Shit." Tucker looked at his sister before pulling her into a hug. "Promise me you won't ride out by yourself."

She hugged him back but didn't answer. It was like asking the wind not to blow.

"Becca, I mean it."

Becca pulled away. "I'll be careful. Besides, I live by myself. Hiding from my life, such as it is, seems a bit of overkill, don't you think? This house is nearly as remote as that ride."

Tucker started to protest.

Jason spoke, "I can keep an eye on her."

Becca crossed her arms. "No." Her ill-fated high school crush on him had left a sizable hole in her heart and meant that Jason was the one man she needed to stay away.

"We care about you and want to keep you safe," Tucker said.

"It's my *job* to keep you safe," Jason clarified.

Jason's words stung her. "Right. I had a scare, but my opening weekend isn't going to happen by magic. I've got work to do. If something else happens, we'll cross that bridge when we get to it, and hope that it doesn't."

"Hope isn't a plan," Tucker said.

"Neither is cowering in fear. I appreciate your concern, really I do. But let's look at this rationally. I was out riding on crown land and stumbled across a couple guys who scared me and who happen to be criminal types. Yeah, that sucks, but we have no reason to believe they wish me harm, or even know who I am."

"The Fischers have been seen quadding in the area on several occasions," Jason reminded her. "The troubling part is we don't know why. You've got a new parcel of land, ride on that instead."

Becca ignored the dig. "It's weirder to think I'm in danger than to think it was a random fluke. I'm fine."

As pep talks went, it was one of her better attempts. But it was true, wasn't it? It was rather arrogant to think she was on the Fischer brothers' radar. They ran guns and drugs and she was opening a luxury ranch eco-inn. Their paths had crossed but there was nothing to suggest they would again. She would finish getting ready and her opening weekend would kick off a successful venture. Everything was going to be fine.

Becca let herself relax for the first time since last night. She almost laughed. She should be focusing her attention on finding a sommelier who would relocate to the rural foothills of the Rocky Mountains instead of worrying about gun and drug runners. Those were two worlds she was sure didn't cross.

# Chapter Nine

Tucker followed Jason out of the barn and fell into step beside him. Jason gave Becca's brother a sideways glance. "Need something?"

"Let's go a bit farther. Becca has the hearing of a friggin' owl when she wants to."

They stopped at Jason's police cruiser before Tucker asked, "What's really going on?"

Jason sized up the man next to him. Tucker was a few inches shorter than Jason with a compact, strong frame. In a bar fight, not that he did that anymore, Jason would want Tucker on his side. Becca's brother was known as being easy going, even a joker sometimes. But Jason suspected his casual energy hid some very deep currents. Tucker held himself coiled, ready. That kind of tension developed over time and for a reason.

Jason pulled out a pack of cigarettes.

"Since when do you smoke?"

"Since I started having to deal with your sister." Jason hadn't smoked in years. Last night he had slipped into the old habit with frightening ease. He lit one and took a long pull, the small ritual providing fleeting relief. Becca left him tied in knots. He didn't like it.

Tucker pointed. "Can I have one of those?"

Jason held out the pack.

Tucker lit one and his shoulders visibly relaxed. "Becca has that effect on all of the males in our family. Well, except our dad. Just don't let her see you with one."

The two men smoked in silence in the early morning quiet.

Tucker asked, "Do you think she's in danger?"

Jason took another pull from his cigarette. The thought of Becca in danger turned him inside out. "I don't know."

"What do you know?"

"Our surveillance hasn't come up with anything concrete besides the Fischers have a newfound interest in quadding the back country. They haven't been carrying anything in or out and the helicopter didn't see anything besides a herd of big horn sheep and a university research site." Jason took another drag on his cigarette. "I wouldn't want the Fischers dogging me. If those guys earned their reputation, they take violence and the crime business to a whole new level. They can strategize and know their way around technology. They are eerily good at what they do."

"Sounds like you respect them." Tucker eyed him as he pulled a drag on his cigarette. "Do you?"

Jason flipped that over in his head. "Respect isn't the word. They sell death. Business acumen is irrelevant when your business is death. Good question, though."

"That was actually a shitty question. Sorry, man."

"It's fine. Sometimes—and I seriously doubt it is in this case—the person a criminal is, isn't the crimes they commit. I don't know, something just isn't adding up with these guys."

Tucker grinned like an idiot. "You're a poet. I think we just had a moment. Hey, that kind of rhymes."

"No it doesn't. And we didn't just have a moment."

"You're a frickin' ray of sunshine, you are," Tucker said, still grinning.

Jason ignored that. "Becca should keep her head down for a while, not that she's ever been accused of being a social butterfly. It helps she doesn't make an easy target. Your sister is tough as nails when she wants to be, Gabe is former CSIS, you're CPS, and everyone in this part of the province has heard how Colt punched a charging grizzly bear. You guys make most sane people think twice." He should take his own advice. Becca Tanner was off limits for any number of reasons.

"When you put it that way, we're a pretty bad-ass family." Tucker sounded like a proud kid. Jason hoped policing never took that innocent wonder away from him. Still, Jason felt an obligation to warn him, "Don't underestimate the Fischers or take anything for granted. I've been wrong about people before."

"Not often. Your work on the Blackthorne case is still used in recruit classes."

Jason waved off the compliment. "That was just right place, right time."

"What was last night?"

"Wrong place, wrong time."

"You *are* a fucking poet."

"I've been called many things, but you are the first ass to call me that."

Tucker asked, "You know who would want to call you that nasty name you found scratched into your truck?"

Jason shook his head. "Nope. It's not the Fischers' style. I've got a few regulars who point out I don't match their expectations of what a law enforcement officer's pedigree should be."

"Is that the official company lines? Because you don't talk like that."

"Something like that."

"You'll really keep an eye on my sister? You guys hate each other."

"It's my job to protect everyone," Jason answered. It rankled that he still felt anything for her.

"And?" Tucker prodded.

Jason shrugged. "How better to annoy your sister than to be in her hip pocket?"

"Whatever works as long as you keep her safe. She'd never let one of us ride shotgun, or tell her what to do"

"What sister would?" Jason retorted.

At the sound of boots crunching both men turned. Becca was walking towards them, her steps almost stomps. "What are you doing?"

Jason watched Tucker transform into a sheepish sibling, caught doing something he wasn't supposed to. "Jason and I were just talking about the situation."

"And inhaling carcinogens while you do it helps? You promised."

Tucker rolled the cigarette between his fingers, pinching off the ember at the end. "It's out. My bad."

She turned to Jason expectantly. "Those carcinogens aren't good for you, either."

He took another drag before slowing exhaling the smoke. She waited, patient and defiant.

Jason pinched out his cigarette without finishing it. He ducked into his cruiser and pulled out his finished to-go coffee and dropped the butt inside. He held it out to Tucker who did the same.

"How unexpected, a man who can clean up after himself." Becca started to turn but stopped. "Thank you." With that she headed back to the barn.

Jason called out after her, "I'll stop by after my shift. Will you have the coffee on?"

She didn't turn around but waved her middle finger as she walked away.

Tucker laughed. "You guys need your own reality show."

Jason put his sunglasses on. "That's the last thing we need. I'll keep you in the loop." He got into his cruiser and fired up the engine. As he drove away Becca's nagging words rang in his ears.

*Those carcinogens aren't good for you, either.*

No woman besides his mother had ever chastised him for smoking. No one had cared enough.

# Chapter Ten

José Martinez waited to officially enter Canada, though his flight had landed ninety minutes ago. He had made it through the maze of border security kiosks, entering what details he would share into what he knew was a woefully inadequate database. Now he was in a larger room, a series of zig-zagging rows organizing the hundreds of people waiting to clear customs.

There were better ways to travel, just less easy to explain—he wasn't here officially.

José resisted a sigh and rolled his wheel bag another few centimeters. He was almost to the border guard windows. He let his gaze circle the large room. Overly stylized welcome signs in various languages greeted him, as did repeatedly posted rules. In English and French, travelers were alerted to the country's cannabis and firearm rule, as well as alcohol, tobacco, and shopping allowances. It appeared Canada's border security took their assignment of collecting proper duty fees seriously.

His attention caught again on a man in line ahead of him. At a glance, the man looked ordinary. His stature, coloring, and attire were similar enough to dozens of men in line. Yet this man's clothing was too well cut to be off the rack, and he carried himself like a two-legged predator. José would know. He took a discreet photo of the man, emailing it to his encrypted account before deleting it. It could be nothing.

José heard his name. A young border guard at one of the windows was talking to the man he'd photographed, and calling him by José's name. José was close enough to see the border guard let her fingers linger when she handed him back his passport. It was an overt invitation. The man accepted his passport.

He turned, still smiling, before looking directly at José. He pointed at him, his fingers cocked like a gun going off. The motion was brief and no one else in line seemed to notice.

The man left and the line moved forward. He reminded José of Fernando. His little display was a move meant to intimidate; José just didn't know what he was supposed to be intimidated about. He'd never seen the man before.

"Passport and printed declaration form," the border guard asked, sounding bored.

José handed over both.

The border guard punched in a few keys on his computer. He gave José a hooded look before he typed in a few more commands. "Where are you coming from?"

"España…Spain."

"Where are you going?"

"Banff."

"Business or pleasure?"

His task was neither. In the end he let money decide. He wasn't getting paid for this errand. "Pleasure."

The guard punched a few keys and another border guard walked up. "Come with me, please. Bring your bag."

José let his voice sound curious and cultured, when he said, "Did I do something wrong?" This wasn't his first time being brought to a back room at a border crossing.

The guard led him into a locked hallway and turned into a large room. Several metal tables were spaced apart. "Please put your bag on the table."

José complied and waited. The guard put on gloves and searched José's bag, rifled through his wallet, and finally searched his person. José knew he wouldn't find anything. Still, he couldn't resist saying, "If you told me what you were looking for maybe I could help you find it."

The guard kept José's wallet but nodded towards the open suitcase in disarray. "Bring that."

His belongings were strewn across the table. José packed his belongings with care before zipping his suitcase closed. He took his time. Finally, he followed the guard to another room. This one was small and had a single table and two chairs.

"Have a seat."

José rolled his eyes. Tedious. Border guards were tedious.

When the guard left, José checked his phone. The image had gotten a hit. The man was Del Fiennes, one of his brother Fernando's former crew members. What was he doing here?

Forty minutes later a woman came in. With brisk movements she closed the door. She sat across from him, a small stack of papers and his wallet in front of her.

She clasped her hands together. "So, are you the real José Martinez or the imposter?"

José sat back. This was going to take a while.

# Chapter Eleven

Becca eyed the bottles of wine lined up on her large kitchen island counter. "Tell me again why I need a sommelier?"

Lillian Kensington was elegance, grace and grit. She was the most sophisticated person Becca knew besides the Wolfgrams, her architects. Perhaps more importantly, she also had experience with violent, dangerous criminals. And had lived. Raised in wealth and privilege on a family estate in the United Kingdom, she had followed her conscience to the darkest places of the globe. As a conflict and war correspondent, she had built her career fighting to raise awareness of injustices to prompt global action. She had routinely put her life in danger to help protect innocent lives around the planet. Her role led to covert courier work for MI6 until a shattering betrayal ended her career and nearly her life. Lillian had slipped into Becca's life a few months ago when against some serious odds, she started dating Becca's brother, Colt. Becca had adored her ever since.

"Want to talk about last night first?" Lillian sat beside her, radiating a confidence Becca could only dream of.

Becca played with a cork. "Not really. I'm trying to remember how to feel normal."

Lillian smiled. "Well darling, your new normal is expensive grapes. Your target demographic will pay out the nose for the glass of wine your sommelier tells them to drink. Get a master sommelier and they will pay even higher. For its markup, wine needs a relatively small space and even the young wines have a long shelf life compared to say, flying fresh lobster in on a regular basis. Basically, having a good sommelier in the right restaurant is like a license to print money."

Becca listened, trying to wrap her brain around what Lillian was saying but she was confused. "Why again do rich people pay people to boss them around?"

"Your clients pay *experts* to make decisions for them. It's subtle, but there's a difference."

"So it's not just a glass of wine?"

Lillian gave her head a small shake. "It's never just wine. You are selling an experience."

"I know I'm in the luxury business but it all just seems so…frivolous."

"Its relevance is relative; to your clients, it's most assuredly relevant. Like it or not, your business is telling people what they want, giving it to them, and charging them an enormous amount for the exchange."

Becca dropped her head into her hands. "What have I gotten myself into?" No one had ever taken her seriously, not her father or her mother, not her brothers, not even herself.

She hadn't given them much to work with.

Becca hadn't been able to pick a single major and had graduated from university with triple majors in restoration agriculture, ecology and political science. Her parents, both died-in-the-wool conservatives, had not approved of her choices. It didn't help that her brothers were all accomplished in their own right and that she had looked up to them with the hero-worship only a younger sister could have. After their parent's spectacular divorce, each of them had scattered, chasing their own dreams, and she had been left alone, wondering where her family was and what she was supposed to do next.

Armed with her shiny new degrees, she had dried her tears, bottled her insecurity, and accepted a job at a small soil restoration consulting company in Germany. It gave her the stability and structure she needed, if not the warm fuzzies of home. Home didn't exist anymore, she had reminded herself; it had been sold off in the divorce. She had been feeling particularly lonely when she saw an ad for a luxury inn in Estonia. The pictures had looked so warm and inviting, like a real home people could rent but without the drama. With the exchange rate in her favor, she cashed out her savings and made a plan to do the same in her beloved foothills. She would build her own damn home.

Lillian gave Becca's shoulder a comforting squeeze. "You're building your future. That takes courage which you have in spades."

Becca sat up. "I'm terrified I made a mistake."

Lillian wrapped her arms around Becca. "My life blew up, hell *I* almost blew up, but those mistakes led me to soul-deep happiness with your brother." Lillian pulled back and looked at Becca, her eyes bright. "The woman I was before the *unfortunate incident* would never have given Colt a second glance. Now I can't imagine my life without him. Darling, pray for mistakes, that's where the magic happens."

Becca felt the sting of tears behind her eyes. "Sounds weird, but I'll try." She eyed the bottles of wine again. "How about I make us some tea?"

Lillian laughed. "Your tea is awful."

Becca ducked her head. She really did make awful tea.

"How about I make us a spot of tea and we go over the list of resumes again? And if it's not too presumptuous, I can help you with your international marketing."

Becca took a breath to object, but Lillian shook her head. "*Shh*, don't even say it. Your refusal to accept help is precariously close to self-sabotage. That you even asked for help today is enormous. You are stuck with me."

"Did you *shush* me?"

Lillian broke into a radiant smile. "I simply highlighted that you need to tweak your strategy."

"You run circles around Colt, don't you?"

"We run circles around each other," Lillian corrected with a secret smile and got up to make tea. Becca watched as Lillian filled the kettle and put it to boil, soothed by the cozy ritual. She sighed deeply and admitted, "Last night scared me."

Lillian looked up from spooning loose tea leaves into a pot. "It might be nothing."

"Maybe." Becca toyed with the cork again. "You know what's weird? I felt safe with Jason and the guy hates me." She still couldn't believe she had asked him for help last night. Lillian was right, she never asked anyone for help. Fear was turning her to mush, irrational mush. Still, she asked, "How did you get over trusting the wrong person?"

Lillian was quiet and Becca rushed out, "Sorry, that was a really personal question."

"It took Colt." The kettle started singing. Lillian flicked open the spout, silencing it, but kept it on the burner. When the water came to a rolling boil, she turned off the burner and poured it over the tea leaves in the pot.

Becca sat back. "I think I know why I suck at making tea."

Lillian smiled. "So you're a coffee woman. I devour your coffee; I can't even drink mine."

Becca loved that about her. She was brilliant and kind. "So back to my brother, how did he help?"

"It wasn't until I started trusting Colt that I forgave myself for trusting Fernando. You see, Fernando's betrayal shook my faith in myself. That was more damaging than any treason tribunal could ever be. Your brother helped me trust myself again."

"You are talking about *my brother*, Colt?" Becca got up and pulled down two beautiful hand-thrown mugs.

"The one and only." Lillian poured them both mugs of steaming tea. "Besides, I have this theory. I needed my life to blow up so I could heal. I was in bad shape. Years of reporting on atrocities and trauma took a serious mental toll. I think that's how I fell for Fernando in the first place. When everything was blowing up, I had to face reality. I simply wasn't me anymore. In trying to help other people I ended up losing myself." Lillian lifted her shoulder in a dainty shrug. Her casual commentary on life-shattering events belied her strength and grit.

Becca asked, "Can I be you for Halloween?"

Lillian's laughter filled the kitchen. It was like audible sunlight. She passed a mug of tea to Becca. "Only if I can be you. You're stronger than you realize."

"That remains to be seen."

Lillian smiled over the rim of her mug. "Want to go over sommelier resumes, international marketing, or Officer Chasseur?"

Becca choked on her tea, splashing hot liquid down her sweater. "Ow, ow, ow." She pulled the plush fabric away from her body to avoid getting burned or soaking her t-shirt underneath and squirmed out of her sweater. She mopped her hands with her soiled sweater in disgust. She crossed the room and fired the sweater into the laundry room, tugged the laundry room door closed and returned to her seat.

"So not Officer Chasseur then?" Lillian asked drily and held up the tea pot. "More tea?"

"Not if he was the last man on earth." Becca pushed her now empty mug forward for a refill.

Lillian filled Becca's mug before picking up a small piece of paper. "So I can just toss in the rubbish bin this stickie note here with his name and mobile on it?"

Becca snatched the note. "Tucker gave this to me. He thought I might need it."

Lillian sipped her tea to hide her grin.

"For safety," Becca insisted. She pulled out her phone and added Jason's number to her contacts.

In her haste she accidentally pressed his number. She swore, repeatedly pressing the red disconnect button.

"Shit! He's going to think I called him."

"You did call him."

"Traitor," Becca grumbled.

Lillian's eyes widened and Becca realized her faux pas. "Sorry, sorry. Oh my god, I didn't mean it like that."

"Relax, I teased you first. My goodness, you are wound a bit tight. You remind me of me. Come on then, let's get some work done. How can I help?"

Becca sat back down on one of the kitchen island stools and opened her laptop. A few clicks later and she had the right digital folder open. "Somewhere in this folder there must be a decent sommelier that I can afford and who will relocate to balmy southern Alberta." Becca closed the lid. "Who am I kidding? No one wants to move to southern Alberta."

Lillian sat down and pried Becca's fingers off the laptop. "I did. I lived in a fairy-tale estate house in England and chose to move to a condo in Canada's hinterland."

"We're not—"

"It tells a better story, love." She opened the lid, assessing the resume titles. "Any restrictions?"

"As long as they do their job right and I can afford them, I'm not going to be picky about the rest."

"This is a bit delicate, but since your head chef is a recovering addict..." Lillian let the rest dangle.

"Good point. No history with drugs." As an afterthought she added, "And no guns, either. Last night sucked."

# Chapter Twelve

Jason knocked on the door to his mom's trailer. The yard was tidy, her truck freshly washed. The window boxes he had made for her still were up, though their flowers were now dead and brittle after the hard frosts. Next spring, they would be vibrant again. His mom loved gardening with her annuals. She said wild splashes of color always made her feel better.

A cold breeze blew in over the back forested ridge. A few of the poplars in the yard still had leaves that rustled frantically on their branches before letting go, a ribbon of golden leaves that only the wind could wave. The wind stopped as suddenly, and the leaves dropped like confetti.

The door opened. "Jason! Come in, come in."

His mom held the door and he scooped her in a quick hug. "Hi mom. Wow, something smells good." He closed the door behind them and automatically took off his boots.

"I just pulled blueberry muffins out of the oven." Rose stood back and got a good look at him. "I always love seeing you in your uniform—what's wrong?"

Jason squirmed under her attention. "What? Nothing's wrong."

"That didn't work when you were a kid, and it doesn't work now." She turned and headed the few steps to the kitchen. "Come on, I just put coffee on. You can tell me all about it. Then you can help me fix that fence."

He smiled and followed his mom into the kitchen. He took his regular seat around her small kitchen table while she headed to the counter. His phone beeped. Becca Tanner was calling.

His mom called over her shoulder, "Go ahead and answer that."

"Naw, that's okay. It's just work stuff."

She placed the coffee and tin of muffins on the table and sat down. "Dear, 'just work stuff' doesn't have you making that face. But no matter, you'll tell me who you are avoiding when you're ready."

Instead of answering, Jason poured them both coffee from the carafe and mugs she brought over.

"Is she pretty?" His mom's smile didn't reach her cautious eyes.

"Nothing for you to worry about, mom. It's nobody."

"I always worry about you. You're too kind-hearted, too easy to get hurt." She added milk and sugar to her coffee and stirred.

"So are you, mom."

After his parents had split up, his mom had had two violent boyfriends. One had the decency to drink himself to death within months. The other was still alive and still terrorizing people. He floated in and out of jail, getting knocked around a little harder each time. The guy was not liked on the inside any more than he was on the outside.

Sons wanted to protect their moms. If they couldn't, they wanted retribution. Jason sent up a silent prayer for Clint Steel. Without his patient insight pointing him in the direction of a career where he could help others, it wouldn't have taken much for Jason to step onto a very different path.

"Oh honey, that's ancient history. Eat a muffin, those blueberries are from Eloise."

"Mom—"

"Ancient. History." She softened her tone and explained, "I'm a different person than I was then. I've done much soul healing since then. This isn't easy for me to admit, but you need to hear it. I now understand I was punishing myself for leaving your dad. I still loved him; I just couldn't live with him anymore. Guilt and pain are awful teachers, but I learned. Now, eat your muffin."

Jason dutifully selected a large one and began eating. Rose did the same. They spoke of the weather and sipped their coffees. After several minutes of conversation his mom finally laughed.

"What," Jason asked, showering the table with crumbs. "Oops, sorry."

"Oh my, she must be something."

"Who?" Jason asked again, licking butter off his fingers.

"The woman who has you so bent out of shape."

"Why do you think it's a woman? It could be work, you know."

"You have a different face when work is bugging you. No, this is a woman. She must be something else."

"You don't know the half of it," Jason muttered.

"So tell me."

Jason was not going to discuss Becca Tanner with his mother. "Do you have those old pictures of grandad?"

"Of course, dear. Why?"

Jason didn't have an answer. "I don't know. You keep talking about Becca, and I was just thinking about our land that she bought."

His mom laughed. It was a beautiful sound. She didn't laugh enough. It distracted him and he wasn't ready when she busted him. "I didn't say Becca, did you say Becca?"

Jason felt his cheeks grow warm. "My mistake." Becca was in his head. She always just slipped in, no matter how hard he tried to keep her out.

"So that's who has got you tied up in knots. Good for her."

"Mom!" This was not where he expected the conversation to go.

"I swear, I've never seen two people work so hard to pretend they're not crazy about each other."

"She's crazy alright, but not for me."

"My dear, you're constantly brushing her off, how would you know?"

Jason didn't mention it was for self-preservation. He and Becca just didn't work, not that they'd actually tried it. Years ago, in high school he had thought they both felt the same way. That was the only reason he had poured his heart out to her in that letter. Her response had been a sharp dismissal. They had been at odds ever since.

Jason needed to change the subject. "About those old photos?"

"Give me a day or two. Stop by later in the week and we'll go through them. I'll put the coffee on."

"Thanks, mom." He got up to go.

"Thanks for checking in on me."

"I wasn't checking in, I'm helping with the fence, and visiting."

"Yes, dear. Well, keep popping in for visits, then, it puts my mind at ease. I worry about you, too. You and me, we're all that we have left."

# Chapter Thirteen

Becca stood in her private study long after the sun had set. Her hair was still damp from the quick shower she had taken and the soft flannel shirt she had put on was getting wet. Such were her days, pin-balling from one task to the next until late into the night. She needed to slow down, but not yet. She still had work to do.

Becca moved to light a fire in the office wood stove. The guest rooms and her bedroom had fireplaces that turned on with the flick of a switch. She couldn't bear to put one of those in here. Some people prided themselves on their kitchens or rec rooms but for Becca, her private office was her pride and joy.

She let herself savor the simple task of lighting the fire. Kneeling, she held match to crushed paper and kindling and watched as each sliver of stick caught.

The slow, tentative flickers spread until they had grown into a proper fire. If only she knew if she was building something as tangible as the fire now warming her, nestled securely in its perfect place. She had no idea if she was creating something real and lasting, or wasting everyone's time, particularly her own. She looked around her at what she had built so far in this single room. More library, than office, this room held her collection of books and her up-cycled winged-back chair, perfect for snuggling up in and reading. The antique floor lamp threw soft, inviting light.

A mountain of paperwork waited on her desk and tacked to the cork board in the kitchen was her to-do list, three pages long with addendums on sticky notes. It was more work than a single person could possibly expect to achieve. More and more, she was feeling like her business plan was a foolish gamble rather than a sound business investment. Her dream of making something of her life—something that her parents could be proud of, instead of taking pot shots at her hippy career decisions—had led her here: bone-tired and wondering if she had enough gas left in her emotional tank.

She had managed to build an elegant, carbon-neutral accommodation. Reclaimed materials accounted for forty percent of the building supplies; they were central to the design element of giving the new build a feeling of graceful longevity. The architects she had worked with were a brilliant husband and wife team originally from Germany. What they took for granted as common-place in sustainable building practices, renewable energy, and sustainable luxury—from building orientation, to high output solar panels and gray water tanks—had been a revelation.

They had also suggested Becca market outside of North America. So far, the majority of her bookings were guests from Japan, Spain, Germany, Britain and India. Still, self-doubt ate at her constantly. She needed higher occupancy numbers. The meagre bookings starting at the end of the month took turns inspiring elation that anyone had chosen her eco-inn, and despair that she had gambled blood, sweat, tears and capital, and lost.

The doorbell rang. The events of the night before flooded into her mind, and she was acutely aware that she was alone in the large empty ranch house. Frowning at her watch and the late hour, she hesitated. She had never felt scared by herself.

Now she did.

Several muffled knocks sounded.

She tried to force her legs to move, to at least peek out a front window but they remained firmly planted. Her phone beeped and she jumped.

It was a text from her brother. *Let Jason in.*

Relief replaced fear. Then anger. He had told her he would check on her and she had told him not to. Anxious to not be alone but feeling unreasonably grumpy with him, she sprinted through the house to the front door. She peeked through the side window. Jason was indeed standing on her front porch. He was on his phone and looking pissed. Hating herself for it, she flung the door open, grabbed his arm and pulled him inside.

# Chapter Fourteen

Jason looked up from his phone as the front door was flung open. Becca grabbed his arm and pulled him in. She slammed the door behind them and locked it. A dozen scenarios rocked through him. "Are you okay? What's happened?" Why didn't he check on her sooner? Why didn't he answer the phone when she had called earlier?

"What? I'm fine." She dropped his arm and crossed hers. Her hair was damp.

"Becca?"

"Want some coffee? I have decaf." She turned and crossed her large foyer and headed down a hall. It was the first time Jason had been inside Becca's new inn and he couldn't help staring. Large wooden beams framed high ceilings while tall windows let in starlight, giving the impression of the outdoors inside. Multi-textured furnishings and thoughtful touches finished off the effect. He had never seen a rough-plank coffee table look elegant or want to touch plush plaid throw pillows. It was an impressive, lovely home. It had the bones to make a successful inn fit for even the most discriminating guests.

"You coming?" Becca called.

Jason took off his boots and followed, acutely aware of how humble his background was compared to this decadence. The kitchen matched the rest of the house with luxurious furnishings paired with practical use from the large exposed beams to the state of the art appliances. This was a working kitchen, not simply a show kitchen. Jason watched Becca start to make coffee. He wasn't ready to sit on the stool she offered.

"What was that all about? Has something happened?"

Becca pushed the button on the coffee grinder. Finally, she stopped and transferred the grounds into a French press. "What do you mean?"

"You yanked me into your house."

When she didn't say anything, he prodded, "Will you tell me why?"

She looked up at him then. "Can you pretend for like a second that you don't hate me?" When Jason nodded she continued. "My hands haven't stopped shaking and I've felt jittery all day."

Jason relaxed. "That's a completely normal response to a startle like you had."

"A startle? Jason, those guys had guns for killing people. I mean a hunting rifle for sustenance is one thing, handguns are another. I didn't sleep last night, I doubt I'll sleep tonight. Yeah, I had a fucking *startle*." She stopped and grabbed the edge of the counter.

"I didn't mean to minimize it." He watched and waited.

The bluster went out of her. "I'm scared. I should be fine, but I'm still scared. I don't like that. I looked them up last night, big mistake. All day I just kept waiting for something bad to happen. I seriously don't have time to be paralyzed in fear and that's what it feels like right now, paralysis."

"Did you talk to your brothers? Both Tucker and Gabe will have experience with adrenaline like this."

Becca shook her head. "No way. I can't make heads or tails of my reaction and I'd just talk in circles. They don't hiccup at danger; how could they understand? Besides, then they'd worry about me more than they already do."

Jason pulled out his wallet and fished inside for a card. He offered it to Becca. "There is a hotline you can call."

Becca glanced at the card but didn't take it. "I already called it. Colt's girlfriend Lillian suggested it. Worst phone call of my life. They kept asking if I was suicidal. When I told them I wasn't, they didn't know what to do with me. I don't know what to do with me." She laughed then and clapped a hand over her mouth.

Jason wasn't sure what to do with a hysterical Becca.

She stopped and held up her hands to him. "They're not shaking anymore."

Jason tried to sound encouraging. "That's a good thing."

She stared at them in wonderment before looking up. "I feel safer with you here. You, of all people."

"Gee, thanks."

"Would I be the person *you* run to?"

The kettle whistled and saved him from having to answer. Jason crossed over to the stove and shut it off, happy to have something to break the building charge within him. When he would have poured the boiling water into the press, Becca put her hand on his arm. "Just a second. Wait for it."

He looked down at her, she was standing close. Her forehead could touch his shoulder if she just leaned a little more in. "What am I waiting for?" he asked in a whisper.

"The water to cool a moment. We want hot, not boiling water, otherwise the coffee burns—" She stopped talking when she looked up at him. She held his gaze. "Jason?"

"Yeah?" He held his breath.

She whispered back, "The water should be good now."

He looked at her, a bit unhinged, and exhaled. He poured the hot water over the ground coffee beans. Becca refitted the top of the press and fished a crocheted cozy out of a drawer and slid it in place. "In four minutes we will have sublime coffee."

"I didn't realize coffee could be sublime," Jason said dryly.

"Bite your tongue."

"I'm used to just drip, you know. Or instant in a pinch."

"Take the olive branch."

"Is that what this is?" He forced old memories aside.

Her stomach growled then, loud enough for him to hear it. "My appetite is back! Are you hungry? I haven't been able to eat anything all day. Now I'm starving." She crossed the kitchen and went rummaging in her large walk-in pantry.

"I'm fine."

Talking to Becca was an exercise in patience. He needed her to focus so he could ask his questions and leave. Jason leaned against the counter and waited for her to come back out. Finally he asked, "About today, it was alright? You didn't see anybody out of the ordinary?"

"Do you count?" Her voice was muffled.

"I'm serious."

Becca popped her head out. "So am I. Two days ago, you hadn't said boo to me unless it was to snarl. Now we're having coffee in my kitchen and so far it hasn't turned into a knife fight." She ducked back into the pantry.

"I mean did anything weird happen?"

She walked out of the pantry holding two boxes of organic macaroni and cheese. "Why do you have to be like that? I'm trying not to freak out and then you say shit that makes me think I should be freaking out." She handed him the boxes. "Here, start these."

"Seriously?"

She held up a hand. "Stop complaining, I'm getting more stuff ready." She started pulling out salad fixings from the refrigerator. "I will answer all of your questions, but not on an empty stomach."

"You're a fucking tornado, you know that, right?" Jason muttered but started making the macaroni and cheese.

Becca's brows knitted and she looked thoughtful. "You mean like a force of nature?"

"Chaos. I mean you are chaos."

She shrugged. "Better than I thought you'd say."

She made a salad while he finished the macaroni and cheese. It felt weird to be in her kitchen, making himself at home. If cooking for someone else could feel homey, that is. She set the table with placemats and cloth napkins. He couldn't tell if it was for his benefit or if she always set it like that.

"You're off duty, right? Want a beer instead of coffee?"

A beer sounded good, but he shook his head. She poured coffees along with two glasses of water and sat down. When he didn't take a seat she said, "I know you said you didn't want to eat, but you're making me nervous standing." She helped herself to salad and pasta. When he sat down and did the same she said, "I didn't notice anything or anyone different around here, but I didn't leave the ranch yard today."

"Have you noticed anything unusual over the last little bit? Anything that stands out?" He took a bite of salad. "Wow, this is good."

Becca smiled. "It's the arugula. Shows off a bit."

Jason looked away; her smile still had the ability to sucker punch him. He really didn't want to be the sucker he was in high school.

Becca dug into her pasta, happily munching away until she stopped cold.

"What is it?" Her face had gone white, and he saw her hands were shaking again.

"Last week a man stopped by asking about Tucker. He said he was an old classmate or something. I had been trying to get my stupid printer to work and was only half listening. I didn't recognize him then."

"Why would that be unusual?"

"It was one of the Fischer brothers."

# Chapter Fifteen

Christopher waited in the inky black night, patient. He blended into the yard perimeter without fuss. His truck was out of sight a kilometer away. There were several yard lights on to be wary of, isolated halos of light in the otherwise black night. Their glow just reached the spruce and aspen poplars circling the large yard of the inn.

The wind gusted, releasing a litany of dry leaves. Like brittle paper, they rustled. The wind swirled and two brushed his face, their earthy fragrance clear and raw. He checked his watch. Officer Chasseur had left Becca Tanner's sprawling ranch house nearly two and a half hours ago and the lights on the main floor had flicked off minutes after. The lone light visible in a single second story window had only been dark for the last forty-five minutes. He had been sure the Mountie was sleeping with the Tanner woman, but now he wasn't so sure.

He didn't like being surprised. In his line of work being surprised was a good way to get yourself killed.

Christopher waited another half hour. He had time. He had already bugged her father's home and laptop earlier in the evening when Bruce Tanner had obligingly taken his former mistress-turned-wife out to dinner. By all accounts, the intel Austin had tracked said Bruce Tanner was a slick one. He was severely mortgaged, routinely blurred the line of what was legal in his businesses, paid dirty politicians and law enforcement to grease any snags, including the nasty drug habit he'd picked up. There was also intel that Bruce Tanner had fathered a child with a mistress decades ago that he had been keeping a secret from his children, and both his past and current wife. Christopher had never wondered about his parents' love or integrity. They were good people and had died way too young.

Yet it was Bruce who was the one accepted within society and Christopher—who paid cash, didn't turn cops or political swine, didn't use the poison he ran, nor misuse women—lived in the margins. Christopher had the decency to know he wasn't fit for civilian circles. Bruce Tanner hadn't figured that out yet. Bruce was a dark fucker. If he got in Christopher and Austin's way, he'd be a dead dark fucker.

It was time. Christopher made his way around to the back. High hedges blocked him. Their tall, partially bare branches rose like interlocking sentinels. In the darkness, he followed the edge for a few feet. They were massive and from his earlier reconnaissance he knew they protected a large garden. It wouldn't take much force to push his way through, but he resisted. His body would leave a sizable hole in the dormant hedge, raising questions. It was easier when no one knew to look for answers.

He circled the structure until he found the gate. It easily slipped open, and he followed the mulched garden path to the back door. In the darkness he could make out the silhouettes of raised beds. He had a heightened sense of smell, and the late-season garden was a riot of scents. While the rich sweetness of long-fallen Saskatoon and raspberries played on the wind, he let his hand graze across several bushes. From the smell he would guess they were sage and rosemary bushes.

In the raised bed, a small carrot patch. The tops felt withered to the touch, the bodies poking out of the soil. Until recently, climate-controlled indoor grow-ops were his only point of reference. Now he knew the yard was in zone two-b. Even in the dark, he knew it took substantial effort to grow a garden like this here. He took the wooden steps at the backdoor two at a time and waited.

Only silence met him.

And the barest whiff of vanilla.

It took Christopher longer than he expected to best Becca Tanner's locks and alarm. They were substantially better than most, and the lingering scent of vanilla—and memories of his mom—had fractured his focus. Finally, he let himself into the mudroom off the kitchen. A small nightlight cast irregular shadows. His peripheral vision caught the imminent threat and without hesitating he charged the back door.

A second later he came face to face not with an un-known assailant, but rather a man's jacket draped over a cheery wreath. In the near darkness his brain registered the unorthodox coat hook and he blinked, regrouping.

He waited again but the house remained silent, wrapped in the stillness that only sleeping houses held.

With a focused calm, he went through the house depositing wireless bugs. Surveillance was a finicky art and one he rarely had to practice. He took his time to do it right.

He finished the kitchen and living room before taking the stairs up to the second floor. A loft overlooked the living room with reading areas and a small library. He positioned another bug and moved on to the guest rooms before letting himself through to the private quarters and the Tanner woman's room. It was the only door partially closed.

He listened just outside the door. She was snoring softly, almost like a purr. He slipped through the partially open door and stopped. He stood still for several long moments and just watched her. She looked serene. And vulnerable.

Suddenly she shifted in her sleep and kicked her feet. He stood still, waiting, watching. She called out and he tensed, ready to attack.

She was dreaming. Murmuring something urgent and intangible, she spun again, restless, locked in the throes of her mind. From the looks of it, it wasn't pleasant.

He had stopped dreaming a long time ago, although he didn't know if nightmares counted as dreams.

Christopher gave her a final look before he set another bug and slipped out of her room. He made his way downstairs and found her office. Her laptop sat on her desk and he lifted the cover. It wasn't locked. It was open to a website. A grainy picture taken from a closed-circuit camera stared back at him. It was an image of him.

He dropped into the desk chair. Not what he had been expecting. He scrolled and read. It was a British news article from last year. The only part of the article that was true was that the charges hadn't stuck.

Christopher checked her browser history and found numerous searches on him and his brothers and RCMP Officer Chasseur. So did a website on international marketing, a recipe for both steak and vegan tacos, and the Canada Energy Regulator website. He noticed a second browser tab was open and he clicked on it.

It was on sommeliers.

Well hell, he thought. He might just have to kill her.

# Chapter Sixteen

Jason woke up in a cold sweat, adrenaline spiking through his system and a bone deep fear gripping his attention. Nothing moved in the shadows of his room, and he heard only the sound of silence. Throwing off the covers, he got up and checked his phone. Three-thirty in the morning and no new notifications.

Something had woken him up.

He threw on a pair of pants and a t-shirt and prowled through his house. Nothing was amiss, but still, he couldn't shake the feeling of danger. He checked his phone again. Nothing. He looked outside his windows. Quiet darkness greeted him.

The urge to see Becca was strong. He picked up his phone again, but something stopped him from texting.

Should he drive over? What if something was wrong, what if she needed help?

He paced his small house, uncertain. If she was in danger, he needed to help. If she wasn't, barging in on her in the middle of the night could destroy whatever fragile truce they had created over her mac and cheese.

He stopped.

The frantic indecision had eased. He no longer felt on fire with danger. He would see Tucker in the morning meeting—they were working on a joint drug task force—

and assign him the role of babysitter. It wouldn't be creepy if her brother checked in on her.

The decision made, Jason turned back to his room. The leftover adrenaline was still buzzing through his system like a hangover. He swore. There was no way he was getting back to sleep tonight. He headed to the kitchen and made himself an instant coffee. Standing in his kitchen, he brought the mug to his lips. As soon as the hot liquid touched his mouth, he remembered how good Becca had smelled when she had taught him how she makes coffee. He slammed his mug down on the counter like he had been burned. The instant coffee tasted like ass compared to her brew.

He picked the mug back up and sat at his kitchen table. He opened his work laptop and opened the notes he had made on the Fischers. Was he missing anything? He logged in to see if any new entries had been recorded in the drug and arms files databases.

He got a ping. An Austin Fischer had applied for a patent for a marijuana strain, outlining a growing process that produced cannabidiol, CBD, with a potency that rivaled opioids.

Jason sat back. That couldn't be right, it would be impossible.

Or was it?

He had taken biochemistry what seemed like a lifetime ago. His professor had mentioned that a drug the public could get their hands on was as important as the high. She had also discussed the complex economics associated with the versatile marijuana plant. Powerful lobbyists from a host of organizations wanted to keep the versatile, cheeky plant considered a severe public hazard.

South of the border, schedule I drugs were considered to have no medical use and a high potential of abuse. As such, marijuana was a hell of a lot harder to research for medical uses as a schedule I drug, than schedule II opioids are. Was the belief that opioids were better at pain management than CBD simply a product of research gaps and drug bias?

Jason wasn't a granola loving tree hugger like Becca, but dismissing inconvenient data was a recipe for disaster. Like the bizarre assault on scientists pushing the alarm bell on the avoidable climate crisis, it was no different than dismissing the possible medical applications of marijuana.

The opioid crisis was a fucking disaster. Could it have been avoided, too?

He hadn't thought of that class in years. Jason scrubbed his face with his hands and remembered. As a painkiller, CBD attached to cannabinoid receptors, jamming cell communication in different parts of the body. A person overdosing on CBD might get a headache, up chuck or be paranoid, but it wouldn't push the kill switch on the autonomic functions of their body. CBD simply did not react with the body that way.

Opioids did. Opioids attached to opioid receptors, including, among others, the high concentration found in the brain stem that regulated the autonomous body functions like breathing and heart rate. That's what made overdosing on an opioid so lethal. The drug pushed a shut-off button on the part of the body that told your lungs to breath or your heart to pump. If you didn't die, opioid use fucked with your brain chemistry, and it was a guessing game when it would blow up a body's ability to carry out normal functions. How different would the opioid crisis look if people would have had access to CBD for as long as they have had access to opioids? The possibilities were staggering.

It was too much to consider, that it all could have been avoided. Jason stood then, tipping over the kitchen chair. Work memories slammed into him.

*Frothing bubbles. Death foam. Too late.*

The first time he had seen an opioid overdose it had looked like a quiet, deadly volcano only instead of lava, foamy, frothing bubbles fizzled out of the victim's mouth.

Jason very carefully picked up the chair, tucking it under the table.

He had seen too many opioid overdoses, arriving too late to help. He had attended too many drug-altered violent domestic disturbances. He had seen scores of strangers hit rock bottom only to bounce. Because that's what happened. Opioids dropped people. Hard. How many times could a person hit bottom, over and over again?

*Bounce, bounce, bounce.*

Jason looked at his hands. What could he do now? How could his hands help someone now? That's how he pushed through when he felt stuck in the mire from work.

Rubbing his eyes, he picked up the mug of coffee and took a sip. It was ice cold. Sputtering, he dropped it and it shattered it into several pieces.

Squatting, and careful not to take a step lest his bare feet find a shard, Jason picked up the largest pieces. Setting them on the table he reached for another, and a different memory flickered. This time from his childhood. Holding the piece of broken ceramic, he thought of another.

With renewed purpose, Jason quickly cleaned up the broken mug before heading down to his sparse, unfinished basement. A treadmill and universal machine filled one side. He headed to the single set of shelves opposite his washer and dryer where a few boxes were stored. He rummaged through the first two. An old, folded letter caught his attention. Closing his eyes, he forced useless memories down. He crammed the folded paper into his pocket and kept searching. He found what he was looking for in the third one. With care, he pulled out the swaddled parcel and headed back upstairs.

Once settled at the kitchen table, he pushed his laptop back, making room, and gently unwrapped his treasure. The rusted metal box was as he remembered. The lettering on the outside was still pitted and indecipherable, the lock springless and the hinges delicate. Inside was a small cloth parcel. With care he unwrapped the cloth. Still resting inside were the treasures he had found as a boy. A small ceramic shard, what looked like a small broken hatchet head, metal balls that could have been gun shot, two brass buttons, a medal in the shape of a crescent moon, and trinkets that could have been part of a bridle or hardware.

He lifted the small copper band. As a boy the simple ring had held little appeal but now he looked at it with new eyes. It could have been a woman's wedding ring. The ring looked delicate in his large hands, and he tried to imagine the woman who may have worn it. Did it slip off on accident or did she take it off? When she had died, why wasn't she buried with it? A small book was at the bottom, its pages empty, any ink was long faded or washed away. The artifacts lay quiet, their secrets lost to time.

He remembered the day he had found these. He had been off playing as he was wont to do and the partial clearing along the fast-flowing river was one of his favorite places. It was far enough away he knew he wouldn't be bothered by anyone yet close enough he would still be home in time for dinner. He had left early, it had still been morning. His grandfather had come over to help fix something, there was always something that needed fixing. His dad and grandpa had started arguing nearly immediately. Jason has slipped out, grabbing an apple on his way and was as quiet as he could be so as not to attract attention.

He had fallen out of a tree. His apple had slipped out of his pocket, and he had lunged for it only to lose his balance. He remembered the sound he had made when he landed. It was a dull thud. He had been dazed and more than a little scared to try to move anything. As he lay on the ground, blinking, his fingers felt different than the rest of him. He wiggled them and to his amazement they rolled over something metal. Excitement replaced fear and he sat up. His hand had hit the corner of the metal box. He dug it out of the silty soil that was half burying it. A book lay inside though the river had likely bled away any ink on its pages long before he found it. He spent the rest of the day exploring and had found the rest of the treasures, though at the time he didn't realize they were artifacts.

When he had returned home that day long ago, his dad and grandpa had still been arguing and he had simply tucked all his treasures away. As little boys do, his attention had lit on something else, and he had forgotten all about asking his dad and grandpa about what he had found.

A few years later it was too late. His grandfather had died; within a few short years his father died, too.

But not before selling that tract of land.

Old anger surfaced. It had taken him a long time to save up enough to buy it back. The price of land in the foothills was steep, but it would have been worth it! His mom would have been so happy. Instead, Becca's father had come in with a bid just high enough to be too competitive for Jason. For Becca. Daddy's little girl. Becca swore she hadn't known about Jason's offer, but how could she not?

His laptop pinged. With a keystroke he called up the notification. Bruce Tanner had pulled Austin Fischer's patent request. So had a Del Fiennes and a José Martinez.

A glow of color was just lighting the horizon when Jason was done filling out the legal paperwork before running international checks on José Martinez and Del Fiennes. Martinez was the older brother of a Fernando Martinez, an international double agent killed last month in the foothills. No further details were listed. Del Fiennes' file was larger. He was an independent mid-level drug and arms dealer jockeying for upward mobility.

What the fuck was Becca's dad into?

# Chapter Seventeen

Becca sat at the desk in her study, her laptop open in front of her. Her finger was hovered over the send button and her stomach was in knots. Lillian was curled up in the study's wingback chair with her own laptop perched in her lap. Becca had acquiesced and the two had been working all morning pulling the final content together for several international marketing campaigns for Becca's dude ranch eco-inn.

"My finger won't hit send," Becca admitted.

The sound of the doorbell interrupted them.

"Are you expecting anyone?" Lillian asked.

Becca shook her head but stood. "I'm sure it's fine. I'll go see who it is."

She headed into the public area of the large ranch house and made her way to the front door. Lillian followed at a discreet distance. Becca looked through the window. A tall man she didn't recognize stood on her porch. He held his sunglasses in his hand. She turned to Lillian and shrugged before opening the door.

"Becca Tanner?" The man asked.

"Yes. How may I help you?" He didn't give off necessarily bad vibes, but he didn't feel reassuring, either.

"I'm actually looking for a place to stay. Do you have any vacancies?"

Becca blinked. Not what she had been expecting. Nor was his *Castellano* accent. "I'm sorry, no. We don't open for a couple weeks yet. I can recommend others, if you like?"

Lillian had moved close to the large living room window that overlooked the front porch. From her peripheral vision, Becca noticed Lillian kept to the bank of translucent curtains bundled to the side of the tall windows, giving her a fair view of the porch while censoring her own identity. Lillian was not smiling.

The man paused. Finally, he smiled. "No, thank you. All the best on your opening." He turned to go.

Automatically, Becca responded, "Thank you."

The man nodded and turned again. This time he stopped and looked at the window where Lillian stood. For a heartbeat Becca wasn't sure what was going to happen. But he simply put his sunglasses back on headed to his vehicle. It was a luxury rental. And electric.

Becca closed the door. "Do you know him?"

Lillian stared out the window. "I'm not sure."

"That was a *Castellano* accent, right?"

"Yes." Lillian didn't elaborate.

"I only started running ads in Spain last week. That's a quick turnaround. Think he's for real?"

"Probably. Come on, you have an email to send."

The two women made their way through the public area of the inn and back into Becca's private office.

Becca sat down. She looked at her laptop before looking at Lillian. "My finger still won't hit send."

Lillian had resumed sitting in the overstuffed wing-back chair, one of her legs hooked over the arm, the other tucked under her. Her own laptop was balanced in her lap. She looked completely at ease, elegant even curled up as she was, and unruffled. She always looked like that. Becca wished she had a fraction of Lillian's confidence, grace, or sense of style.

Lillian asked, "Are you nervous investing that amount of money or that it'll work?"

"Both." With her launch imminent, Becca was second guessing every decision she had made and every dollar spent. She could do anything with a horse or a hammer in her hands. Over the last two years her business plans had required her to build tangible results—a house, a barn, clearing trails, training horses. It was relatively easy to believe in yourself when you could see the fruits of your labor every day. But actually *running* a business that counted on other people choosing her venue above all others made her doubt everything.

"Your marketing campaigns are routine for this publicist, she knows what she's doing. Are you getting hungry?"

"Yeah, I guess. I'm not worried about her; I'm worried about me. I don't know if I know what I'm doing." A familiar fear of failure washed over her. "Why did I ever think I could run an inn?"

Lillian closed her laptop. "Because you want to, so you decided to. Becca, this isn't rocket science. You've thought this through, and your business plan is sound. Plus, you're passionate about it. You're sharing your love of the land and showing that luxury doesn't have to mean abusive planetary practices. You're selling sustainable luxury. You got this."

Becca didn't add she also just really wanted to know where home was, so she had built her own. Lillian's faith in her couldn't have come at a better time. The older woman had been a lifesaver.

"I don't know what I would do without you these past few months. You're why I have any bookings at all, your content writing and photos are works of art and your historical research may yet reroute that pipeline. You've added significantly to the historical record while at the same time translating it so regular people actually understand what you're talking about. You bring everything to life."

Lillian leaned over and squeezed Becca's hand. "My dear, your family brought me back to life."

Becca looked down as she remembered harsh memories. Finally she looked up. "You saved my brother when he was kidnapped. Sometimes I still get so scared. I know the chance of it happening again are like being struck by lightning, but sometimes lightning strikes twice."

"And now the Fischer brothers appear to have set up shop nearby. Are you sure it was one of them that stopped by before, asking for Tucker?"

Becca nodded. "I think so, but it's entirely possible my mind is playing tricks on me. I-I just don't know."

Lillian eyed her. "How are you holding up?"

Becca shrugged and picked up her pen, fiddling with it.

"Have you talked to Clint about it? He's got such a grounded outlook. That man nurtures just being in the same room."

Becca smiled. Lillian was right. Clint, though he had no family of his own, had been instrumental in their lives. Neighbors while growing up, they had all run to Clint when they were hurt or needed advice. He had as much compassion as he did integrity and grit. Becca and her brothers would have been lost growing up without him around.

"Not yet."

"How's Officer Chasseur?"

Becca dropped the pen cap. "Fine, I'm sure. Why do you ask?"

Lillian's smile was as wise as Eve's. "Darling, I've got eyes. Besides, he seems a stand-up chap, not to mention completely gorgeous."

"Lillian! What about Colt?"

"What about him? Your brother and I agree, you're totally smitten with your Officer Chasseur. He's a good guy, you should see what's there."

"He's not *my* Officer Chasseur," Becca grumbled.

"That's what I said about Colt and now look at us, we can't keep our hands off each other."

Becca jumped to her feet. "That's my cue to make lunch."

"Hit send first."

Becca made a face but tapped the laptop's keyboard, setting in motion a gamble she hoped would pay off.

"Feel better?"

"I feel like I'm going to puke."

"Nah, you're just over hungry. Let's go."

The two women headed to the kitchen and Becca asked, "What is it with you and food lately?"

"I enjoy your cooking," Lillian murmured.

"Said no one ever." Now *Tucker* was a proper chef. Why he had become a police officer when he could cook like an angel was beyond her. Colt and Gabe could hold their own in the kitchen, but Becca had learned the basics and left it at that.

"Must be the company then, and sorry about the over-share."

"There are worse things than being crazy for my brother."

Lillian paused. "I'm crazy for all of you. I meant it when I said your family brought me back to life. Thank you for that."

Becca was still getting to know Lillian. Originally from England and a war correspondent and MI6 courier, she had moved to Canada a few months prior after a major scandal that had involved international spies, the foreign affairs office, and her stellar career imploding. She had been covering the Calgary Stampede, arguably a hefty fall from her journalistic grace, and had been assigned to interview Becca's bull-riding brother, Colt. Becca had never seen her brother so happy. Lillian was gracious and lovely, if still a bit intimidating.

The two women enjoyed a simple meal of butternut squash bisque out of a Tetra Pac, and toasted French bread. "How about a coffee on the front porch before we get cooped back up in the office?"

"Sounds lovely. Could I ask for decaf, please?"

"I can't believe I'm saying this but good idea; caffeine has become a little too much like water for me these last few weeks." Lillian rose to help, but Becca waved her off. "I'll meet you on the front porch. Go enjoy the sunshine. There are blankets in the waterproof box out there. It's supposed to snow this weekend."

Lillian's eyes bugged. "It's September."

"Welcome to western Canada."

"Right. Blankets are routinely kept on the porches here. Got it." Lillian headed out the kitchen towards the front door.

The water hadn't even boiled before Lillian was back in the kitchen, her phone in her hands. "Are you expected a package?"

"What?" Becca turned from measuring coffee beans. "What's wrong?"

"There's a letter-size package on your front porch with no address. Are you expecting anyone to drop something off?" Lillian's voice was dead serious.

"No."

"I'm calling it in. Please don't panic but the last one of these I saw had a bomb in it."

# Chapter Eighteen

Jason sat in one of the detachment's briefing rooms, reading glasses perched on his nose. He was flipping through a large bound volume of the *Criminal Code of Canada*. The wall behind him was covered with information and images of the two living Fischer brothers and the crimes they were considered persons-of-interest in, as well as the three deceased brothers and their convictions, mostly theft, possession, assaults, and impeding investigations. A large smart TV hung at the end of the room and another monitor was suspended from the ceiling and blinked with updated tasks. Detective Tanner walked into the room. Becca's brother had made detective a few months ago but this was the first time Jason had worked with Tucker on a case. The RCMP coordinated with CPS when necessary. The Fischers made it necessary. A task force had been established to curtail the erupting violence in the area and the Fischers were the lead suspects.

"Tanner, glad you're here, man."

Tucker nodded, pulling his laptop out of his bag and putting it on the table. "Chasseur, what's the word?"

"Any idea why one Christopher Fischer would ring Becca's doorbell asking after you?"

"*What?*" Tucker let out a string of expletives. He dropped into a seat across from Jason. "Explain."

Jason filled Tucker in on what Becca had remembered, adding, "She thought it was Christopher Fischer based on the photos she's seen online, but wasn't sure. Whoever it was stopped by weeks ago and she admitted she had been preoccupied and wasn't really paying attention."

"It doesn't make any sense. Why would they come asking for me?"

"She did say there was a chance she was remembering wrong."

Tucker's usual smiling face was somber. "Ever wonder what happened?"

"What do you mean?"

Tucker pointed to the board. "Five brothers raised by their mom, a school teacher, until she died. Looks like breast cancer and she couldn't afford the trial pharmaceutical treatment option available. She died waiting for her traditional surgery appointment."

"Christ, that is awful. Wouldn't her insurance cover the trial treatment? I thought teachers had great health benefits?"

"She taught at a private school. No union. Her kids went there tuition-free, that might explain why she taught there. When she died they were booted out. Harsh." Tucker pointed at the board. "What's that? That's new."

Jason looked up. "One of the uni's found out Christopher Fischer and his mom were taking sommelier classes together before she died. They must have lied about his age if he joined her?"

Tucker shrugged. "I guess? I know how to pair wine, but I've never looked into sommelier classes." He turned to his laptop and pulled up a file.

"Anything in there about the father?" Jason had known the Fischer brothers' parents had died a long time ago, but he hadn't considered following the deeper family angle Tucker was tracing.

Tucker scanned the document. "He died five years before she did. He was a heavy machine mechanic. It says here he was crushed while on the job. The operator who caused it was high at the time. Dang, that's a one-two punch for the boys."

"The Fischer boys have spent fifteen years terrorizing a lot of people," Jason reminded him.

Tucker looked up. "I know, but most of the time there's a reason." He read further. "After their mom died they were placed with an aunt. She turned them into social services, said she couldn't handle them. They bounced around in the system. No one would take five boys, so they were split up. Looks like that's when they started the family business, to afford to stay together." Tucker whistled. "Hashtag after school special, you know? Besides the whole brutally violent part."

Jason looked over at Tucker over the rim of his glasses.

Tucker's mouth tipped into a grin. "Was it the hashtags? Because Becca says they're too much."

"Becca's right. Where the hell did you learn to talk like that? Because it wasn't in any police detachment."

Tucker shifted in his seat. "I watch a lot of cooking vlogs."

"Why?"

Pink actually creeped into his cheeks. "I like to cook, alright? A man's got to eat for fuck sake. And not all of us are content barely knowing how to boil water like my sister. That woman has no idea how to cook."

Jason thought Becca cooked just fine. "I'm not knocking it. Vlog away." He waited a heartbeat. "Hashtag after school specials stopped like a century ago."

Tucker threw a pen at him.

"What else does it say?"

"One brother took meth and drove his car off an overpass in Vancouver. He managed to kill himself and derail a commuter train." Tucker leaned forward, reading. "Wow, no train deaths. It looks like the second brother to die was killed in a shoot-out with a rival gang in a Toronto suburb. Four responding police officers were injured from people throwing...small appliances out the windows at them." Tucker looked up. "Is that for real?"

Jason nodded. "I've heard Toronto police have a complicated relationship with their community."

"Your idea of complicated sounds complicated." Tucker resumed reading. "The most recent Fischer brother to die overdosed on fentanyl in downtown Calgary. That was last year. The two brothers remaining, Christopher and Austin, run the family business. Looks like they work across Canada and the United States. Recent intel suggests they have entered the international scenes in France, Germany, Spain, South Africa, Peru, Chile, New Zealand and Australia."

Jason picked up the pen Tucker had thrown at him, thinking. "That's a lot of random drug references for a couple of brothers."

"Huh." Tucker looked thoughtful. "Those are all wine exporting countries."

"Is that a thing in the drug and arms world?" Jason had never heard a connection.

Tucker shrugged. "I've heard of pockets of violence in France associated with some vineyards."

"Seriously? It's just wine."

Tucker threw another pen at him. "Philistine, bite your tongue."

Jason thought he sounded like his sister.

"Whatever. Is there any drug connection with the family before the mom got sick?"

Tucker shook his head. "No, except their aunt was arrested for buying pain killers from an undercover police officer a week before she surrendered the boys."

"Is she still alive?" Jason asked. The background information he had been originally given had not mentioned the aunt.

Tucker typed on the laptop in front of him. "Yes. She is currently living in Florida after writing a tell-all on the five boys. It was made into a movie."

"Are you serious?"

"I couldn't make that shit up. That is seriously fucked up. I'm surprised they haven't offed her."

Jason frowned. Tucker had a point. He had tracked the Fischers for years. He was familiar with their list of assumed offenses; however the history of repeated and unjust abandonment was news.

"Was there ever a libel case?"

Tucker shook his head. "Doesn't look like it. The Fischers are mid-level players in the drug and guns scene and with an overly violent reputation when dealing with rival gangs or anyone who gets in their way."

"And?"

"And they've never been convicted, but have a tell-all book and documentary about their gruesome exploits? Something doesn't add up. Is their reputation earned or marketed?"

"You think their reputation is fabricated?"

"Maybe," Tucker answered slowly. "I doubt they'd be working with the woman that orchestrated the brothers being split up, but it's possible her tell-all gave them leverage to expand without actually earning their notoriety."

"And criminal types read true crime?" Jason wasn't convinced.

"No idea. Maybe they're just playing the hand life dealt them the best they can?"

"You voted liberal, didn't you?"

"You forgot the bleeding heart part. Or dirty hippie. I get that one a lot, too. Regardless, something's weird with these guys." Tucker tapped on the keyboard in front of him. "I'll check the call logs, see if anything pops for your warrant."

Jason liked Tucker. In another world where he wasn't constantly squaring off against his sister, they would have been friends.

Jason returned to looking through the *Criminal Code of Canada*.

Two uniformed officers walked into the war room. They nodded to both Jason and Tucker and sat down at one of the empty laptops. In a few minutes the printer in the corner started up.

Jason reread the passage he had found and slid the heavy book towards Tucker. "Think this would work? It has some parallels to the Frank case."

Tucker looked up from the call logs he was scrolling through. He read the passage. "That should fit to get a warrant for surveillance at least." Tucker looked up as one of the officers scooped up the freshly printed images and started to tape truck photos to the growing collection on the wall. "What's that?"

Jason glanced over before turning back to his warrant notes. "That was the message left on my truck the night I ran into your sister hightailing it from the Fischer brothers."

Tucker swore. Jason didn't bother to lookup. "Not the first time, won't be the last."

"You think it was the Fischers or someone working for them?"

Jason shrugged and started a new page of warrant notes.

Tucker prodded, "Doesn't that make you mad?"

Jason took off his reading glasses. "Of course it does, but that's irrelevant. Getting mad will burn me a hell of a lot more than whoever scratched that crap into the truck paint." Tucker looked ready to argue but Jason stopped him. "We'll catch whoever did it, or not. It's part of the job."

"That shit ain't right," Tucker grumbled.

"That's the job." Jason put his reading glasses back on. His phone pinged and he swore. "Your sister just got an unmarked package."

# Chapter Nineteen

"For the hundredth time, I didn't know you were working the case." Becca stood, arms crossed, inside her living room ready to throttle her brother.

Tucker threw up his hands in frustration. "Will someone talk some sense into my sister."

"Does it come with mind reading skills?" she snapped back. "Because the last time I checked, you worked for the city police, and we are nowhere near city limits. Hence the Mountie."

Jason cleared his throat. Both Tanner siblings turned and demanded in unison, *"What?"*

"The affection is commendable but mind if I ask a few more questions? Becca, last night you said one of the Fischer brothers came to your door last week?" He had his notebook and pen in hand.

"Yeah, he was asking about Tucker."

That set Tucker off again. "For the love of god, Becca, why didn't you tell me?"

Becca shouted back, "I said I forgot! At the time I thought he was one of your lame friends. If I had known he was an international arms and drug dealer, I would have mentioned it." She checked herself and in a lower decibel continued, "I was trying to get my stupid printer to work and just wanted the guy at the door gone. I didn't let him in, although he asked."

Lillian walked into the room carrying a tray laden with tea, cups and biscuits. "Tea anyone?" She set the tray down.

Jason cleared his throat. "Tell me about the package."

Lillian looked up from pouring. "Becca, do you want me to tell it?"

"Yes, please." Becca let herself drop onto the sofa next to Lillian but not before she heard Jason mutter, "A voice of reason, thank you."

"I heard that." Becca glared at Jason. She was more than a little put out her brother was doing the exact same thing.

For his part, Jason didn't roll his eyes. He merely said, "Let's listen to what she has to say, shall we?"

Becca crossed her arms. "He means stop yelling at me, Tucker."

"Pretty sure that's not, in fact, what he meant," Tucker fired back.

It was Lillian who cleared her throat this time. Both Becca and Tucker dutifully shut up. She handed Becca a cup of tea before starting. "Becca and I had been working all morning indoors in her private study setting up an international marketing campaign. We didn't hear or see anything unusual until a man stopped by asking if there were vacancies."

"Did you recognize him?" Jason asked.

Becca shook her head. "No. The only thing I remember really was that he had a Spanish accent."

Lillian hesitated, "I saw him through the front window but through the sheer curtains. I couldn't place him, but I might have seen him before. Becca told him she opened in a couple weeks. He did not accept her offer of recommendations for nearby alternatives. He left and we went back to her study to work. At lunch we decided to have our coffee outside on the porch, that's when we saw the envelope. Becca contacted you, Jason, and I called nine-one-one."

Jason was writing in his notebook. "Why did you call nine-one-one? Most people would have just picked it up and opened it."

Lillian answered, "The last unmarked package I saw had a motion-sensitive bomb in it."

Jason stopped writing. "I'm sorry, who are you, again?"

"Lillian Kensington." She said it formally, her English accent crisp. Becca knew that was Lillian's armor voice.

Tucker piped in, "You know, Colt's sweetheart."

"Could this package have been for you?" Jason asked.

Lillian waved off that idea. "All the people that wanted me dead are dead."

Jason stopped writing again. "Help me out here, guys."

"Don't worry, I didn't kill them." Lillian smiled and asked, "Tea?"

"I'm going to need a bit more context," Jason said, looking between the three of them.

Becca might have imagined Lillian's shoulder's drop, but she knew Lillian really didn't like talking about it. Becca filled in, "Lillian was a war correspondent and courier for MI6. A double agent, Fernando Martinez, did some really bad shit and tried to take Lillian down with him. He failed, she was not convicted of treason, he broke out of prison, chased her here, kidnapped Colt, tried to kill her, he died instead, the end. Can we move on?"

Jason's attention had been piqued. "You were there that night? Your niece called me the night Colt was kidnapped."

Lillian blinked and Becca would bet she was fighting not to cry.

"I was there, but I doubt my name made it into any reports."

"Why?"

"People with higher security clearance than I make those decisions."

Jason processed that. "Do you know a José Martinez?"

Lillian stared hard at him. "Fernando's older brother's name is José Martinez, why?"

Before Jason could answer, footsteps stomped on the front porch and two loud raps sounded before the door was flung open.

Colt, Becca's brother charged in. He immediately zeroed in on Lillian and swept over to her. He knelt next to the couch where Lillian was sitting ramrod straight. His wide hand spread protectively over Lillian's abdomen. "Are you okay? How's the baby? What happened?" He didn't seem to notice the room went silent at his declaration.

Lillian cradled Colt's bearded cheek in her hand. "We're fine, darling." She tilted her head pointedly. "So is your sister."

Colt swung his gaze to Becca, his eyes filled with worry.

"You guys are having a baby?" Becca asked, a little stunned. "I'm going to be an auntie?"

Colt looked at Lillian, who nodded. Becca swooped them both in an enormous hug. "I'm so happy for you two! Lillian, that's why you've been constantly eating! You're preggo!"

Tucker stuck out his hand to shake his brother's. "Wow, congratulations. Why didn't you tell us earlier?"

Becca looked at Lillian and smiled. "First trimester."

Lillian and Colt both nodded.

Tucker looked confused. "I don't know what that means." He turned to Colt. "How do you know what that means?"

"Kinda my world now. You would be shocked at how much I've learned about babies recently."

"Congratulations," Jason said. He had a thoughtful look on his face and Becca wondered if he ever wanted children.

Another knock sounded on the door. Before Becca rose to answer it, Jason moved. "I can get it."

A uniformed constable handed Jason an envelope and a small report before leaving.

"What's that? That's not the package," Becca said.

Jason scanned the small report he was holding before answering, "The original has been cleared of any biohazard or incendiary concerns but has been taken as evidence." He scanned further before looking at Lillian and Colt. "Any idea how it has your fingerprints on it?"

Colt looked confused. "What's in it?"

Jason slid a stack of photocopies out of the envelope he was holding. He laid them out on the coffee table.

Lillian's teacup made a thud as she nearly dropped it setting it down. "Those look like our research notes that were stolen when Colt was kidnapped." Lillian grabbed Colt's knee. He wrapped a protective arm around her and dropped a kiss on the top of her head. She visibly relaxed in his arms.

"What research?" Jason asked.

"We looked into the historical record of Becca's land."

"My dad's land." Becca clarified, darting a look at Jason. She moved the tea tray to a side table to make more room. Jason didn't look happy. Becca tried not to let her hands shake when she spread the copies of notes, photos, academic journal copies and marked up maps out across the coffee table. She could feel the ice rolling off Jason. With all of the recent tension and possible danger, she had forgotten all about this research. Jason was going to be pissed.

Lillian scanned the items. "This doesn't make sense. These are Colt and my research notes, but Fernando was the one who stole all of this when he kidnapped Colt. He's dead. Who could have possibly gotten their hands on it from him? All of his crew were either deported or dead, too." She looked at Jason. "Why did you ask who José was?"

"He came across our radar." Jason made some notes.

"To my knowledge, Fernando and José did not get along." Lillian paused. "Do you believe otherwise?"

Jason shook his head. "Did this Fernando have anything to do with arms dealing?"

Lillian nodded. "In Europe. I hadn't heard anything about him expanding into North America, though."

Becca dared a look at Jason. He was still frowning. He stepped forward and picked up a photocopy from a book that had a grainy picture of an old man. "What is all this for exactly?"

The room went quiet. The tension between Becca and Jason was palpable. Becca met Jason's hard gaze head on. "There is a proposed pipeline project. I want it to avoid the Frost River tributaries. We were looking for something that would flag at least a more in-depth assessment."

"Why?" Jason's voice had an edge.

"Besides the obvious of protecting heritage and environmental resources?" she asked. "There is also the practical. No one will want to stay at an eco-inn with a pipeline bisecting the supposed pristine part. We want them to reroute."

"Those tributaries are on the land I wanted back in my family."

"Yes." Becca didn't know what else to say.

Jason held up the grainy picture. "So, your Hail Mary is using *my* family's history? This is my grandfather." He swung his gaze to Tucker. "Det. Tanner, can you finish up here?"

Tucker looked startled at Jason's glacial tone. "Sure, you need to be someplace?"

"Anywhere but here. You're now on babysitting duty." He dropped the photocopy on the pile and walked out.

# Chapter Twenty

Jason heard the front door open behind him; he made it three steps down the porch stairs before Becca flew in front of him. She put her hand on his chest to stop him.

He kept walking.

Facing backwards, she misplaced her foot on the next step and started to fall.

He grabbed the hand on his chest, catching her weight before she could tumble.

They stared at each other.

When she had her balance, he dropped her hand and sidestepped around her on the stairs and jumped down the rest. He nearly made it to his cruiser before she wedged herself between him and the car, her hand back on his chest.

"Will you just listen to me?"

He gave a cold laugh. "Jokes on me, again. Hell, I thought we were actually getting along."

"We were, we are!"

"No, you're using my history to protect your investment. That's not getting along, that's business. That's *self-interest*. You're just like your father."

Becca recoiled. "I am nothing like my father."

"Just keep telling yourself that, maybe someday it'll be true. Now move, I need to get back to work."

"I'm not," she insisted.

"Prove it," Jason challenged.

Becca stared, unable to. From the look on her face, she knew it, too. "Go to hell."

"Told you, I live there. Your dad made sure of it."

She looked ready to say something but changed her mind. She just stepped aside. That pissed him off as much as anything. "You never fight when the going actually gets tough, do you?"

"That's not fair."

"A lot of things aren't fair; I've never considered the truth one of them. Why am I not surprised you do?"

"I don't want to fight, Jason."

There it was. That's what always stuck. Years ago, he had been ready to fight for her, regardless of her dad's threats. He had hoped she would be willing to fight for him, too, fight for them. But she wasn't. She had shot down his foolish hopes with slicing clarity. When would he finally accept she would never care enough to fight for him? It dawned on him he did have a type. He needed someone who would be in his corner. Becca wasn't even in her own corner.

She gave him one more long look before she walked up her front porch stairs and in the front door. She didn't look back, and he realized that Becca didn't actually give a fuck if he saw her point. A few token protests, sure. When he didn't come to heel, she moved on quick enough.

Jason got in the police cruiser. It took everything he had not to slam the door. Becca had enough family, why did she have to use his? He had stood in her living room, watching as she was surrounded by her supportive, loving siblings while she leveraged his family history to protect her investment. He had the moral high ground here, so why did he feel so shitty?

His phone pinged with an incoming email. Attached was the digital file of what was spread across Becca's trendy coffee table. It had been a mistake he received it; it wasn't considered associated with the task force. Protocol dictated he delete the file.

Jason scrolled through it instead. He stopped scrolling when he saw a map and enlarged the image. It took only moments for him to recognize the location. Pocketing his phone, Jason started the car and headed back to the detachment. He knew why they hadn't found anything.

They were looking in the wrong spot.

# Chapter Twenty-One

Christopher Fischer watched the unfolding drama through high powered binoculars and a bank of wide windows. He was set up in a copse of trees that provided the necessary cover and site lines. He adjusted the ear bud playing the live audio surveillance feed coming from the inn's front room. It wasn't often he was surprised. Today had been full of them.

The Tanner woman had called the police when she'd found the package he had left. She didn't move or touch it. In Christopher's experience civilians lived in blissful ignorance until it was too late. Becca's friend Lillian Kensington was no civilian and was proving to be an unfortunate wealth of information. That's how things got messy fast; when the wrong people knew too much. Lillian had been there the night Colt was kidnapped and Fernando died, but everything had happened fast and in dim light. Would she recognize him or Austin?

A commotion drew his attention. Officer Chasseur was storming out of the house with the Tanner woman running after him. Christopher hadn't bugged the front porch so he couldn't hear what they were saying but the tension between the two was palpable even from his distant hiding spot.

"What is it?" Austin, Christopher' younger brother, asked without looking up from his laptop. He was sitting cross-legged on the ground at the back of the copse of trees, his laptop resting atop his legs. He looked out of place. Still focused on his screen and periodically punching in numbers, Austin asked, "Those two sleeping together, yet?"

"No, they're not banging on the porch, they're fighting."

Austin pulled out one ear bud and held it up. "This shit's better than TV. That Lillian chick is knocked up."

Christopher ignored him; that detail was currently irrelevant. Until it wasn't.

"We should bug her phone, too, if you can swing it."

"Becca or Lillian's? Because I can't tell if you're creeping on them or think they have intel."

Austin flung a rock at him. "Fuck you, I didn't mean like that."

Christopher easily sidestepped the projectile. "The Tanner woman does need a bit more pressure."

"You gonna kill her when it's done?"

The nonchalance of his brother's question bothered him. Christopher was only as violent as he had to be to protect his family and assets. "Maybe. I don't know." An uncomfortable possibility rose. "Seriously, you're not sweet on her, are you?" That could complicate things.

"What? No, all I meant was don't you ever get sick of blood?"

Christopher stilled. "You want out?"

His younger brother looked up and asked in disbelief, "And do what?"

"You're good at chemistry and prototype guns."

"With zero experience I can speak of unless I want to get arrested. Who am I going to work for, the fucking government? Cooking drugs or bombs for them is not exactly getting out of the business. Believe me, not the first time I've looked at my limited choices. Fuck you, anyway. What's with the twenty questions?"

Christopher looked at his brother, careful to keep his face neutral. "You know we need this to work. This will change everything."

"Yeah, I know." His brother popped the ear bud back in and stared at the screen on his lap.

Christopher hadn't realized how on the edge his brother was. He would be wise to pay closer attention; now wasn't the time to wish what might have been. Hell, he hadn't chosen this path, either. Life had dumped it on him, and he had dumped it on his little brother.

As the silence stretched the tension built between them. His phone vibrated with an incoming email. Christopher pulled out his phone and swore. "Why am I being offered an interview for the sommelier position at Becca Tanner's inn?"

Austin glared back. "Because you're a trained sommelier. Take the fucking interview instead of spending the rest of your life fucking gutting people for a living. Shit, for the older brother sometimes you're really fucking dense."

"That was one time!" Christopher reread the email, trying to imagine himself in the role.

"Think she'll get the pipeline rerouted or postponed?"

Christopher looked up. "I don't care as long as she

gets it off our line. She's certainly motivated enough for her own business reasons."

Austin added sarcastically, "And that's why she's still alive."

They needed that crown land empty. Christopher wasn't sure how to trigger Becca Tanner into a more robust opposition to the pipeline, but he hoped his package of historical maps and photos might spur her into action. She was an anomaly to him. The women in his world were controlled through addiction and fear. They partied, used, sold, and turned tricks. Once, when he was a lot younger, he had tried to help one. He had witnessed a young sex trade worker getting knocked around by a john. He had never considered himself a do-gooder, not since his mom had died, and his aunt had left them to the system. But it didn't feel right to let that shit go. It had felt good to break the guy's jaw until he felt the hot sting of metal in his back. The prostitute had stabbed him, screaming at him that now she wasn't going to get paid.

He and his brothers hadn't grown up on the street, but they were fast learners. He hadn't helped another since.

Christopher lifted the binoculars again, but no new movement interrupted the inn's front yard.

"We can still go to one of the First Nations. They'd have a better chance of getting a pipeline sidelined, or at least rerouted."

"Too risky. Murder on a reserve still barely makes the news, but a murder of someone on a reserve that could possibly be linked to a pipeline? That shit would be a media field day. No, I think the death of an over-mortgaged, lonely, workaholic woman would be much easier to explain. No one would suspect that kind of woman would have anything to do with a pipeline's approval or cancelation. Remember, kill when necessary—"

*"And executing good planning makes it unnecessary.* I got it. You've been spouting that shit since before my balls dropped."

The two went back to their uneasy silence. Austin's laptop started quietly beeping.

"Turn the fucking sound off," Christopher snapped.

Austin looked up, dazed. "We actually did it."

Christopher lowered his binoculars. "For real this time?"

Austin shot him a annoyed look before pointing to his screen. "Fuck you. Can't you get excited? The math finally works. We still need to confirm the potency of the field tests match the projections, but we did it. Bro, we did it."

It wouldn't bring any of their brothers back, but it should bring a crushing financial blow to the fuckers whose drugs killed two of them. "Good. It'll be fun to watch these dominoes fall." His phone rang. "You know Bruce Tanner?"

"Isn't that Becca's dad's name?" Austin asked.

Christopher took the call.

"You have five seconds."

"Oh, I think you'll want more than that. This is Bruce Tanner." When Christopher didn't say anything, the guy continued, "I own the land you seem to have taken an interest in."

It was Crown Land, but Christopher didn't correct the dipshit. "And?"

"I can make your pipeline headache go away or get bigger. Your choice. How much are you willing to pay for it to go away?"

Christopher had few personal rules. Never allowing him or his brother to be intimidated was one of them. Neither was revealing his hand too early because of pride. Besides, if he had to, he would kill the guy. "How much was your other offer?"

"How'd you—" The older man sputtered before catching himself.

Too late. Christopher smirked. It had been awhile, but being underestimated made things way easier. "Give me a number."

"I don't have to give you anything," Bruce Tanner snapped. He hung up.

Christopher snorted. Chump. A professional would never lose their cool like that, especially in front of an enemy. Arrogant fuck. Bruce Tanner would not last long playing with the big boys.

"What was that all about?" Austin asked.

"I think Becca's dad has an offer to take us down. The dick wanted us to counter the offer, but I think I flustered him."

"Of course you did, you're an asshole."

"Only when I have to be."

"You shot that guy's kneecaps last month."

"What choice did I have? He ran off with our product before paying." It's not like Christopher enjoyed that part of the job. And the creep lived.

Austin rolled his eyes. "He was still in the parking lot. You're an asshole."

Christopher shrugged. His brother may have a point. Christopher was getting more violent.

"Who could be Bruce's other offer, the Spaniard is dead?" Austin asked.

"Double check Bruce Tanner isn't the player, would you? Becca seems innocent, and pliable enough. We just have to gauge when to apply enough pressure. She'll break."

Christopher almost felt sorry for her. Nothing on their surveillance indicated Becca knew anything about what her father was into—and with that guy's closet of skeletons, he was up to something. Becca's dysfunctional relationship with her dad wasn't Christopher' problem; but finding out how big of a problem Bruce Tanner was going to be was.

# Chapter Twenty-Two

B ecca picked up another towel and snapped it aggressively before folding it.

Her mom tsked. "Now dear, you'll give yourself frown lines."

"Not really caring at the moment, mom." Becca snapped another towel. They were standing in one of the upstairs guest bedrooms folding new towels for the guests she hoped would come pouring in. Her mom had shown up unexpected with breakfast burritos and smoothies.

Samantha frowned herself, but picked up another towel and folded it with a significantly more dainty hand.

"Sorry mom. You're trying to help, I know." Five days had passed since Jason's damning words had sliced a hole in her conscience. Was he right? She had always thought of history as the responsibility of everyone and belonging to no one. It had never occurred to her that access of history—particularly that many generations past—would be limited to blood descendants. Becca gently added her folded towel to the tidy stack and picked up another from the basket. "How have you been? I've been so busy lately we haven't really had much time to hang out."

"Yes, well, I hear you have time to spend with your father."

Becca noticed her mom was folding with considerably more force. "What are you talking about? I haven't seen him in weeks."

"I overheard Shelly, that waitress at the diner mention the three of you were in last week for lunch."

"I haven't eaten out in months. Who was supposed to be our third?"

Samantha dropped the towel she had been folding and fumbled to retrieve it. "I've decided I won't speak her name."

Becca's gut tightened. Five years later and her parent's divorce still had aftershocks. "Mom, Shelly is mistaken. I wasn't in the cafe last week, let alone with dad and his, um, the third one."

"Shelly has no reason to lie."

Becca waited for her mom to look before she reminded her, "Neither do I."

Samantha harrumphed. "Which chef did you decide on, again?"

"His name is Roman. He was out of Vancouver, then Whistler. I'm lucky he accepted. His credentials are incredible, if a bit tarnished. I still need a sommelier, though. I don't know wine well enough."

"Won't Roman do that kind of stuff?"

"To attract the demographic I want to, they will expect a proper sommelier and wine cellar to match. I need world class food and he needs a second chance."

"What does that mean?"

Becca stopped folding towels, hesitating. "The only

reason I scored Roman is because he is a recovering alcoholic and addict. No one wanted to touch him in BC, he's burned too many bridges."

"Do you think that's a good idea?"

"I hired him, so yes, I think he's a good idea."

"I'm not comfortable with an addict living here, Becca."

"He'll be in the staff dorm. Mom, I wouldn't have hired him if I thought he'd be an issue."

"Staff dorm, please, that's a cabin with bunkbeds."

Becca pivoted. "Lillian has given me the contacts for a few sommeliers that might be able to consult a few times a year. I got a few resumes emailed, too."

"That sounds nice dear, but folks aren't that choosy out here."

Becca clamped down on her impatience. "Yes, but my target demographic is."

Samantha flipped over the discreet label on the towel. "One hundred percent organic cotton, for a towel. Are you kidding me?"

Becca snatched the towel out of her mom's hands. "Yes. Welcome to eco-tourism."

Samantha tsked again. "You kids spend money on ridiculous things. When does your housekeeper start? Opening weekend is a couple weeks away, isn't it?"

"Eighteen days. She's able to start in a week." Until Becca knew if she actually had something to worry about with the Fischer Brothers, she did not want any of her help starting early.

"You could use her help now."

"I know that. But she's the one I want and that's when she can start."

Samantha harrumphed. "Seems to me like you are forgetting you are the boss."

"I'm not forgetting anything. I just have a different way to do things than you."

"Or your father." Samantha laughed. It wasn't kind. "He'd have a fit if he knew your housekeeper was setting her own start date."

"Dad and I barely talk, not much chance of him having one thing or another to say about it." Their relationship had iced further when Lillian had come into their lives. Her contacts had uncovered a possible connection between Bruce Tanner and the man who had shot Gabe five years ago.

"How is your father and his trollop?"

"I literally just said I never talk to him." Becca folded another towel. She knew it had been a bad idea accepting her mom's help.

"Yes, I suppose you did." Samantha was quiet. "How are his treatments?"

"Fake."

"I don't understand."

"He faked having cancer. Before you ask, I have no idea why. He doesn't actually talk to any of us. If we hear boo, it's from Meredith. You have every reason to hate her, but she's trying a hell of a lot harder than dad is." She didn't add *or you typically do.*

"He never tried very hard. I am sorry you kids had to deal with that."

Becca's head snapped up. Samantha finished folding the last towel of the load. "Where do you want these?"

"Linen closet at the end of the hall please." Becca reached for the next laundry basket piled high with sheets and pillow cases.

When Samantha returned she handed Becca something small, about the size of a small bumblebee, and black. It had different compartments and two oblong holes. "I found this on the floor in the hallway. What is it?"

Becca accepted the small object and turned it around several times. "I have no idea. Thanks, and thanks for your help."

The smile Samantha gave Becca was real and reminded her of the woman her mom had been years ago; it was all too rare these days. "Of course dear, I said to myself, 'how is that child going to get all that work done by her lonesome?' Why you don't even have a man to help, not that your father ever helped me out around the house."

"Mom, don't start—" Becca would never tell her mom that apparently Bruce helped Meredith around their house.

But Samantha had kept going. "Sure your father would pay for help. I do remember when that Chasseur boy had come up to house asking if we wanted our driveway shoveled for five dollars. Can you imagine? That drive was huge. Who works that cheap? Your father said yes, but then sent Tucker, Colt and Gabe to play in the front yard to watch him work. When they tried to help him, your dad sent them back inside. Then he shorted the kid."

Becca blanched. "Do you mean Jason Chasseur?"

Samantha waved her hand. "Yes, that's right. He's a Mountie now, isn't he?" Samantha's demeanor turned coy. "He certainly grew up. I'd like a chance to watch him play in my front yard, or back yard, or my—"

"Stop."

"What? Can't a woman have fun?"

"Not like that."

"Sounds like you're sweet on him." Samantha reached for a sheet. "Your father would be livid his meddling didn't stick."

Becca picked up the other end of the flat sheet and they team-folded. "What are you talking about?"

"Don't you remember? When you kids were in high school and that Chasseur boy came sniffing around, your father told him in no uncertain terms you weren't interested."

"Mom, what are you talking about? Jason and I never went out in high school." Not that she hadn't desperately wanted to.

"That's because your father made sure of it. He can be very nasty when he wants to be, always has." Samantha took the folded edge from Becca and crisply ran her hand to flatten the material even more. She laid it on the bed and reached for another one.

"But you married him, surely he must have been different then?"

The look Samantha gave Becca was pitying. "You kids,

you're too idealistic, your plans too grandiose. I grew up dirt poor. Your father was my meal ticket out. He was ambitious and shrewd enough to pull it off. And he did."

"You guys didn't love each other?"

Samantha gave a cold laugh. "Oh I thought we did. I was the happiest girl when I walked down that aisle. The man of my dreams *and* he had money. I was living my happily ever after. Two hours later I walked in on him with one of the bridesmaids. Cliché, right? Five hours later and with everyone liquored up I heard I had been a dare meant to piss off his own father."

"Oh mom—"

"No, it made me stronger, tougher. I came from nothing, just poor ranching stock in a time when the giants of ranching were making something of themselves. Now my family has money from oil, but then we were squandering. I am who I am today because of your father. He might not be nice, but he's a hell of a teacher. And I took him to school in the divorce." She gave an unladylike snort. "He's either actually in love with her, or she has something he wants. That weakness was my leveraging point in court."

Becca was trying to process all of the revelations. "Have you ever been in love, mom?"

That stopped Samantha short. "I stopped believing in love a long time ago."

"Then why do you ride me to find a man?" Becca had naively believed her mother didn't want her to grow old alone, or something innocent, like in those cheesy movies.

"Because the men have the power, dear. When you control a man, you control that power. It gets our foot in the game we never would have been invited to as a woman."

"Do you really believe that?"

"Of course I do, I've lived it my whole life."

# Chapter Twenty-Three

Jason watched the paramedic close the ambulance door. He turned to Officer Cooper. "Escort the ambulance to the hospital."

"By myself?" asked the rookie officer, ever mindful of following orders but with a definite charge in his voice.

Jason nodded. "Officer Yang is riding in the back of the ambulance if you need her, and you can always call me if need be."

Officer Cooper nodded eagerly, but then hesitated. "This was a bad one, wasn't it?"

Jason nodded. "We got here in time."

"Sometimes we won't, though, will we?"

"No, sometimes we won't." Every time Jason was on a call like this one he pictured the hell his mom went through. After his parents' divorce, she had two violent boyfriends. "You go ahead. I'll be right behind you guys."

Jason watched as the ambulance, followed close behind by Cooper, pulled out of the rural driveway. The victim inside would make it. This time.

The yard was now quiet. He was alone. It had been an ugly domestic assault, violent and way too common. Calls like these always left him feeling raw. He swiped at his face before getting into his own cruiser. Four more calls had come in. He radioed in and was dispatched. Sirens on, he switched gears and headed to his next call. It would be at least twenty minutes before he could get there. He'd find out then if it would be soon enough.

His cell phone rang over Bluetooth. It was Becca. She had called him every day like clockwork over the last five days. Ever since he realized her angle, and called her out on it. He resisted the urge to throw his phone and simply punched the decline button instead. Five seconds later it rang again. He swore until he saw it was Tucker. He clicked it on. "Chasseur here."

"Jason, it's Tucker."

"I'm not babysitting your sister tonight. Find a new idiot."

"What? No, we have a new problem. Wait, why not?"

"Why'd you call, Tucker?" Jason knew he sounded impatient but he had had a restless night of little sleep followed by hell's own shift.

There was a charged pause before Tucker pushed on. "Remember when Lillian said everyone that wanted her dead, already was?"

"Yeah."

"The Spanish double-agent's brother cleared customs in Toronto five days ago." Thoughts of Becca exploded into Jason's mind. Why hadn't he answered any of her calls? "What are you talking about? What does Becca's friend Lillian have to do with a Spanish double-agent?"

"Are you kidding? Only the biggest bust in Alberta history and the only one we've gotten to team up with CSIS and MI6 for. And you actually met the woman in the eye of the storm less than a week ago. Don't you read the national newsletter?"

"No, why, do you? I didn't work the case. If it was that important it should have been in a memo, not a newsletter. And your sister's recap of Lillian's past was hardly a debrief." He had read the cryptically taciturn original report, but it hadn't mentioned Lillian at all, and any reference to an international spy was hazy at best. Her niece, Sophie Kensington and Craig Cameron had called him — not nine-one-one — the night Colt was kidnapped, but Jason had been on a series of other horrific calls. After, he had followed up, but Colt was safe and the single perpetrator deceased. Jason had dropped it.

"You're impossible," Tucker said before filling Jason in on the headline-making case.

Jason connected the dots. "Let me get this straight. Lillian was a British war correspondent who also couriered various communications for Scotland Yard and MI6. She had no idea she was being seduced and duped by a Spanish double-agent trying to intercept the information she would carry back and forth. When the spy was exposed, she was cleared of any wrong-doing. But the spy escaped and tracked her down here, in Canada last month. *He* was the one to kidnap Colt, died, and his brother just cleared customs?" And stole Lillian and Colt's research that included Jason's family history.

"Yes."

"Why didn't you just say so?"

There was a long pause. "See now, I can't tell if you're kidding or not."

Jason checked his rear-view mirror. "I'm kidding."

"Right. Anyway, we have limited intel on the Spanish agent's brother. Get this, the guy has diplomatic immunity."

"Why did he say he was here?"

"Pleasure. The timing could just be a coincidence, but that's hard to believe, though. The tabloid coverage in Europe was relentless. I think everyone and their dog know Lillian Kensington is in Canada. She comes from an incredibly well-connected family. She was a big deal even before she was tried—and exonerated—for treason."

"The rest of the world thinks Canada is Toronto, Montreal, and Vancouver. Do you think this Martinez guy is traveling from Toronto to here? Is this a credible threat or are you seeing problems where there aren't any?"

"You didn't let me finish. There's another guy. We think a man named Del Fiennes used José Martinez's credentials to get in moments before the real José came through customs. Fiennes is a known arms dealer with suspected drug connections. I'm sure he'll look at a map."

Jason straightened. Both José Martinez and Del Fiennes had pulled patent information on the Fischers. "Guns and drugs, that sounds like the same circles as the Fischers. Why did Border Services allow him in?"

"That's the really weird part. There was no flag on José Martinez's name. When Del Fiennes used José Martinez's credentials, he looked legit, and no one questioned him. Moments later, when the real José Martinez tried to clear customs, he was picked up."

"The guy with diplomatic immunity was picked up? What did he do?"

"He waited patiently. How weird is this? Who waits patiently with border security when they have that sort of clout?"

Tucker had a point. "What's his status?"

"He's an unknown. His credentials don't come with an explanation, but his brother died last month trying to take out my soon-to-be sister-in-law and kidnap my brother. In Canada."

This shit was worse than trying to follow a movie. "I'm almost at my call, anything else?"

"It was the head of Jordemorden Central Security and Intelligence Center that reported the buzzer on Fiennes — none of our databases flagged him."

"What the hell is a Jordemorden?"

"It's a where, not a what. Jordemorden is a country off the coast of Denmark. The Danes and French fought over it for centuries until two royal kids apparently fell in love with each other and ran off together before their parents could marry them off to anyone else. The couple received their own country as a wedding present."

"How in the world do you know that?"

"Can I get a, *what's the Internet for a thousand* please?"

Jason gripped the wheel. Tucker had Becca's sense of humor.

When Jason didn't respond, Tucker continued, "The Jordemorden guys called our Border Services a few minutes ago. It gets worse. Del Fiennes — the guy impersonating José Martinez — the details in his record of entry are gone."

"What do you mean gone?"

"Empty. Zero. There's nothing there, it's all gone. Border Services was hacked."

There were too many maybes and all of them bad. Was Del Fiennes or José Martinez after Lillian or the Fischers, and if so, was Becca in any collateral danger?

He heard Tucker clicking away on the other end of the line. "Looks like both of our services are in the loop, you should have gotten your update."

"I was just at a call and nearly at my next. I haven't seen any updates yet. Do you know where Becca is now?"

"Hang on. I'll track her phone."

"Does she know you track her phone?"

"Of course not. I connected our phones when she ran after you on the porch."

Jason slowed and turned onto the next Range Road. His call was less than a kilometer away.

It was Tucker's turn to swear. "She's at my dad's and Meredith's."

"So?"

"My dad likes to engage in psychological gunfights...and he might have had something to do with Gabe getting shot five years ago."

Jason swore. *"What?"*

"I know, our family is seriously fucked. Bruce doesn't know we suspect anything. Becca's smart, she'll stay safe. It could all just be nothing."

Jason gripped the steering wheel tighter. "Didn't a John Doe get shot at his wedding a couple months ago?

What the fuck is your dad into?"

Tucker answered quietly, "I don't know, man. I don't know."

Jason blew out a breath. "Can you warn Lillian that Fernando Martinez's brother is in Canada?"

"I called Colt. Lillian had already been apprised by her government." Tucker paused. "I've never had international law enforcement types give a heads-up on a case before."

Jason had. "It's never good news when they do."

Fuck. How big was this?

# Chapter Twenty-Four

Becca pulled up to her dad's sprawling Calgary house. This particular urban neighborhood reflected sophistication and privilege. She tried not to shudder at the over manicured trees. She loved gardens, but these were trophies. There was a difference.

She stepped down from her truck and checked her hands to make sure they were clean. She had meant to change before making the drive into town, but she had lost track of time. There was no way she was getting stuck in rush hour traffic to change clothes for her father. She figured this would take no more than ten minutes, or her dad would throw her out in five. Becca didn't think she could stomach anything longer.

She rang the doorbell. As she waited, she wasn't sure what she should do with her hands. She wasn't used to vibrating with this much anger. She didn't have to wait long. A tall, graceful woman answered the door. She was wearing country club chic, a coordinated tracksuit with matching runners. Becca would bet three months' mortgage those shoes had never ran anywhere.

"Can I help you?" Meredith's voice was melodious without a hint of disapproval.

Becca stared at the older woman. She wasn't sure what to expect, but not being recognized wasn't it. "I need to speak with my father."

Meredith paused a half second, then recognition dawned. Her smile seemed genuine when she graciously opened the door wider. "Rebecca, of course. Do come in." The older woman saw Becca settled in what could only be described as a parlor before saying, "I'll just get your father, dear. Would you care for a cup of tea or coffee?"

"No, thank you."

Meredith paused at the doorway. "It is nice to see you."

Becca managed an uncomfortable smile. When Meredith left to find her father, Becca let out an exhale. She was in the lion's den. The angular dark gray chair she was sitting on was more trendy than comfortable. Becca's eye was drawn to the geometric designs on the throw pillows. The pattern matched the curtains. This was what a show home looked like. Her heart sank a bit. She had consulted an interior designer for her inn, but she hadn't asked for trendy. Her very expensive furnishings were ranching meets boho. Well, to her they were expensive, to her dad and Meredith, it was probably what they spent in this single room. Two true crime books were on one of the end tables and the only personal items in the room.

"Becca, what a surprise." Her father, Bruce, stood in the doorway.

*But not a nice surprise.*

"Dad, you look well." For someone who faked having cancer.

Meredith came up behind Bruce. "Yes, he does. Would you two like any refreshments?"

Becca wondered if a scotch counted.

"Coffee please," Bruce said.

"I'm fine, really," Becca repeated.

Meredith kissed Bruce lightly on his cheek before heading to the back of the house. No doubt that was where the kitchen was. Becca had never been past the front door before.

Bruce crossed the room and settled back on a gray loveseat. Becca noticed the geometric patterns were also on the rug. "I see you didn't dress up, but must you wear barn clothes to town?"

"Yes, dad, I was working. Taking time to change for you would put me in rush hour traffic. You always told us to work smart."

Bruce looked cross. "Why are you here?"

"Jason Chasseur. Did you buy the old Chasseur place out from under him?" Becca realized she was holding her breath.

"What are you asking about that piece of trash for?"

"Name calling, really?" Becca asked, before Meredith stood in the doorway again. "Darling, do you want de-caf?"

"Of course," Bruce smiled indulgently.

Before Meredith could leave, Becca called out to her, "Is it common for your social circles to call those with less money *trash*?"

The older woman's hand flew to her chest. "Why of course not dear. Who said that?"

"Your husband, just now."

"Don't listen—" Bruce stammered.

Meredith looked at Bruce with considerably more

backbone than Becca had ever seen her show. "Fix it," she said firmly before turning and walking back out.

"Now look at what you did." Bruce accused.

"Told on you with your latest? Yeah, I'm a real ass."

Bruce was indignant. "Meredith is my wife."

"She's got more steel than we thought, good for her. I believe she said *fix it*. Answer my question, did you know Jason Chasseur had placed an offer on the land?"

Bruce remained silent.

"What's your beef with him, anyway? And what did you tell him in high school?"

"I did what any father would, kept him away from you."

"What are you talking about?"

Bruce's smile was unconscionably cold and for the first time, Becca felt uneasy, not simply annoyed at her father.

"I told him I'd have his father arrested if he went anywhere near you again. I did anyway, with pleasure."

Becca was appalled. "That's outrageous, even for you."

"What was I supposed to do? He kept coming around and you were such a silly little girl, spouting your environmental and human rights nonsense. You were the worst kind of impressionable. It was only a matter of time before he knocked you up."

Her father's words were a sharp slap. With dead calm she spoke, "I wasn't sexually active in high school, you ass. When exactly did you knock up Doris Stone? She's quite a bit younger than you. Was she still in high school?" Becca, Colt and Tucker had only just found out about Tanner Stone, her half-brother. Poor Gabe had accidentally found out when he was a kid. Bruce had terrorized Gabe into keeping quiet for years.

Bruce paled. "Quiet!" He glanced furtively at the hallway Meredith had disappeared down. "How did you find out?"

Anger flashed in Becca, stronger than any unease. "About the half-brother you hid our entire life? Tanner was what, too real for you? A living reminder that your choices impact other people? Hell, created other people you never claimed? Hard to keep a secret like that."

"You have no right."

"Of course, she does." Meredith stood in the doorway. She set the tray she had been carrying down with crisp force. Her eyes sparked with anger when she looked at Bruce. When she turned to Becca, they softened. "Rebecca dear, you probably should have this." Meredith handed her an opened envelope. It had a pipeline company logo in the corner. "If you wouldn't mind, Bruce and I have a lot to talk about. Including how not to insult women. Would you mind too terribly much if we cut your visit short?"

"You read my mind." Becca reached for her purse. She looked up, meeting Meredith's gaze. "Thank you."

Meredith only nodded.

Bruce eyed the envelope. "Why did you give her the pipeline notification? *I* own that land."

"No, *we* own the land. The three of us. She's the one actually using it. It impacts her the most. Besides, you will be too busy explaining why you didn't care to share you have another son."

Becca slipped out the front door. She wasn't sure if she was more angry or hurt. She always felt like such a fool after seeing him. She kept hoping her father would come around. That he'd care. Love her. She wiped at her wet eyes. Fuck him. She and her brothers had Clint. He cared. That's all people needed, someone to give a damn.

Meredith had surprised her. That brought an unexpected smile. She had always judged Meredith harshly. Becca had her reasons. The woman had chosen to have an affair with Bruce. It was the final straw that had split her parents. Shattered Becca's world. She had been looking for home ever since. Had even built her own, goddamnit.

Becca climbed into her truck. Meredith wasn't the root of her family's dysfunction. Her parents' relationship had never been solid. They weren't actually even particularly nice people. If not Meredith, it would have been some other woman. Or man. Her mom could have gotten fed up and strayed. That thought made her sad. Her mom had never been loved by a man. That shit wasn't right.

Becca remembered the letter. It wasn't good news.

# Chapter Twenty-Five

"*S it.*" Meredith had never taken that tone with another living person in her life. She had never felt like this before in her life; quite frankly she was beside herself. Becca's visit had shaken her. She knew Bruce could be selfish, even narcissistic, but recently his actions had been firing alarm bells.

Bruce obediently sat on the plush living room furniture. The room was bathed in the early setting sun. The golden light was at odds with her rising anger. She was so mad she didn't know where to start.

He leaned back and rested his arm across the back of the couch, completely at ease. "Darling, it was a mistake. One I paid eighteen years for. I did my part. It's over. I don't know why you are allowing yourself to get so worked up. Becca is like that, always needling where she doesn't belong."

Meredith held up a manicured hand. "Stop."

Bruce sat up straighter, affronted by her tone, but kept his mouth shut.

She started pacing as she talked. "I know our relationship started under dishonorable circumstances. We had an affair. No matter how you rationalize it, it was not right. I have endeavored to make amends with your children, if not your ex-wife. I know you love me; I don't doubt that. But I do object to your choices in this. Kids are not financial tokens that you cash in and out, and Becca is certainly within her rights to call you on your secrecy."

"Honey—" Bruce started to stand up.

"Sit down. I'm talking." Meredith had never been this mad before. "You gave up your right to speak first. You had over five years to tell me about Tanner. *Five years, Bruce.* I'm the one talking now. You gave up that right remaining silent. Children need our love, our attention and care, certainly more than a cheque." She stopped short and looked at her husband. He was a stranger. The last few months she had been increasingly wary. "I'm leaving. I have to go."

Bruce stood, trying to embrace her. "Don't you think that is an overreaction? You don't want to do that, darling. Don't let my kids come between us."

"Your kids aren't coming between us, the truth is." Once the words were out she wished, just for single moment, that she could snatch them back. She wanted to snap closed the Pandora's box she had opened months ago and forget she ever saw what was inside. But her life had just irrevocably changed. She couldn't pretend anymore. The man she fell in love with was not a good person. She had ignored it for years. The last several months it had gotten worse. "I know you had your reasons for every single one of your choices. I just don't have to keep pretending they are the right ones." She headed towards the hallway.

"What are you saying?"

She turned. Her husband didn't look broken, far from it. He looked contemptuous. An icy feeling swept up her and she wondered if she was in danger. This was what she had been pretending she wasn't noticing. She pivoted. "This has been all too much. I need to go to my art class; it'll help clear my head. I don't want to be late."

Just like that, the darkness he had let slip vanished, but the moment had shaken her. The last few months she hadn't been crazy, he was…dangerous.

The polished charm was back in place when he said, "Of course, my dear. Shall I order something in for when you get home?"

"Don't you remember, I promised Ruth I would stay with her while she's on her juice detox. She started this morning."

"She's a grown woman."

Meredith gave him an indulgent smile. "Who is sensible enough to ask for help when she needs it. These are like a girls' holiday for us, minus the mojitos of course. Don't worry, we'll talk when I'm back home."

Bruce's mobile beeped.

"You get that. Don't worry about me." Placated, Bruce answered the phone and Meredith slipped down the hall. She stopped in the first room, her office. She had already packed to stay with her friend, but she would take the few minutes to grab essentials. It had never occurred to her to prepare a proper get-away bag.

Meredith collected her passport from the top drawer of her desk, along with the credit card in her maiden name she had kept even after they had married. She paused when she heard Bruce talking. She could hear him plain as day, he must still be sitting on the couch on the other side of the office wall.

*"I've been waiting for your call. I have information on Christopher and Austin Fischer. What's your price?"*

Meredith stopped herself from gasping. Her book club had read another true crime book last month. It was a tell-all—a poorly written one at that—about the Fischer brothers.

What was Bruce into?

Meredith did gasp then. She had left the book in the living room. The Fischer brothers were on the cover. What publisher wouldn't market that? Naughty or not, both of them were undeniably handsome. She needed to get it before Bruce noticed she had a book on the very men he was trying to sell out.

She cocked her head; he was still on the phone. Without questioning herself why, she grabbed his passport, too, along with her old-school address book, before silently making her way down the hall. He couldn't get too far without his passport and her address book contained all of their shared banking passcodes. She picked up the bag she had packed that morning, threw a few more articles of clothes in it, her laptop, and added her favorite and most expensive jewelry.

She waited. She heard Bruce heading towards the kitchen. Meredith darted down the hall and scooped up the books on the end table. She slipped out the front door. Her car was in the driveway. She had never been so happy to drive an electric car as she was in that moment. She started the car with barely a whisper. Reversing out the driveway, she dared a look.

Bruce was still on the phone.

# Chapter Twenty-Six

Clint's truck was in the drive. Becca checked the barn first before making her way across the yard and knocked on the back door. The ranch house was old, more of a cabin than a proper house. It sat on a small rise, nestled by larger foothills but still with one hell of a mountain view and natural protection from the bracing winds that thundered through. A small stream flowed nearby, adding to its charm and practicality. The outside was as clean, tidy and rough around the edges as the inside. Just like Clint.

The back door opened.

"Becca, what a lovely surprise! Come in, come in." Clint ushered her in and closed the door. "I was just about to have an early dinner before I finish fencing. Are you hungry? There's plenty."

Becca smiled. She had always felt safe and welcome here. "Famished. I missed lunch."

Clint set another place at the table while Becca washed up. She pulled out the letter Meredith had handed her and sat down.

"What's that?" Clint sat, too, and ladled chili into Becca's bowl.

"Notification of the route selection of the proposed pipeline."

"I take it it's not good news?" Clint asked, spooning chili into his own bowl. He pushed a plate of sliced bread towards her. "Here. I baked that this morning."

She let her face drop to her hands a moment before she sat up straight and rubbed her tired eyes. "Thanks, this looks amazing." She reached for her knife and the butter. "Maybe I can market it as part of the scenery." Her voice broke, though, betraying her fear. "What am I going to do Clint? What if all this was a horrible mistake?"

"My dear, if it is then you'll pivot. You're not the first person to have doubts about a business venture. Cut yourself some slack. Besides, one pipeline tie-in does not fail an inn. What's really bothering you?"

Becca looked up. "How well do you know Officer Chasseur?"

"Jason? Pretty well. Why do you ask?"

"Mom said something about dad and him." Becca pushed her chili around her bowl.

Clint's spoon stopped. "That could cover quite a bit of ground. What specifically are you wanting to know?"

"In high school, what did dad do to Jason?"

"Have you asked your dad?"

"Yes."

"Have you asked Jason?"

"No."

"Why not?" Clint's voice was patient yet firm.

"It's complicated."

"So un-complicate it."

"It's not that easy. He hasn't taken my calls in five days—"

"Is the man worth it?"

Becca stared at Clint. Was he playing matchmaker? This quiet, sensible man in front of her had been the most grounding adult figure in her life so she answered honestly.

"I hope so."

Clint smiled. "Well, honey, you're worth it, too. So uncomplicate it. Anything else?"

Becca dug into her chili and explained her three-page to-do list. In between bites she pulled it out and spread it out on the table between them. "Can you help me distinguish between the have-to-haves and the nice-to-haves?"

Clint pulled out a pair of reading classes. "Well let's see then. How are you holding up with everything? Tuck filled me in."

"It's kind of surreal, like I must be watching it happen to someone else. I'm too boring for something like this to happen to."

"I don't think that's how it works, honey, and you, my dear, have never been boring."

Becca gave a half smile at Clint's kind words. "It isn't financially feasible for me to postpone opening weekend if I don't have to. I won't put my staff or clients in danger, but right now I don't even know what the danger is exactly. So, I'm on my own. I'm going to knock as much off this final to-do list as I can. If my opening weekend happens, I'll be as ready as I can be." Becca dropped her face into her hands again and mumbled, "I really hope this all doesn't blow up in my face."

Clint smiled. "Kiddo, that's a lot to shoulder. Let's have a look, then." He slid the list over and pulled a pen from the kitchen counter. In fifteen minutes he had taken her three page list and whittled it down to half a page. "Honey, that's all you need."

Becca stared at the shortened list. "You kept the experiences and trimmed the stuff.'"

"Simplify, my dear. Get down to the essence."

Becca knew he was talking about more than her to-do list. "I have no idea where to start."

Clint's voice was kind when he asked, "If you trim out all the stuff?"

Becca finished, "What do I want to experience?"

"That's my girl." He picked up the pipeline envelope. "Is it a hydrogen pipeline?"

"I—I just assumed it was just another oil or gas one."

Clint pointed to the return logo. "Those guys have shifted focus and are developing their hydrogen network. With Banff decarbonizing so fast, other communities are following. Have a look. No one wants a right-of-way going through their backyard, but that particular one may be more on-point for your eco-tourism business than you realize."

Becca dropped her spoon with a clatter. Clint smiled and handed her the envelope. She had skimmed it when she was sitting in her dad's driveway, but this time she read it. "Holy shit, it is a hydrogen pipeline."

Clint shrugged. "Times are changing. Domestic demand is building, and the foreign hydrogen markets were already opening up, b-before Russian oil was banned." Clint's voice broke. Becca knew an old school friend of his had been killed in Ukraine. She placed her hand on his arm and squeezed.

He patted her hand and cleared his throat. "Hydrogen is a game changer."

Clint rose, picking up his bowl and spoon. "I'm sorry to leave you, but I best be on my way. I dawdled making that bread and now I'm behind getting that fencing done. Stay as long as you like."

She jumped up. "I'll get those; you cooked. And thanks, Clint, I appreciate the ear."

"Anytime kiddo, anytime." He headed out the back door. Becca sat alone for long minutes, considering what he had said. A hydrogen pipeline, that changed things. And between Lillian and Clint, it felt like everyone thought her and Jason were a thing. If they only knew. Problem was, regardless of their history, she was pretty sure she wanted to experience Jason.

# Chapter Twenty-Seven

"T hat wasn't a day or two." Rose Chasseur looked at her son.

Jason squirmed under the maternal scrutiny. "I've been busy."

Rose waved him in, shutting the door behind him. "Or you've been avoiding me."

"Maybe." Jason sniffed. "Are you making homemade pizza?"

"I needed to lure you home somehow. It'll be ready in a bit. Come on in."

"Sorry. We're understaffed and work is...brisk."

Jason hung up his coat and toed off his boots, before joining his mom. She sat in an old plush chair in the living room. His parents had been older when they had him, much older than his classmates' parents had been. He eyed her, covertly, trying to notice if she was slowing down or needed help. She still had the energy of women half her age. Rose was the most active adult he knew, except maybe Becca.

He took a seat on the sagging but comfortable couch near her. The room wouldn't win any design challenges, but it was warm and inviting. As soon as he sat down some of the tension he had been holding eased. Ever since she had moved here, his mom's house just made him feel relaxed.

A large shoe box sat on the coffee table in front of them. "Is that it?"

"It is, so go ahead." Rose sat with her legs curled under her in her favorite chair, her elbow on the armrest and her chin resting in her palm.

Jason opened the lid. His stomach gave a little flip flop. A large photo rested on top. It wasn't his grandpa. The man looking back at him was a mirror image of himself. Except the eyes, those were harder. It was his father's service photo. The first time his father had ever gone to the United States was to enlist in the U.S. Army. The Vietnam War was waging, and his father had chosen to sign up. "I still don't understand why he did it?"

His mom's smile was sad. "Your dad was as restless as they come. In those days that's what young men did when they couldn't sit still long enough to not get in trouble. Canada wasn't in a war, so your dad drove to Montana. Americans didn't mind Canadians enlisting back then. The Vietnam War had been going on for years by then, everyone realized the horror. He still joined." Her voice was soft. "Go on, pull everything out."

Jason picked up the photo of his dad. His father had been a hard person to know. He placed the photo of his dad on the coffee table. A bundle of handwritten letters tied with a faded blue ribbon were under the photo. He gently pulled them out. "What are these?"

"Love letters."

"Beg your pardon?"

"For a long time, letters were all we had. Before he was captured. I didn't tell him how I felt before he left. That's not what good girls did. I was only fifteen, he had just turned eighteen. I was too chicken to follow my own heart. I was scared, I guess. What would people think? We cared a lot about that crap then." She swung her legs down and picked up the photo. "He didn't think I could love him, someone so wild and with so little to his name. He had no money to go to school, not that that would have done him any good, he was too restless to sit still in a classroom. We were just friends because we didn't think we were allowed to be anything more."

"So he joined a war?"

"Don't judge too harshly," she chided. "The war was his ticket out of here. He had a hard go of it here. I couldn't fault him needing to go somewhere. Anywhere but here. It was only through those letters that we shared how we truly felt about each other. We just didn't know he wouldn't be whole when he came back." His mom set the photo down and reached for the packet of letters. "You can read it, him slowly breaking."

Jason realized then his mom was a mystery to him. Maybe more so than his dad was.

Rose ran her finger along the ribbon holding the letters together. "He signed up so he wouldn't have to see me marry someone else. Women, especially poor women like me, were expected to do two things, marry young and have babies."

"Yet you waited for him. Why didn't you marry someone else?"

Rose gave a small laugh. "I grew a backbone. I didn't want anyone else, I wanted him. So I waited." Rose looked out the window. "Then he was captured. The war was over and still he didn't come home. I got cryptic letters from him after he had escaped, he was trying to make his way back home yet so very fearful he would be captured again. When he finally did make it home, he was a broken man. Not all of him survived that war. That's why you came along so late. We took things slow once he did come back."

Jason hesitated. "Why'd you stay as long as you did, I mean once he was back?"

"I loved that man every single day of his life, broken or not. I still do."

Jason kept listening. They should have had this conversation years ago.

"When you came, years later, we thought we might have a fresh start, and we did for a while. We weren't perfect, but we both loved you very much."

"He never told me." Jason's stomach rolled and he tried to clamp down the lid on what he was feeling. Emotions sucked.

"I know. He loved you though." She pulled out another bundled stack, this one of old photos. Some were grainy with age; others only had a slight patina. They looked at pictures and Jason listened as his mom spoke of each one. Nearly a half hour had gone by before she pulled out a tattered image. It was similar to the one Becca had in her file.

"That's grandpa Chasseur, right?"

Rose smiled. "He's an older grandpa Chasseur than the one you're thinking of. He was your great grandfather's grandfather. His name was Armand Chasseur." She pulled out another grainy photo. It used to hang in his parents' living room and was identical to the one Becca had. "This one is your grandpa Chasseur, grandpa Oscar Chasseur."

Jason compared the photos. The men could have passed for the same person. "That's eerie."

"How do you think I feel? Sometimes looking at you is like looking at a ghost you look so much like your dad." Rose held the photo closer. "It is remarkable how much they look alike. Your father's mom gave these to me. He wasn't interested in the past. Neither were you over the years, that you two had in common."

"I'm interested now."

"I'm glad. Understanding your roots sometimes answers the question marks in your life."

"I don't have questions."

"That's fine." Rose smiled. "Someday you might."

Jason had a strong relationship with his mom, but some things a man kept to himself. He pulled out a few loose letters in the box of memories. "What are these?"

"Your great grandparents wrote to each other, too."

"I had no idea I came from such a chatty family."

"Wait until you see what's next." She reached inside the shoe box and pulled out a fabric-wrapped object about the size of her hand. With great care she unwrapped a small, rough-worn leather book and handed it to him. There was no title. He realized why when he opened the cover. It was a journal.

Carefully he turned a couple pages. "It's in French."

"Mostly."

"Whose is it?"

"It was Armand's; I'd say it's yours now."

Jason could read passable French and the handwriting was tidy enough, yet he still struggled to make out several of the words. He turned another page and saw a striking hand-drawn map. The craftsmanship was nothing short of true artistry. He turned the journal to face her. "That's incredible."

Rose nodded. "There are several other maps in there. I can't read French, so I'm not sure how helpful it will be, but I hope it helps you and that Tanner girl."

"Becca knows about this?" The joy of discovery he had been feeling dampened.

"Now don't you start. Her friend Lillian stopped by maybe a month or more ago. Such a nice, well-mannered young woman. She had a lovely accent, too, though I suspect Becca's brother Colt has his hands full. That woman has spunk. I like her."

"You met Lillian Kensington; she was here? Are you okay?"

"Why wouldn't I be? She was a lovely."

"Mom, she had an assassin after her." Jason closed his eyes. His mom would be the death of him from simply worrying about her.

"That nice young woman? Whatever for? She must be okay; I saw her at the market just last week. It breaks my heart what you kids have to put up with these days."

"She's fine. The assassin isn't." Jason pinched the bridge of his nose. "Mom, do me a favor, don't make friends with people with assassins after them."

Rose sat up straighter. "I will do no such thing. I'm too old to worry about such things and you just said the assassin was taken care of. Anyway, I like Lillian. I like Becca, too. That's why Lillian was here, to try and help Becca. Lillian didn't get a chance to see the journal, though, she had gotten a call, some sort of emergency."

"Mom, I am not helping Becca—"

She interrupted him. "Now don't you start. You've been sweet on Becca for years, not that the young woman would know it with all of your ridiculous bluster."

"I'm not sweet on her."

His mom rolled her eyes. "I need you to take these to her, to borrow of course. Or maybe you could make her copies. Yes, that would nice. I've been meaning to show a professor at one of the local universities. That journal might be interesting to them, too."

Jason pushed the memorabilia away from him. "I'll take copies to any professor you want, but I'm not helping Becca. You don't know what she's done."

Rose pushed them back. "Accepted the land her daddy bought for her? The nerve of a young woman these days. Building a business from the ground up, by herself, and you're what, mad she didn't check with you first? Why would she do that, dear, when you've only given her grief? So her dad helped by buying her some land! I'd buy you land if I could afford it. Would that make me a bad mom?"

Jason shifted in his seat, uncomfortable at his mom's words. "You know how long it's taken me to scrape together enough to buy our land back. Then she just blows in with her daddy's money."

His mom placed a gentle hand on his arm. "Are you mad at her or her dad?"

Jason shook his head. "It's not that easy."

"Sure it is. I don't know what happened all those years ago, but I see how she looks at you. Still, after all these years and the hard time you keep giving her. I love you but you're an idiot. That woman is crazy about you and you're crazy not to at least see where it goes."

How had the conversation turned here? "I'm telling you, she doesn't like me like that."

Rose patted him on the shoulder before standing. "You are as oblivious as your father was, God rest his soul. Don't wait as long as we did. I don't have many regrets in life, but I regret not telling him earlier how I felt."

Jason had had no idea. "I remember you guys divorcing a lot more than any affection between you."

"Divorcing someone you're still in love with does not bring out the best in anyone."

"He was hard to love." Jason looked at the stack of love letters. How much of his parents didn't he know?

Rose leaned down and hugged him. "As hard as he was, he loved you. Never forget that. He was hopeless trying to express it, but never doubt your father loved you." She kissed the top of his head before messing up his hair like she used to do when he was a kid. "I'm going to go assemble pizza. Dinner should be ready in fifteen minutes."

"Thanks mom." After she left the room he stared at the memorabilia, thinking about what his mom had said. He reached for the journal again and gently flipped through it. It was a weird thing seeing one of your ancestor's handwriting. His map sketches were even more surreal, the man had talent. Jason wondered again about the old journal he had found as a kid. Or it might just be a book. Pen and ink or printed ink, both would likely be prone to fade in the elements.

"Pizza's ready," his mom called from the kitchen.

"Coming," Jason called back. He put everything carefully back into the box, no closer to knowing what he was going to do with it.

# Chapter Twenty-Eight

"Jason, please, we need to talk. Call me." Becca thumbed off her cell phone and looked out her back kitchen window. The message was the sixth one she had left for him in as many days. She couldn't blame him for avoiding her, but this was getting annoying. She needed to talk to him. It didn't feel right leaving things after their last encounter. She felt awful. And he was the police for godsakes! Weren't they supposed to hear you out? Listen to the truth? At least there hadn't been any further run-ins or concerns with the Fischers.

When her phone rang in her hand, hope flared. "Jason?"

A mechanical voice sounded, "Stop the pipeline."

A cold shiver went through Becca. "What? Who is this?"

The eerie voice repeated, "Stop the pipeline."

Sustained internal tension shoved fear out of the way. "It's a hydrogen pipeline. Do you know how hard it's been to get Alberta, not to mention Canada, to shift our energy futures? Are you kidding me? Stop a hydrogen pipeline? Why don't you ask me to club a baby seal or burn down the rainforests while I'm at it?"

Silence met her outburst.

"Hello?" Becca asked.

*Click.*

Ohmygod, what had she done? Of all the times to get on one of her rants, why the hell did she pick the time she was being terrorized by god only knows who? Fuck.

This time Becca called nine-one-one. She was feeling a bit hysterical as she waited for the rural officers. Thirty-five minutes later an RCMP cruiser finally swung into her drive. It wasn't Jason who got out. From the looks of him, the young man was barely out of nappies. Once inside, he fumbled with his notebook and dropped his pen twice. His radio went off, disrupting him. And he forgot something in his car.

Becca perched on the edge of one of the couches, waiting. She had called Tucker after making the call to nine-one-one and wished he was here instead of the young pup in front of her. She re-crossed her arms and tried not to scream. The poor kid was clearly nervous. She needed a fucking rock right now.

"Okay, now I'm ready." He flashed a dazzling smile, his pen and paper ready.

Becca hoped her tone was gentle when she asked, "You look pretty enthusiastic, how long have you been an officer?"

The young man straightened on his chair. "This is my first solo call, miss."

His blissful eagerness to help dampened the bite of her strained nerves. "Well, you passed the first test, calling me miss instead of ma'am."

"I have four older sisters," he explained.

"That'll do it." Becca went on to detail—slowly—the weird phone call, and the letter Meredith had given her about the pipeline project running through her land. Once the initial excitement of his first call dissipated, the young man was surprisingly thorough and clear-headed. He asked astute questions and gave Becca time to remember and talk things through. When they were done she said, "You're pretty good at that. You make a fine officer."

The young officer beamed. "Thanks. Officer Chasseur was my training officer."

"Is that a good thing?" Becca had no idea Jason's reputation in the RCMP.

"Are you kidding? That guy is a legend." Another cruiser thundered into the driveway. "Speak of the devil."

Becca watched through the window as the devil himself slammed his car door and took the porch stairs two at a time. Rapid-fire knocking pounded on her front door.

Taking her time, she got up and opened the door. "Yes?"

He stopped, as if suddenly aware she hadn't granted him permission to enter. "You were supposed to call me."

"I did. Repeatedly."

"I meant about something like this."

"Really? How'd you know the other times I called *weren't* an emergency?"

They stared at each other. Finally Jason asked, "Can I come in?"

Becca opened the door wider. She hated that she felt better with him here. She turned and left him at the door.

She heard it close behind her. The next few minutes consisted of the officers talking and Becca clarifying any questions Jason had. He flipped his notebook closed. "Good work, Cooper. Write your report and I'll check in with you at the detachment tomorrow."

Officer Cooper looked between Becca and Jason, hesitating. The undercurrents boiling between her and Jason were palpable. If they could bottle the energy crackling between them, Alberta would have a whole new energy boom.

"Can I get you anything else, Officer Cooper?" Becca asked.

"No miss." He gave a nervous glance in Jason's direction before asking her, "Do you need anything before I go?"

"Nope. After you leave I'm just going to kick your training officer in the junk."

The younger officer's eyes widened. He darted another look at Jason. "I can't let you do that, miss."

"Fine. Then I guess we're all done here. Thanks for your help. I promise not to assault Officer Chasseur."

Hesitating, Officer Cooper held out his hand. Becca shook it enthusiastically, hoping to undo some of the damage she had no doubt just done and walked him to the front door.

The young officer left in a hurry, leaving her alone with Jason. He stood silent, waiting for her to make the first move. She had no idea what to do.

# Chapter Twenty-Nine

When Officer Cooper left, Jason heard Becca lock the deadbolt before heading down the hallway to the back of her house. The setting sun had dipped behind the front range, leaving everything in the darkening living room in long shadows. Jason waited there, unsure what to do. He had gotten here as fast as he could, terrified he would be too late. This time he had simply missed Becca's call, not avoided it, and she had every right to be pissed at him.

Still, he had never attended a call where the victim ignored him. He turned towards the front door to leave, already writing the protection detail request in his head when he heard her scream. Jason sprinted down the hall and ran into her well-lit kitchen. Becca was holding a knife.

"What's wrong?"

Becca was staring at the backdoor, the knife shaking in her hand. "You're still here?"

"Yes. Why did you scream and why are you holding a knife?" Jason managed to keep his voice steady.

Becca looked at him. She set the knife on the counter and stepped back. "I thought I saw something."

"What did you think you saw?"

"Nothing." She grabbed a tea towel and wiped her hands. She tossed the towel on the far side of the kitchen island before turning them up and staring at them. "Why do palms sweat when you're scared?"

"No idea. What scared you?" Jason slowly moved around the large island counter, looking for danger and needing to be closer to her in case he needed to protect her.

Becca finally looked at him, before cocking her head to the side. "Stop it. You used that same voice on my horse. I'm not going to fall to pieces."

Jason knew a minefield when he heard it. Still, he added, "No one would judge if you did."

"I'll remember that." She shook her hands out and exhaled. "Why'd you stay? You've been avoiding me all week."

"Why'd you scream?"

Becca pointed to the back door. "Tucker left his stupid jacket hanging on the wreath on the door. I *told* him the difference between a decoration and a coat hook." She crossed her arms defensively. "It looked like a person."

Jason crossed to the back door, transferring Tucker's coat from the wreath to one of the empty hooks adjacent to the door. *She was safe.* He let himself relax a little.

She fired a barbecue lighter down the large island counter in the center of the room. It stopped a few inches from the edge he was standing closest to. "Make yourself useful."

"Why do you keep feeding me?"

"I'll send a bill if it makes you feel better. Mind firing up the barbecue? I hate washing pots and pans."

Her spunk released more tension within him. "Sure." Jason scooped up the lighter and headed for the back door. She came around the large island counter towards him. He stilled.

She reached around him, and he held his breath. A moment later light flooded in front of him, illuminating the back deck.

"That should help," she said.

Jason stood there, unhinged while she flipped on a damn light switch.

He nodded and grabbed the doorknob. Once outside, he crossed the now-lit deck to the professional sized grill. It was huge. Jason opened the cover and lit a single burner. He heard the backdoor slam. Becca dropped a plate with two steaks on the side table. "I like mine medium." She left a bottle of locally brewed lager next to the plate of steaks before heading back inside.

Jason grilled the steaks as the last whispers of the sunset faded into night behind the line of mountains. The fall night was cool but not cold. He looked around. The deck was as oversized as the grill, meant to accommodate large groups. It opened out to a large garden. Beyond, trees ringed the yard. Farther still, what looked to be a greenhouse stood quiet in the near darkness. It wasn't hard to imagine Becca's inn full of satisfied diners sharing bottles of expensive wine and fancy hors d'oeuvres before gourmet entrées and artful desserts. They'd laugh and toast special occasions on this very deck, charmed at their Canadian vacation and the quaint mountain setting.

He flipped the steaks and took a sip of beer. What was he doing? Becca Tanner might as well handcuff him. All she did was tie him in knots anyway. He should be running as fast and as far away as possible. Deciding to do just that, he finished up grilling the steaks. Jason headed back inside, ready to make an excuse and get the hell out of there.

A small feast awaited. He slid the plate of steaks and the barely-touched lager next to a large garden salad and steaming roasted potatoes. "For a woman who says she doesn't know how to cook, you put out a decent spread."

"Why do you think I still get a dinner invite a couple times a week from family? Tucker would never make me his brownies again if he knew the truth." She held out a plate to him. "These potatoes are leftovers from him. Let's eat before we start arguing; I need my strength. You are seriously hard to deal with."

"I meant it looks amazing."

"Oh. Sorry. I'm off." Becca climbed onto the stool and rubbed her face with her hands.

She looked tired. He thought about what his mom said. Opening a business was hard enough, now she had any number of criminal types dancing too close. Instead of leaving, Jason took a seat at the island counter next to her. He asked the first thing that popped into his head, "You don't like eating in your formal dining room?"

She smiled. "Too formal."

They filled their plates and started eating. Jason fidgeted on the stool. His gear belt was catching with an awkward pull every time he made the slightest movement. He took it off and laid it on the counter.

"Did you really ask the caller if he wanted you to club a baby seal?"

Becca finished her bite. "I agree under the circumstances it wasn't my smartest move, but I was angry. Shifting to hydrogen is a big deal. There are enough naysayers. I can't just keep quiet and obedient over something like this."

"No, I don't suppose you could." Jason didn't always agree with Becca's politics, but he admired her integrity. The thought of Becca quiet and obedient gave him chills.

They finished their dinners in an oddly companionable silence.

Becca sat back. "I totally needed that."

"Stress can be pure hell on a body."

Becca smiled and rubbed her stomach. "I was talking about the steak."

"Right. Sorry."

Within a few minutes they had the table cleared and the dishwasher running. When his phone rang she nodded. "Take your time."

Jason turned and accepted the call. Listening to his boss, he walked to the other side of the large kitchen and stopped at a cork board on the wall. A photocopy of a three-page to-do list was tacked in place. Only half or so of the tasks were crossed off and a quarter were highlighted. His mom was right, Becca was up to her eyeballs in work and doing it alone. He wrapped up the call as quickly as he felt prudent. Finally, he turned around. "About not calling back—"

He was talking to an empty kitchen. Jason hesitated a moment before walking to the left of the back door. A lockable door was open to a hallway. He went back and retrieved his gear belt. Putting it back on, he headed through the open door to the hall. Halfway down, French doors opened into a sunken medium sized room. Jason descended the two stairs into the room. It looked like a study. Floor to ceiling bookshelves lined two walls, and tall windows, their curtains pulled tight, lined the last wall, opposite the large doorway. Becca sat curled in the single wingback chair next to the wood stove, reading in the soft halo of light the discreet floor lamp threw.

Jason didn't know what to say. "What are you reading?"

She straightened in her chair, swinging her legs down, and tossed the book on the single side table. "International marketing. My business model is high end quality, not quantity."

"What do you mean?"

"Think box seating versus general admission. Selling a few box seats makes the same amount as dozens of general admission tickets. I have a finite number of fancy rooms with large overhead. If I want to make this successful, the international crowd is where it's at. Canada is becoming a priority destination for an eco-friendlier, under crowded fresh air experience. This place checks all the right boxes—well, minus the jet fuel." She was quiet a moment. "I just have to make sure my target demographic knows this place exists."

It stung sharing his family's land with a bunch of tourists. "Do you want me to search the house before I head out?"

"Have a seat." The only other chair available was the one at her desk. She must have felt his hesitation because she added, "Please."

Jason passed her and rounded the large desk. He dropped into the surprisingly comfortable wooden office chair. Bars of sturdy wood, curved with a skilled hand framed the back. He wiggled in the chair, impressed. Craftsmanship such as this was rare. "Nice piece."

Distracted, she answered, "Thanks. It's an antique." She looked tired. Jason thought again about what his mom said. Opening a business sounded like a significant amount of hard work with no guarantee it would work out. Add to those inherent risks, now Becca had any number of criminal types dancing too close. The last week had taken a toll on what must have been already pressed nerves. By the sounds of it she had been pushing pretty hard for the last two years, spending her savings on the down-payment for the inn's mortgage.

As an officer he had a union and a pension. He didn't think a hell of a lot about retirement because as long as he didn't screw up, his was reasonably secure. He had no idea how his civilian friends stomached the ups and downs of working in a boom and bust economy. He supposed that's why Becca was so adamant about renewables; diversifying made sense.

She rubbed her eyes and sat forward. A moment passed, maybe two, before she clapped her hands on the tops of her legs and stood.

"You okay?"

"Yeah, I just wasn't ready to be alone yet."

That made sense. Jason eyed her as she moved behind him. "What are you doing?"

"I just need to get something."

Becca reached for something on the shelf behind the large desk. Instinctively he reached to cover his sidearm. Becca moved again, this time placing one hand on the back of his chair and reaching the other around his shoulder. She placed an object on the desk in front of him.

Her mouth was close to his ear, her breath warm on his cheek when she asked, "Can you fix this?"

A three-inch bolt with an incorrectly threaded nut rested in front of him. Jason relaxed and lifted the metal pieces. "Sure, do you have a pliers and wrench?"

*Click.* Cold metal wrapped around his right wrist. When Becca stepped left, he reached for her with his free hand. He knew his mistake the second he made it. Still behind him, she had leverage on her side and with a hefty, fast tug, Becca pulled his left arm behind him and slid the second metal bangle home.

"Are you fucking nuts?" Jason tugged against the metal restraints and tried to control his temper.

"No, I'm desperate."

Jason strained against the cuffs again, his large shoulders not helping his leverage any. He worked his arms and wrists trying to get purchase against the cuffs. "Do you realize how many laws you're breaking right now?"

She moved closer then, nearly straddling him. He stilled. When she put her hands on his shoulders and leaned over to peek behind him, the lower part of her torso pressed against his nose.

*"Is this necessary?"* His voice was muffled against the soft flannel of her shirt.

"Just making sure they're on right."

"First kidnapping job?"

"You know, I've never kidnapped anyone." She stepped back, her hands no longer braced on his shoulders. Instead, she held her crossed arms tight against herself.

"You mean before me."

Becca looked at him a long time. "Yeah, before you. I just want to talk."

"About how you stole my family's land?"

"My bank account would disagree."

Jason rotated his wrists again. He knew it was futile, yet he still tried to find a weakness in his restraints. "You stole my chance to buy it."

"I didn't know you had put an offer on the land, I swear to you. Please believe me."

"Or what? You're going to leave me in these handcuffs? You're coercing my forgiveness? Why don't you try *earning* it, Becca." He strained against the cuffs. *"Goddamn it."*

Becca's face blanched. "Ohmygod, what was I thinking? I can't believe I did that, that wasn't fair." She moved close, unlocking the bangle on his left hand and clicking it shut on her own wrist. Becca held up their joined wrists. "Better?"

Jason stood slowly. It hurt to see how sad yet hopeful she looked. He said her name.

She was looking up at him now, her head tilted back. "You always walk away."

"Becca, please, not now. I don't want to hear it—"

"I didn't know the nasty things my dad said to you when we were kids."

She was too close; Jason wasn't ready for this. "Becca stop. Unlock the handcuffs."

"I wouldn't steal from you. Or knowingly steal your chance at your family's land. And I'm sorry my dad was so cruel to you in high school. That wasn't right."

Her face was mere inches from his.

"Right's got nothing to do with life," he whispered.

"Please don't think so little of me. I've had my head down, trying to launch on time. I swear I had no idea you had put in an offer." Becca dropped her head, looking down. "I don't even know why my dad did it. He wasn't speaking to me at the time."

Jason cradled her cheek with his free hand, tilting it up. She turned into his hand.

The front door opened and a voice called from the foyer: "Becca, you okay? I just heard about the phone call."

It sounded like Tucker, Becca's brother. Jason opened his mouth to call out, but Becca pressed her fingers against his lips. She stretched and with a tap of her foot, turned the floor lamp off. Darkness engulfed the room. It took a moment for his eyes to adjust to the slice of light coming down the hall from the kitchen.

Becca held her body still, her fingers still pressed against his mouth, but he could feel her chest rise and fall.

*Sweet Jesus.*

"Becca, you home?" Tucker was making his way to the back of the house.

Becca shifted, and replaced her fingers with soft, warm lips.

Jason didn't hesitate, he kissed her back, hungrier than he meant to. Her hand cupped his jaw as his tongue found hers.

The overhead light flicked on. It would have blinded him had his eyes been open.

"Woah!" Tucker snapped the light back off. "I saw nothing. Didn't know you had company, sis."

Becca sighed. "Turn the light back on. It's not what you think."

*"It's worse,"* Jason muttered.

Tucker stayed just outside the door. He did not turn on the light. "That's okay, just wanted to make sure you were okay. I heard about the phone call. Um...right then...you're in good hands, I'll just go—"

"Your sister has me handcuffed. I'd appreciate if you'd supervise the unlocking."

Silence met his request.

Finally Becca grumbled, "When you put it that way, it sounds ridiculous. Like I've got a sex dungeon or something."

Tucker turned the light back on and slowly entered the room. "You guys are not joking, are you?"

Jason held up his and Becca's joined wrists.

Becca shifted. "I needed to talk to him, and he always walks away before I'm done."

"So, naturally you handcuffed him. Where's the key?"

Becca pulled the key out of the front pocket of her jeans.

Tucker snatched it out of her hand. With a couple quick motions, he released her and Jason and asked, "What was the kiss supposed to be then?"

Becca shrugged. "You showed up, so I had to silence him."

"Makes total sense, you *had* to kiss him." Tucker smirked and handed Jason his cuffs and key.

"Um, he kissed me back."

Tucker held up his hand. "I really don't need to know the play-by-play. Now that I know you're safe, I'm hungry. What do you have to eat? Do I smell steak?"

Becca darted a look at Jason, her face no longer giving anything away. "Sure, come on."

By the time they filed into the kitchen, Jason felt reasonably certain his heart was no longer plastered on his sleeve.

Becca skirted around him with nervous energy. To her brother, she said, "The steak's gone but there's a fresh loaf of French bread and I have some of the German salami you love." She finally met his eyes. "Jason are you still hungry?"

He was. He could still taste her on his lips. But he just shook his head.

Tucker beelined for the fridge, humming to himself. He pulled out the salami and mustard, then snagged the French loaf from the far counter and made himself a sandwich. Between bites he asked, "What happened with the phone call?"

"Some mechanical voice called and told me to stop the pipeline. Like I have the power to do that."

"Didn't Lillian find historical reference to an old fort back there or something?" Tucker asked, rewrapping the bread and putting away the salami and mustard.

Jason stilled. Images of his childhood whispered through his mind.

"Colt was kidnapped before they found anything concrete enough to reroute a pipeline. And certainly not before I need to open to start paying back these business loans. By the way, it's a hydrogen pipeline."

Tucker looked up. "Oh, that kind of changes things for you, doesn't it?"

Becca nodded. "This time. The next one is anyone's guess. With the price of oil back up, the tap is back on. Paused projects are firing back up."

"The Lynn Site is there and ranked an HRV-1," Jason reasoned. "I thought the size and uniqueness of that particular archaeology site and the available options to route around it had always dissuaded pipeline development."

"The site was destroyed by the 2013 flood. The HRV-1 trigger is still there, but that specific site is now considered a non-issue."

The stretch of land that meant so much to him might actually be lost for good. "Are you serious?"

"Look, we both love that land. It's part of your history and my future. I co-own the title, but not the mineral rights. Until I finish paying my father back, he is primary on the title. He wants the development. Whoever is leaving me creepy messages wants me to stop the pipeline and is probably the same person who left Colt and Lillian's stolen research on my doorstep. So it seems safe to say that the 'bad guys' want our legitimate help stopping the pipeline. Question is, why do they care?"

Jason had a dark thought. "Let's say the pipeline doesn't go through. What worries me is what happens after? If it's the land the Fischers are interested in, Becca will be a liability to them. Her guests will be riding out on the very land they don't want anyone snooping around on."

"You *are* a dark fucker." Tucker shot a look at his sister, no doubt gauging how she was handling the speculations.

Jason didn't like it any more than Tucker did, but if he was right, she had to be warned. "Hazard of the job. Besides, what would you do in their shoes?"

"Shit. It does make sense."

"So I may or may not be safe as long as I'm still useful? Great, I'm going under before I even open. Mom and dad were right, opening my own business was a hare-brained idea."

Tucker crossed the room and put his arm around Becca's shoulder. "You know that's not true. Mom and dad are never right, about anything, ever."

That got a tight smile from Becca. "Thanks for the solidarity, bro."

Tucker looked up at Jason. "We do have another option."

"What's that?" Becca's eyes had turned hopeful.

Jason answered for him. "We catch them first."

Becca grabbed the tea towel she had discarded earlier and started wringing it. "Not to sound unsupportive, but haven't you guys been after them for years? What makes this time different?"

*Your safety. You make this time different.*

He looked down instead of answering and saw a small black object sitting on a bright sticky note pad on Becca's large island counter. It had been under the tea towel, and he hadn't noticed it. He picked it up. "Where did you get this?"

Becca looked over. "My mom found it in the hallway upstairs. I don't know what it is."

Tucker moved closer and Jason held it up. Tucker started to say, "Good god, it's a—," but Jason clamped his hand over Tucker's mouth. He held his other index finger to his lips and Tucker nodded. Jason removed his hand and grabbed the pen next to the sticky pad, scribbling a note. He tore off the piece of paper and held it up to Becca.

*Your house is bugged.*

# Chapter Thirty

Becca's first reaction was fear. Someone had been in her home and was spying on her. Oh god, had they been in her house when she was home? She hadn't noticed anything amiss, but she'd been so distracted lately. Her stomach dropped. She had lived alone for a long time and thought nothing of walking around naked. Was that thing audio, or video, too?

Fury battled with fear. How dare some asshole shatter her security and peace of mind. This was her *home.*

She plucked the note out of Jason's hand and placed it on the butcher block island counter. Without a word she went to the counter next to her stove. A lovely pottery crock held assorted wooden spoons, spatulas and one meat tenderizer. She seized the weapon before snapping a cheery pumpkin tea towel off the long horizontal oven handle.

Back at the island counter, she folded the tea towel in half and set it on the island. Becca held out her hand, palm up. Without a word Jason dropped the offensive gadget into her hand. She placed it in the center of one side of the folded towel before carefully folded the towel over again. With the might of Thor, she slammed the meat tenderizer down, hard.

Again and again, she hit the small lump inside the towel.

*Bam, bam, bam.*

Every whack released stores of pent-up anger she hadn't even been aware were there.

Jason and Tucker didn't say a word.

*Whack, whack, whack.*

Finally, Becca slammed the hammer down a final time, her outburst over.

She handed the meat tenderizer to Jason and let Tucker hug her. She allowed herself a brief ugly cry, a full sixty seconds.

When Becca opened her eyes, Jason, rock solid and patient, was staring back at her. He turned on the stove fan and in a hushed voice said, "We shouldn't crush all of them."

Despite herself, Becca felt a smile tug. "Too much paperwork?"

"Something like that."

Becca stepped away from her brother and rubbed her eyes. In her own hushed voice she said, "I'll grab a few things then stay at Clint's." Her brother opened his mouth, but she stopped him. "I'll be fine there and I'm not driving all the way into the city tonight."

"I'll drive you then," Jason said.

Becca wanted nothing more than to collapse in his arms and let him take care of everything. Instead, she said, "No, thank you. I'll be fine at Clint's. I'll need my truck tomorrow anyway."

"We don't even know if he's home," Tucker reasoned.

"He was fencing, I'm sure he's home by now, it's dark. I'll be fine." Becca could at least get herself to Clint's. "I'll even let you know when I get there so you know I'm safe."

She ran upstairs and threw together a quick overnight bag. Was she being watched now? She would stay at Clint's until her home could be swept for more surveillance devices and she could manage to get her own surveillance cameras installed.

She lifted her fingers to her mouth. The feel of Jason's lips were burned into her memory. She had dreamed about that moment for years, yet never in her wildest fantasies had it included danger. That wasn't her fantasy at all.

Becca paused. She was being an idiot. Her house had been bugged. Pining over someone who didn't like her, let alone love her, was ridiculous. She needed to focus on surviving whatever the hell was going on long enough to open her inn and pay off her stupid, gigantic mortgage.

Becca finished packing and headed downstairs. Jason and Tucker were waiting for her outside. Tucker pulled her into another hug. She hugged him back and tried not to cling.

She pulled away and turned to look at Jason, trying to find the right words. Nothing brilliant came to mind. "Sorry I kissed you."

He stared back at her. "We checked your truck. It looks clean."

Bugs, he meant more bugs or tracking devices.

"Thanks." Her voice sounded brittle, even to her. She hadn't thought to look on or in her truck. "Good night then."

She climbed woodenly into her truck and hoped Clint was home. She wasn't sure she could handle whatever surprise came next.

# Chapter Thirty-One

Jason stood in Becca's driveway watching her taillights blink a moment before pulling out onto the range road towards Clint's ranch. Tucker pulled out a pack of cigarettes and held the pack out to Jason. He hesitated a moment before withdrawing one.

Tucker lit his own before handing the lighter to Jason. "So, you and my sister. I did not see that coming, but I'm not surprised."

Jason exhaled. "She handcuffed me, then kissed me to shut me up. That hardly constitutes a thing. Besides, she's immune to me."

"Not even close, but that's your problem to figure out."

Jason eyed Tucker, more than a little curious.

Tucker continued, "Colt and I will get cameras up tomorrow. I doubt I can keep her at Clint's or my condo longer than a night or two. She's scared, but she's put too much blood, sweat and tears into this place to hang back and wait until whatever this is blows over. Whatever the fuck this is. Feels like a storm that hasn't decided if it's going to break or not."

"Some storms never actually break."

Tucker shook his head. "Again, with the poet. I got the green light to hit up some of my old street contacts from my undercover days. I'm going to slide back in and see if

I can find out anything. Somebody's got to know something."

"It's not the worst idea in the world," Jason agreed. "Does your supervisor think the Fischers are likely the ones dogging Becca about the pipeline?"

"No." Tucker's tone made it clear what he thought of that. "Are the Fischers known for using bugs?"

"Nah, but that doesn't mean they don't, just that we don't have any intel on it yet."

Tucker nodded and took another pull off his cigarette. Finally he said, "The last time I went undercover I got stabbed."

"You hoping for a gun this time?" Dark humor had gotten Jason through more than a few intense days.

Tucker laughed. "Sure, why not? I just want to get the poison off the street. It's damn depressing watching people fade away in front of your eyes, or blow out in a single wink."

Jason couldn't argue. Addiction was a bitch. And hard as fuck for so many to kick. "You going out tomorrow?"

Tucker nodded.

Now Jason had two Tanners to worry about.

# Chapter Thirty-Two

Morning light flooded Becca's barn, illuminating shafts of shifting dust. Becca always marveled how sunlight could bring even air into focus. Too bad it couldn't illuminate who had bugged her house. She finished filling the feed pails for each of her horses. Dust and sunlight were still dancing in the stalls. She closed her eyes and listened, trying to turn off the anger that had been erupting since finding the surveillance equipment. She heard soft muzzles pushing oats in pails and the crunch of equine teeth grinding oats. Somewhere a barn cat thumped, no doubt to find a spot in a shaft of sunlight to curl up in. Pixie looked up, her pail now empty and nickered at her. Stürmisch, her favorite gelding, grunted and blew loudly out his mouth. She smiled. She felt safer in the barn than in the house. They hadn't bugged in here. And Tucker had only found audio bugs in her house, not video. She should be thankful for small miracles. She would have to stop walking around naked when she opened to guests, but not just yet. There was something primal being awash in moonlight in your own house. It felt good.

Like kissing Jason last night. Heat that had nothing to do with anger flowed through her. Between the inopportune sensuality waking up, and her anger and fear, she was a storm of emotions. Maybe Jason was right, her force of nature was chaos.

Her smile turned into a frown. She was a nobody in a family of overachievers and had about as much of a chance of stopping a pipeline as catching a comet tail. Why the hell had she been targeted? No one else along the proposed right-of-way had reported being threatened. What was it about *her* stretch of the proposed pipeline route? Had she unknowingly pissed someone off? Besides Jason, of course.

A dark thought flooded her mind. No way. They had their differences and she was convinced he didn't like her. But he couldn't be capable of this, could he?

Pixie nuzzled her shoulder as Becca tried to calm her racing mind. She went to lift her hand to stroke Pixie, but a sharp pain hit her and she clutched her chest, grabbing the stall for support. She didn't know if seconds or minutes ticked by. Becca tried to take calming breaths and leaned into Pixie. She wrapped her arms around her horse and held on. She breathed in the comforting smells of horseflesh and hay. Her big horse stayed still, supporting her and Becca wondered what her breaking point was. Everyone had one. Maybe she had just hit hers.

Making her way out of Pixie's stall, she closed the stall door and let herself crumble against it and slide towards the floor. She just needed to sit a minute. The pain in her chest started to ease. She closed her eyes.

And then someone was calling her name.

She opened her eyes and Jason was there, kneeling next to her. "Becca, can you hear me? What's happened? What do you need?" His eyes were frantic.

Without thinking, she wrapped her arms around him. "Please tell me I'm too young to have a heart attack. Don't let me have a panic attack, either."

He lifted her, his strong arms holding her protective and safe. He set her on a wooden half-cabinet. It was warmer than the concrete floor of the barn. He stood between her legs, his arms braced on either side of her. "You okay? What happened?"

Becca rubbed her chest, feeling groggy. "I was doing barn chores, I remember I was in Pixie's stall and trying to think who I could have pissed off enough to scare me and bug my house, and you were the only one I could think of." Becca lifted her hand to Jason's chest. "That made my chest squeeze tight and I didn't feel well."

Jason's eyes were bleak. "I'd never hurt you Becca. I'm not the one terrorizing you."

Becca hugged him then, hard. "I believe you." And she did. Every cell in her body felt safer with Jason near.

Jason let his hand lift, tucking a strand of hair behind her ear. She turned her head into his hand, savoring the contact. She resisted the urge to kiss him. Instead, she straightened and scrubbed her face with her hands. "I need to get back to work."

Jason frowned. "You just had some sort of episode; you need to get checked out by a doctor. I can give you a lift."

The pain and tightness in Becca's chest had disappeared. "I'm better now." It had been scary, though. She would be wise to watch it. Becca leaned forward, landing on her feet as she slid off her wooden perch. Jason had moved a half step back. She was now standing incredibly close to his chest. Becca looked up at him. "Why are you here, anyway?"

"You didn't answer my question."

"You didn't answer mine," she countered.

"I stopped by Clint's this morning." He hesitated. "I wanted to check that you were okay."

"Oh. Thank you." This time when she felt tingly all over she knew it was all because of the man standing next to her. Ignoring that, she added, "My brothers are putting up cameras today."

"Good."

"I need to let the horses out." She ducked her head and stepped around him.

"I got it." Jason picked up a curious barn kitten that had been winding its way around his legs and handed it to Becca. "You rest. Here. Pet a cat."

"Feline stress therapy?"

"Something like that."

Becca tucked the friendly kitten close to her chest. Immediately she could feel its vibrating purr. Jason pointed to her office. "Go relax."

She climbed back up onto the cabinet instead with the kitten purring in her arms, and watched Jason work. He let her horses out to pasture and mucked out the stalls. He brought two bags of oats down from the loft and topped off the water buckets. Becca couldn't remember the last time she watched someone else work, let alone in her barn. It was deeply pleasurable. She tried not to chastise herself, and instead tried matching her breathing with the wee kitten. It worked if she took one breath to every four the kitten took.

"How are you feeling?"

Becca looked up. Jason was in front of her again.

"Better. The kitten helped. And thanks for your help." She set the kitten down. It darted as soon as its legs hit the cabinet. "I need to mark trails and take GPS waypoints for tourist maps."

"Would you go see a doctor if I marked trails and took waypoints for you?"

"No. Would you help me, though?" Becca held her breath.

Jason smiled briefly. It transformed his face, softening the hard lines and angles. "Why do you think I brought these?" He held up his work-gloved hands. "You're really not going to fight me on it?"

"A police escort while I'm enjoying a new deviant fanbase? I'll even share my sandwich."

"I brought food. I figured it was my turn to feed you."

Becca led the way to her Quonset where she pulled out her quad. Jason helped her attach the trailer into place. Together, they loaded several pre-cut wood posts and the necessary tools. Becca headed back into the Quonset and returned with two helmets. She handed him one. "I only have one quad, but I have an idea."

"The last time that happened I ended up handcuffed." He waited a beat. "Want to talk about last night?"

He meant the kiss.

"Nope."

"Me, neither." He put the full face helmet on.

"We can ride double and borrow one of Clint's." She put her own helmet on and fished the keys out of her pocket. Firing up the quad, she pretended not to like it when Jason straddled the seat behind her, or how good it felt when his arms looped in front of her waist.

She turned her head and he nodded, ready.

They rode in silence, following a double-track through the scrub brush between Becca's place and Clint's. Most of the aspen leaves had turned and the autumn sun made everything glow. She really did love this land. When she had been in Germany she had dreamed of these foothills, certain that moving back would make her happy. She'd been back two years and was no closer to happiness than she had been before.

The ride to Clint's was brief. Her surrogate uncle was outside, working on his old yard pickup truck. He looked up from under the hood and waited until Becca turned the motor off. "Hi kids."

Becca opened her helmet visor and muttered, "I'm thirty years old."

"You both will always be kids to me and thank God for it," Clint answered, his hands still deep within the guts of the old Chevy.

Becca felt Jason shift behind her. "Hey Clint, mind if we borrow a quad?"

Clint looked up again, pleased as pie. "You know where everything is, help yourself."

Jason got off the quad, his hand briefly resting on Becca's shoulder as he leveraged himself off. As Jason headed to the outbuilding, Becca walked over to Clint.

"Can you hand me the nine-sixteenths socket wrench?"

Becca fished out the wrench. She handed it to Clint and leaned over to see what he was doing. "Water hose?"

"Yup, and new belts while I'm at it."

She nodded. "He thinks I'm using him."

Clint worked the socket wrench, making it click. "Are you?"

That stopped Becca. "I've been asking myself that for days. God, how he must hate me."

Clint raised an eyebrow, his hands still deep under the hood. "A man doesn't offer to help a woman on his day off when hate is on his mind."

The faint rumble of the quad engine sounded from the large shed behind them.

He gave a final tug. "That should do it. Can you hand me the belts? They're in the bag by your feet."

Becca bent at the waist to pick up the bag of auto parts. Bent over, she saw Jason ride out of the shed, his head turned towards her. She straightened, realizing she had probably just given him an eyeful. Embarrassed, Becca slapped the package of belts on the truck fender for Clint and ran to fire up her own quad. She heard Clint chuckle but didn't turn around. She didn't want to give Jason a reason to cut his engine, and hurried to start hers. In moments, he was there. Becca gave Clint a quick wave. He looked happy and she could tell he was pleased to see the two of them together. Clint was such a kind man. He had never shared why he hadn't let a woman snatch him up years ago, and it certainly wasn't for lack of opportunity. Perhaps her inn would bring a woman as kind, smart and fun as he was. Then Becca could play matchmaker for him.

# Chapter Thirty-Three

Jason hadn't been quadding in ages. The path they were on was a well-worn double track. The tall grasses on either side of the dirt trail had long turned to golden brown. In the distance Chimney Creek was visible only by the tell-tale clusters of bushy willow. The gently rolling terrain made easy riding and despite everything, he caught himself enjoying the moment.

While they had been picking up the second quad, dark clouds had rolled in. The arid foothills of southern Alberta were at an elevation that was rather responsive to the sun. No matter the season, direct sunshine added significant warmth. Conversely, when you were in the shade the temperature dropped noticeably. Jason eyed the building clouds. If they were lucky, the temperature would stay cold enough to snow. If it warmed up much more, they would likely be getting wet.

Jason didn't mention precipitation to Becca. The woman was strung pretty tight and if anyone needed to get outside, it was her. That's how he remembered her most. When they were kids, she had always been the one who wanted to be outside.

They were just pulling up to the back of Becca's inn. She slowed to a stop at the trail head, a short distance from the back of her ranch yard. She shut off her quad and pulled off her helmet, setting it on the gear rack behind her seat. Jason did the same.

Becca pointed to a spot to the right of the trial head. "I want to get the posts in today and collect the waypoints for the map. This will be our first one."

Jason started unloading the auger and a post. He hesitated. "You called first, right?"

Becca looked up from her phone. "Yes, Officer, I got the appropriate line locates. We are free to dig."

"I didn't mean it like that."

"Relax, neither did I. In this case your diligence is appreciated."

Jason paused. "When hasn't my diligence been appreciated?"

"Don't ask questions you don't want to hear the answers to."

"I'll try to remember that." Jason got to work auguring.

Becca resumed typing on her phone and said, "It's easier if I name the waypoints out here." She looked up a minute later. "Wow, you're fast."

Jason shrugged, oddly pleased. "I worked a couple summers fencing when I was younger." He eyed the extra-long posts. "How high do you want these?"

"Deep enough they won't topple without a concrete base and tall enough I can attach a sign that will be visible from the top of a horse. I got clearance to dig up to five feet, so you have plenty of wiggle room."

"I can work with that math." Jason augured a few more feet before sliding a post in.

"Perfect." Becca pocketed her phone and grabbed a shovel and the level.

Jason took the shovel from her. "I can shovel."

Becca held the post level while Jason backfilled the hole, tightly packing the dirt around the post.

They quadded to the next spot on Becca's list. This time there was a fork in the trail. "After we place one here, we'll head up the north fork first," Becca said. She pulled out her phone to take a waypoint and frowned.

"What is it?"

"I just got a notification. It looks like my dad is trying to log into my business insurance account."

"Why?"

"I have no idea."

"Did you give him the login?"

"I had to add him as a contact for the land loan, but no, I did not give him account access."

Jason didn't trust Bruce Tanner. "Could there be a reasonable explanation?"

"Maybe. I just can't think of what that could be."

"Want to go back?"

"No. These line locates are going to expire and it needs to get done. I'll check on it when we get back."

Over the next three hours they fell into a steady rhythm. He'd start auguring as Becca took a waypoint, notes and occasionally photos for the maps she would design and have printed for tourists to venture out on their own.

Her attention to detail impressed Jason, as did her courage to strike out on her own for what she wanted.

Years ago, Clint had hired Jason to help him build a shed. As they worked, the older man had made an offhand comment about Jason being suited to emergency services work. The comment had caught Jason off guard at the same time it had sparked something inside him.

Now Jason knew Clint did not speak offhand about anything. When Jason was in high school, Clint had dropped a number of career seeds. Policing was the only one that had rooted. Jason's parents had never discussed higher education with him. The only careers he could ever remember briefly discussing with them were ranch hand or rig worker. Clint's comment had changed Jason's life.

Becca stopped at the valley rim and Jason recognized where they were. The contentious land between them spread out below. A gust of wind kicked up and Jason could hear the rustling of a thousand aspen leaves letting go of their branches, swirling past them until the wind died and the leaves dropped. A half-hearted breeze tumbled them once more, before they skittered to a stop.

"The aspen leaves remind me of confetti," Becca said, unloading gear. "Or Christmas balls when they land in evergreens."

Pockets of lodgepole pine and Douglas fir added shades of green across the landscape's otherwise tawny canvas. Wayward dry aspen leaves had wound up in many of their boughs. They did indeed look like golden Christmas balls.

"That's rather whimsical of you."

"What do you mean?"

"You always loved being outside, but I remember you having more of a science bent."

"I can be whimsical," Becca said, a bit defensively. She looked out across the land. Below them rolling foothills of native prairie grassland stretched out, flanked by two meandering glacial streams. Beyond, peaks of the front range rose up.

"This place is paradise, Jason. No wonder you hate me."

Jason gave her sideways look. "That mean you'll sell it back to me?"

"Even if I wanted to I can't, my dad's primary on the title."

"Do you want to?"

"I don't know what I want anymore. I don't even know what's right anymore."

"You having second thoughts about opening on time?"

"More like questioning everything in my life a hundred times a day, including opening day."

"Can you afford to wait?"

"No, but I won't put others in danger so I don't go bankrupt, either."

"Your margin is that tight?"

"I had a nest egg when I moved back from Germany. The exchange rate was in my favor when I moved back. I borrowed what I thought was enough from the bank to make this work, but not so much they'd turn me down. Colt's a silent investor, so I want to minimize his risk. I naively thought if anything came up, financial or otherwise, I could just work harder. My emergency buffer did not include armed criminal types pushing back my opening indefinitely. I really don't want to let Colt down, Jason. He believes in me more than anyone else, myself included."

Jason didn't correct her. A hawk circled high above, riding invisible currents. Jason slid the oversized pole in the hole. Becca held it level as he backfilled. "When my dad offered that land I can't believe I fell for it. There are always strings attached with him."

"What do you mean?"

Becca shrugged. "This month it's the pipeline. He knows it's causing me to second guess myself and the feasibility of this whole thing, and he's playing that. Next it'll be something different. Last spring it was a cancer scare to get us kids to come to heel."

"That's cold."

Becca snorted. "That's my dad. My mom is no saint, either. Her only advice to me was to marry money and then manipulate the crap out of him. Sorry, I probably should have kept that to myself."

"You and your brothers turned out fairly well-adjusted, your lapse in judgement with handcuffs aside."

Becca smiled at the sideways compliment. "That would be Clint's influence. He's always been our rock. When we needed someone strong, he was there."

"Clint's helped a lot of people."

Becca looked him in the eye. "That sounds personal."

"It was."

Raindrops started to fall. Becca eyed the line of steel gray clouds that had materialized and were angling towards them. "That was the last one. Now, if we can just make it back before that storm hits." She pointed at the ominous sky.

They headed back. The wind gusted and Jason had to work to keep his quad steady. The now-empty trailer Becca was pulling buffeted in the strong wind, nearly pulling her off the track. The trailer had been a bit of a nuisance in some of the tighter spots on the trail, but in a wind like this, it could be dangerous. An ill-timed gust could flip the trailer, taking her with it.

Becca motioned in front of her, and Jason looked up. A sheer rock wall rose in front of them. He had no idea what she meant, but he followed. She knew this part of the landscape better than he did.

A few minutes later, he followed her up a small, bushy rise. She cut her engine. He did the same. The rain was pelting them now and they both were nearly soaked. He was following her up a narrow trail until suddenly she vanished. He lunged, worried that she had fallen in a hidden crevasse or worse.

In a moment he realized why he couldn't see her. He hadn't seen it through the bush until the opening yawned before him. Becca had her helmet off and was rummaging in the back of the cave.

He pulled his helmet off, too, and placed it just beyond the rain's reach. He looked around. "What is this place?" A small camp table sported a lantern and pop-up chair. Plastic-wrapped blankets hung from a line that had been anchored into the rock wall, as did what looked like a camping blow-up mattress.

"Peace and solitude." She had an armload of firewood and kindling and knelt at a small circle of stones near the mouth of the cave but well behind the rain line. She dropped her bundle and started arranging kindling and crushed newsprint. "There's more in the back, can you grab another load?"

Jason did as she bided. Kneeling near her, he stacked the firewood load within her reach. "You camp here?"

"Rarely anymore, there's always work that needs to get done instead, but it's a shot of peace when I need to get away."

Still kneeling, he sat back on his heels and looked around. "Yet you showed it to me."

She lifted a shoulder. "We were getting soaked."

He persisted. "Neither one of us would have melted. Why did you let me in?" It was clearly her secret sanctuary. That she had allowed him in made him uncomfortable.

She struck a match and lit the crumbled paper tucked in the kindling. She watched the paper catch. Small orange flames licked up, enveloping the dry kindling. In moments, the kindling had caught, too, and was starting to burn. Becca leaned forward and blew on the fledgling flames, the flames pausing and the embers glowing until she stopped. Then fierce flames burst higher, charged by the rush of air. She added larger kindling, and a few small logs. They caught and she stared at the growing blaze. He didn't think she was going to answer him. Finally, she looked up at him and asked, "Why did you come?"

The wind blew particularly fierce and fat raindrops gusted in. Flames danced, casting her face in the glow of firelight. She looked like a pixie in her element, the heart of a mountain.

Theirs was not an easy truce and this felt dangerously close to intimacy even. He stood. "Mind if I pull the table and chair over to dry our stuff?

"Of course." Her tone was reasonable yet he felt very much like his peace was threatened.

Jason moved the table and chair stiffly before stripping off his quilted plaid jacket. He hung it towards the fire to dry. The thick fabric had done a good job keeping his base layer dry. His jeans were soaked but he was not getting out of those. He offered her the chair.

"Probably not a good idea for me to sit in your lap."

His head flew up at her words.

"Never mind, forget I said anything," Becca stammered. She dropped into the chair, staring into the fire like she was memorizing it for a test. For the first time, Jason let himself consider she might actually feel something for him.

Maybe it was the warmth of the fire or the intimacy of the secluded space, but Jason felt himself thawing where she was concerned. Here, watching the firelight play across her face, it was easy to dismiss all the reasons he thought he should stay away from her.

She looked up, her eyes bleak. "I'm cancelling my opening weekend. It's the right thing to do. It's the only thing to do, actually."

Jason agreed but remained silent. Becca added, "I'll start making the calls tonight." Suddenly she covered her face with her hands and Jason heard a small choked sound. In a heartbeat he was in front of her. He pulled her out of the chair and wrapped his arms around her. Becca held him tight, her face buried against his shoulder. He stroked her hair and held her.

When she pulled back her lips were mere inches from his. He leaned in. She met him halfway. This time when their lips touched there was no hesitation. He tasted her, tightening his arms around her. She brought her hands up, framing his face as she kissed him back.

They stayed like that for a long time, not igniting like the kindling, but burning slow and hot like the logs. After a while, Jason noticed the sound of the rain subsiding outside their warm little world, and he held her closer.

Then gunshots echoed outside.

Still clinging to each other, each drew back and swung their gazes towards the mouth of the cave.

Another round of gunshots sounded. He couldn't be sure, but it sounded distant.

Jason looked down. "Do you get many hunters out here?"

She looked up at him with worried eyes. "Some-times."

Jason still had his arms around her; she still held his face in her hands. He wanted to stay, wrapped in the warmth of her and the cave and firelight, but the spell was broken. "We should be getting back."

She nodded, but didn't move from his embrace. He dropped his head. She kissed him again, claiming his mouth with a fierceness he had only ever dreamed about, before finally breaking away.

They smothered the fire and collected their gear. No more shots sounded.

"Ready?"

Becca nodded, not meeting his eyes.

Their relationship had changed today, he just wasn't sure to what.

# Chapter Thirty-Four

Christopher followed his little brother along the wide creek bed. At this time of year the water was low and it was easier walking on the exposed river rocks than through the bush. They had left their quads some distance away, wanting to avoid creating trails to the test plot location.

Christopher eyed the dark clouds overhead. Through the valley he could tell it was storming to the west of them. He craved the solitude and quiet out here. That the day was overcast and dark only added to its appeal for him. Nature's was a righteous dark, whereas life was just ugly dark.

Austin looked over his shoulder. "That Becca is funny. Club a baby seal, she cracks me up."

"She was pretty fired up. I can't see a hydrogen pipeline making a difference."

"It will."

"What do you care?"

"Fossil fuels are dinosaurs." Austin stopped and grinned. "Get it?"

"Yes, brainiac, I know where oil comes from."

"You're a dinosaur. Energy is changing. After we get this on the market we should look into producing green hydrogen. I'm not crazy about the blue stuff, but pink hydrogen has caught my attention."

"What are you babbling about now?"

"Energy. Keep up, big brother. Why not make some money on something other than guns or drugs?"

"You want to invest in the energy sector?"

"No, I want to fucking own it. The clowns have been picking their asses, whining. *There's no market, there's no demand.* Chumps. You make the fucking market, then sell the shit driving it."

"You're serious aren't you?"

"Serious as a fucking hydrogen-run freight train. People are herd animals, they do what you tell them to do. That's why marketing is a thing."

Christopher couldn't disagree.

"The technology's there, just waiting for someone with a clue. Well, that's me."

"Right now, I need you to focus on opioid-strength marijuana."

Austin shook his head. "What would you do without me?"

If Austin were gone, Christopher would be completely alone. Not something he wanted to entertain. Christopher checked their fake university signage was still up, including the painted rocks forming the university initials. That should look collegiate enough from the air. He jumped down the riverbank and hopscotched across strategically placed rocks until he cleared the shallow river. Austin followed. Test plots dotted the inside curve of the river. Series of white tarps stretched around thick stakes created miniature greenhouses, both protecting and supporting the valuable plants within. Christopher knew soil and land by instinct, but it was Austin who understood the chemistry. They hiked to the next bend in the river. Austin pointed out the newly marked grid for the next season's test. "This spot has nearly identical microbes and matrix chemistry, with minimal microclimatic variance."

"In English, man."

Austin angled his wrist, pointing his finger straight down at the ground. "Plant the pot here."

"How soon until next season?"

Austin shrugged. "Early June if we're lucky. Early July if we're not."

Christopher didn't like that timeline, but nature had him by the balls. To maximize marijuana grow ops indoors, explicit timelines were followed. Growing outside in high elevation with a growing season this tight seriously limited the amount that could be produced from a single plant.

"And you're sure we can't recreate the right conditions indoors?" They hiked back to the current test plots.

"I've tried everything, bringing in the local soil, the local water. Nothing works. I haven't been able to isolate what supercharges the CBD from this specific location. I don't even know why you put a seedling here in the first place. It's crap for growing fragile plants."

"Marijuana grown indoors is fragile. Any plant that grows up outside is way tougher. Besides, you know I put a few grafted ones out here, too."

"Yes, well, the indoor tests of the same strain have marginally higher CBD levels, but nothing that compares to these supercharged outdoor ones. These are weird-ass plants."

Christopher smiled. "It's the land, kid."

Austin rolled his eyes. "Here we go. More *terroir* crap. I thought that only applied to wine."

Christopher didn't take the bait. "You're sure this will work?"

Austin pressed. "That Becca woman needs a sommelier."

Christopher took out his sheers and clipped off a few plants at their bases, gently rolling them in linen before sliding them in the map canister he carried. "Her classifieds are irrelevant to me."

"They shouldn't be," Austin muttered, making notes of what Christopher clipped. "You hate being a thug."

Christopher was losing patience. "My career choices were made a long time ago. So were yours." He held up the map canister. "Tell me again the numbers are actually solid."

Austin's jaw was set, but he relented like he always did. "Yeah, they work. Your little solo garden parties of dropping seedlings in random places hit. The CBD levels from what we've harvested here are crazy elevated, like *opioids*-elevated. That's why they're going to fucking blow up the market. With our babies here, no one has to play Russian roulette for a little pain relief."

Two of their brothers overdosed. But they had blown up their lives before finally blowing up their bodies. "That's why we're doing this," Christopher reminded him.

"Yeah, for the fucking money."

"Don't," Christopher warned.

"What?" Austin's eyes flashed. "They should've put goddamn guns in their mouths, it would have been a cleaner way to fucking off themselves."

"Those are our brothers you're talking about."

"No, real brothers wouldn't do that to family. They were fucking selfish bastards."

Christopher's voice dropped low. "You know addiction doesn't work like that."

Austin ran a hand across his face. "Whatever. Let's not get into it again. They're dead. We're not. We're going to drop this on the market like a fucking tsunami. Everybody is going to want a piece of this." Austin paused. "That's why I applied for a patent."

Christopher stopped. "You did what?"

"Don't look at me like that. Chemists go a lifetime without making a breakthrough like this. I'm not letting some pharmaceutical dickwad hijack our work. Those assholes patent everything from traditional knowledge to their Frankencrops. Fuck that. They're screwing sick people, culture, and poisoning the land. We should win the goddamn Nobel Peace Prize; your neurotic wine terroir bullshit—"

Christopher grabbed for his brother's throat as the sound of bullets ripped through the air. They both dropped to the ground.

He pulled his gun with one hand and reached out to his little brother with the other. Austin was already down, laying on his back, making a weird gurgling sound and clutching his midsection. Austin's torso was a mess of blood and shredded innards.

Christopher crawled over and pressed his hand against the wounds, hoping it was enough pressure to slow the bleeding. Austin croaked, " —applies to marijuana, too."

"Shh." Christopher's hand was soaked. Austin was losing too much blood too fast and they were still taking fire.

Austin grunted.

Christopher avoided looking down at him; instead he scanned the horizon looking for the shooter.

Austin grunted again. They both knew Christopher had to take out whoever was shooting at them, or get them to retreat fast. Austin wouldn't make it otherwise.

*"Fuck."* Christopher got up and sprinted to the tree line, gun firing.

# Chapter Thirty-Five

Clint Steel's horse reared at the sound of shots. They were too close for comfort and way too many fired together. He thought he heard a choked scream.

*Becca and Jason.*

As his horse sprang forward, he kept his seat in the saddle, but just barely. He lost a lot of ground, but managed to bring his mount under control. It would have been a different story if he had still been rewiring fences when the shooting started.

Clint heard a battle scream and the staccato of several shots being fired off. The bush was too thick to see which way to go for safety. Indecision warred within him until he heard a choking gasp. Clint cautiously urged his mount towards the sound. A man was lying on his back. He was too small to be Jason and Clint felt guilty for his relief. The man's hands were clutched to his abdomen. Blood visibly flowed from between his fingers.

Clint kicked out of his stirrups, landing on the ground. He wrapped the reins around a sturdy branch and dropped to his knees.

The man was young. His eyes were wide, and he gave a fresh gurgled start when he saw Clint.

"It's ok, it's ok. Sounds like you've gone and got yourself shot. Let's have a look." Clint kept his voice steady as he talked the man through the checking of his wounds. He gently pulled the man's jacket and shirt back, exposing his abdomen. Several bullets had torn into him and if Clint was correct, the man's intestines spilled out from the overlarge holes. He shrugged out of his own jacket and flannel shirt and as gentle as he could pushed the intestines back in. He pressed his flannel shirt tight, applying pressure to the wound. One handed, he pulled out his SPOT device and activated it. He thumbed a succinct text message and hit send. Moments later confirmation of helicopter support beeped.

"See, help's coming. We just need to hold tight—"

The man's body was laying on something. Clint slid his hand under the man's back and felt cold steel at the same time he heard a click behind him.

He closed his eyes. He knew that sound. He hadn't expected to die today.

"Step away from my brother."

Clint turned his head. "I'm holding your brother's intestines in. He's lost way too much blood. Now, you can shoot me or help me stop him from bleeding out. The helicopter will be here soon."

"Why were you out here?"

"I was fencing when I heard shots. My horse spooked and we saw your brother. He needed help."

The man tucked the gun away and dropped to the other side of his brother's prone body. He looked Clint in the eye and said, "He dies, you're dead."

# Chapter Thirty-Six

Christopher Fischer sat sprawled in an uncomfortable chair in the surgical waiting room, an untouched can of coke and bag of chips in front of him on a coffee table. The vending machines at the end of the hall offered few options. The clock above the door ticked loudly. The police had already been and gone, twice, but a uniform cop had stayed behind and was stationed by the door. Their frustration was visceral. They wanted him for a lot of charges. Some he did, most he didn't.

The door opened and Christopher steeled himself, unwilling to give away his fear. But it wasn't the cop, it was a crying woman, waiting for news on the condition of a loved one. She gasped when she saw him. He looked down. His brother's blood had soaked through most of the fabric of his shirt and a good deal of his pants. He knew he looked like hell but didn't give a fuck what she thought of him.

He held her gaze until she retreated and took the long way around a bank of chairs on the far side of the room. He had been told enough times his eyes were lifeless. Stupid fucks, he felt everything. Something flickered in the corner of his eye, but when he turned his head, nothing was there.

That had been happening too much lately.

Shaking his head, he scanned the room full of families waiting for news, just like him.

The scent of vanilla suddenly assaulted his nose and he suddenly missed his mom so bad, if he wasn't already sitting, his knees would have buckled.

He swiped at his nose and counted the addicts in the room. They stuck out like beacons of easy money. He never bought into the idea that an addict on the street was a piece of shit, while an addict in a nice home was merely self-medicating their stressful lives. He never felt bad selling drugs to the rich and bored, but selling to people on the street was something else. He knew what they were trying to numb themselves from.

The door opened again and a white coat came through with a clip board. The doctor noticed the cop immediately and stopped. Without saying a word she looked down at the chart in her hand and then up. Her eyes found Christopher's and she walked over. She showed no fear, just a weariness that was alarming in its casualness.

"Mr. Fischer?"

Christopher sat up straighter. "That's me."

The doctor sat on the coffee table, avoiding the bag of chips and can of pop. She had positioned herself between the cop and Christopher. In a tone that did not move beyond the two of them she said, "I will take you back in a moment to see your brother. He made it through surgery, but he lost a lot of blood and there are a lot of entry wounds."

"So he's almost dead, I get it. What aren't you telling me?"

The doctor held his gaze. Her lack of fear was unusual. It had an unnerving effect on Christopher. Most men feared him and women always did. This woman was different.

"People handle distress in different ways. Apparently you are already a concern to public safety." The doctor lifted her index finger, indicating behind her shoulder and Christopher's attention was drawn to the uniformed officer. "Are you going to be okay to go back there?"

Christopher made eye contact with the doctor then. As fucked as his life had been, her eyes had seen more. It was right there in front of him. Christopher couldn't help it, he stared, a bit in awe. "Why are you asking me instead of Handcuffs over there?"

"Because I took an expensive class in bedside manners."

Christopher eyed the officer. "No trouble. I just want to see my brother."

The doctor nodded. "That's what I was hoping you would say." She eyed Christopher's bloody clothing. "I'll get you something to change into. Let's go."

They passed the officer and walked through the swinging doors. Christopher's heart pounded and his ears started to ring. The fluorescent lights hurt his eyes and it smelled like death on this side of the doors.

The doctor stopped at a small shelf, pulling a set of visitor scrubs down and handing them to him. "Mr. Fischer, I have been informed you are in the business of dealing arms and drugs." The doctor held up her hand, intercepting Christopher's interruption. "How a man makes his living is up to him. However, as a professional curtesy I'm asking you to consider alternative products. Bullets wounds are pure hell to patch up and overdoses are as ugly as they are avoidable. Both are an unconscionable assault on the dignity of the human body."

Christopher was taken aback. No one had spoken to him like that since his mom, and he had never heard anyone speak of protecting the dignity of a body.

"Are you for real?"

"As real as the four bullets I pulled out of your brother's abdomen. You can get changed in there. There are plastic bags under the sink you can put your soiled clothes into. I'll wait here and then take you to see your brother. Do hurry."

Christopher took the scrubs. In the single washroom, he tugged off his long-sleeved shirt and jeans before cramming them into a bag he found under the sink. Nearly naked, he scrubbed his hands and face. The white sink was a stark contrast to the river of red circling the drain. Frantic, he pulled out several paper towels, trying to push the bloody water down the drain faster. There was so much red. Too much. An anguished cry escaped him, and he heard a knock on the door.

"Mr. Fischer?" It was the doctor waiting to take him to his brother.

"I'm fine, I'm fine. Hang on." Christopher slammed the water taps off and mopped his wet arms and face. His gaze landed on the garbage filled with paper towels soaked with his brother's blood. Christopher was going to be sick. He pivoted towards the toilet in the small space, retching. The shadows under the door moved. The doctor was there, waiting. She let him have his moment and didn't knock again.

Christopher rinsed his mouth before putting on the visitor scrubs and walked out.

# Chapter Thirty-Seven

Jason drove the quad into Becca's ranch yard, stopping at her front door. The sun had set and the early evening air was cold, particularly with their rain-soaked clothes. He flipped open his visor and said loud enough to be heard over the engine, "Go on in. I'll put this stuff away."

Becca nodded and dismounted from the back of the quad. They had stopped at Clint's already and dropped off the second quad. She tugged off her helmet. Her braid had come undone and her hair was a wild mess around her head. She was beautiful.

Jason took her helmet.

"Thanks." Becca looked everywhere but at him. Neither seemed to know what to say since the cave.

Tucker came out the front door. He made an eating motion with his hands and Becca visibly brightened. She gave her brother the thumbs up, and he disappeared back inside the house.

Becca turned, this time looking at him. "Whatever Tucker made you're going to want to eat. See you inside?"

Jason nodded. "Sure."

Becca stepped back. She smiled shyly at him before turning and running into the house. She had done the same thing years ago. Before that fucking letter.

Sarah Kades

Jason drove the quad to the Quonset. He unloaded the gear and trailer and tried not to compare then and now. She had shredded him last time. He was supposed to be smarter now. He checked the trailer to make sure he had gotten everything when he noticed a large river stone in the corner. Bands of pink, blue and gray wound through-out the rock. As far as rocks went, it had visual appeal. He hadn't noticed it before. Becca must have liked it and picked it up. He put it on one of the work spaces in the Quonset.

As he was walking back to the house, trying to think of an excuse to leave, he noticed fresh vehicle tracks through her yard. Shit.

"Did you get a shift in downtown today?" Jason asked Tucker. They were seated around Becca's large island counter in her kitchen. Tucker had made some sort of bisque soup and fresh bread. Jason couldn't remember ever having a meal in a restaurant that tasted half as good, and it was just bread and soup.

Becca lowered her spoon. "What is he talking about? Tell me you are not back doing undercover work."

"Becca, everything's fine. I was just looking to get some intel." Tucker made a slicing motion with his hand. "Ixnay on the freaking out my sister part."

"You promised you were done with undercover work."

"And I was. Until this task force."

Jason looked between the two siblings. Sometimes he forgot to censor himself. "Sorry I brought up a sensitive

238

topic." He tried to pivot. "Did everything go well putting up the cameras?"

"It did. Colt could moonlight installing security systems."

"Where did you end up putting them outside?" Jason took another spoonful of soup.

Tucker rattled off locations. "You should have seen Colt, he shimmied up the back of the house and the barn."

"So you didn't need to bring the truck around to reach?"

Becca pulled at her bread, looking at Jason.

Tucker didn't notice. "Didn't need to, Colt free climbed everything."

Becca spoke, "Jason, what's going on? Those questions weren't random."

Tucker looked up, surprised. "What's she talking about?"

*Jesus*, Becca should be the one in law enforcement. "I saw fresh tire tracks out back and I didn't want to alarm anyone. I was hoping there was a benign explanation."

Becca swung her gaze to Tucker. "Did you guys drive back there?"

Tucker shook his head.

"Can I stay in town with you tonight?" Becca blurted.

"Hell yeah. I'll be able to actually sleep tonight."

At Tucker's declaration, Becca raised an eyebrow. Tucker was too busy eating to notice.

Jason leaned forward. "He's worried about you. It's easier for guys to sleep when we know the people we care about are close and safe."

"Nice mansplaining, but that's not just a *guy* thing." Becca stood. "If you'll excuse me, I have to pack a bag and my laptop. I have several emails to send about postponing my opening."

Less than an hour later, Jason and Tucker watched Becca's headlights flash at the end of the drive before she turned towards Calgary.

Jason held out a pack of cigarettes. Tucker took one and said, "We gotta quit these."

Jason lit his before answering, "I know."

A few minutes later, truck headlights flashed at the end of the long drive and adrenaline poured into Jason's system. What now?

Jason relaxed when he recognized Clint's truck; that is until he saw the older man was covered in blood. Both Jason and Tucker sprinted over.

"It's not my blood." Clint assured them through the open window. "I'm okay."

Officer Cooper was in the passenger seat and leaned over. "He found one of the Fischer brothers shot up."

"Where?" Jason asked.

"At the end of my Chimney Creek lease. I did what I could so he wouldn't bleed out. Stars flew him in to Foothills Hospital. He's near dead, but not dead yet."

Tucker looked at Jason. "They're not affiliated, right?"

"You mean gangs?" Jason shook his head. "As far as we understand they only trust family."

"Any chance the brothers took shots at each other?" Tucker asked.

It was Clint's turn to shake his head. "The other one was ready to blow my head off until he realized I was the only thing holding his brother's guts in."

Tucker stepped forward. "Are you okay?"

Cooper leaned towards the open window. "He did a damn fine job."

The older man looked down at his stained shirt. "Really, I'm fine, none of this blood is mine."

"He means having a gun pulled on you," Jason said quietly. Clint looked older than Jason had ever seen him.

"I've had worse days. I would have gotten here sooner, but I drove his brother to the hospital. They couldn't take him in the helicopter. Officer Cooper escorted us."

Tucker's eyes bugged. "You gave one of the Fischers a ride?"

Clint shrugged. "I figured if he was going to do something, he would have done it when he had a gun pointed at the back of my head."

Officer Cooper looked a little green, then. Jason didn't know if it was one of Clint's finer moments, it just as easily could have been a fatal decision. Jason didn't know if he would have played taxi to the guy who had pulled a gun on him.

"Where is Becca, by the way?"

"Staying at my condo."

Clint nodded. "Good. I hate to say it, but you fellas keep her off that back lease. I don't know what's going on back there, but something bad is brewing." Clint looked down. "I need to get this blood off me. I'm tagging out for the day. Officer Cooper, where can I drop you?"

Jason stepped forward. "I can give Officer Cooper a ride back to the detachment."

Jason realized his mistake as soon as Officer Cooper got into his truck. Jason had printed the file that had been erroneously emailed to him; it was sitting on his front passenger seat. Cooper picked up the folder before he sat down, dislodging a few sheets in his haste.

"Thanks for the ride, Officer Chasseur. I didn't want to be a bother for Mr. Steel." Cooper righted the folder and retrieved the papers that had slid out. Jason could tell the moment the younger officer realized what they were. Copper darted a sideways look at Jason. "These look like Ms. Tanner's files. That was very accommodating of her to share them with you."

"It was." Jason did not correct the younger officer. Becca hadn't mentioned the file since Jason had stormed out of her house after seeing the contents spread across her coffee table. Jason held out his hand.

Officer Cooper hesitated before handing Jason the file. Jason tucked it next to the seat. He knew what he had to do. He would deal with that later.

# Chapter Thirty-Eight

Becca flexed her fingers on the steering wheel of her truck. She turned on the radio and something about a lovesick country girl crooned over the speakers. An image of Jason's powerful body flashed through her mind, followed by an image of the handcuffs. All that power had been leashed so tight. Becca punched off the radio and opened her window a couple inches, leaning her head in the stream of icy air. Danger should not make her biological clock tick louder.

Her phone pinged, lighting up the truck's caller ID display. *Meredith.* Becca reached to decline the call. The truck bucked on the cracked highway and her finger missed the decline button, activating the call, instead. Becca jabbed her finger against the truck's display screen, trying to hang up.

"Becca, dear?" Meredith's voice, usually so annoyingly melodious, sounded brittle through the truck's speakers.

Resigned, Becca answered. "Meredith, hello."

"I was just wondering, that is, if you wouldn't mind so much..." The older woman's voice trailed off.

"What is it?" This was why you didn't take calls from the woman your dad left your mom for. It was seriously awkward.

"I left your father," Meredith blurted.

Becca adjusted her grip on the wheel. "Are you okay?"

"Can I come over?" Becca heard the defeat in the older woman's voice.

"I'm actually in town, I'm staying at Tucker's tonight." Becca cringed as soon as the words were out. The last thing Becca wanted to do, like ever, was hang out with her dad's mistress-turned-wife. Meredith wasn't the first woman Bruce had cheated on Samantha with, just the one he left Becca's mom for.

"Oh, that sounds lovely."

Squirming, Becca forced out, "Would you like to meet me there?" *Please say no, please say no, please say no.*

"Thank you dear. Yes, I would." Meredith sniffled a small, dainty sound. "This means a lot."

Becca stopped herself from pounding on the steering wheel. "Do you know where Tucker lives?" Becca didn't think Meredith had ever been to her brother's condo.

"I have all you kids in my contacts. Christmas and birthday cards, and such." Her voice trailed off.

"You send those?" There was a charged pause before Becca relented. "Never mind, forget I said anything. I'm just coming into town now. I'll be there in twenty minutes."

Meredith leapt at the olive branch. "I'll pick up dinner."

Tucker's bisque and fresh bread had been enough, but Meredith pressed when Becca didn't immediately respond. "I'll get anything you like."

"Sure, how about pizza and a bottle of red wine?"

Meredith voice brightened. "I'll make it two of each!"

Becca could tell the older woman was trying. She sighed. "Thank you, that's Tucker's favorite." Becca thought about the emails she had to write tonight. "I've had a shit-ass day, too, so we'll commiserate."

"I'll bring chocolate."

# Chapter Thirty-Nine

Jason sat at his kitchen table. His quiet dinner over, the dishes done. A cup of untouched tea sat at his elbow. In front of him the box from his mom lay empty, its contents neatly ordered across his table, along with the small box of artifacts he'd found as a kid. Next to that was the printed copies of the file he had been erroneously emailed. When Jason dropped Cooper at the detachment the younger officer had given him a cryptic look before disappearing into the building. This was a breach of the rules and they both knew it.

A crumbled, folded letter lay alone and off to the side. He wasn't ready to touch that one, yet.

Jason pulled the folder of printed files towards him and opened it. He picked up the top sheet—a tidy summary, succinct and well-written—before skimming the contents. Lillian Kensington was a thorough researcher with a talent for prose. It was all there, staring back at him in Garamond, a lively report summing up his family history. It overlapped the mementos from his mom with a shocking number of the gaps filled in. Lillian brought the facts and figures to life. It felt like he would recognize his grandparents should he pass them on the street. It had the uncomfortable effect of feeling like he was sharing his grandparents with strangers and left him feeling exposed. He didn't like that. Still, it had been Clint who first hired Lillian to help Becca. Clint's direct involvement complicated things. When Jason was still young and mad at the world it had been Clint who had pointed him on a less self-destructive path. Clint's participation gave the report undeniable credibility. Jason set the file aside, unsure how he was supposed to feel.

Gently, he picked up his several-times great grandfather's journal. He hadn't been raised sentimental and didn't expect how unsettling it would be to hold something so ancestral in his hands. The cover was cracked and stained. What were those discolored spots? Could have been water damage, maybe even just dirt. He didn't think it was blood, although one stain looked suspiciously like a thumbprint. He tipped the cover open revealing soft pages that were fragile but not as brittle as he had expected. It carried the distinct smell of old books. To him, this was what old smelled like. Jason had ridden with another officer once who had discussed in great detail the uniquely old smell of hospitals. Jason had listened with half an ear but internally dismissed the older officer's assessment. Old didn't smell like heavy duty cleaners and stale air. Everyone knew old smelled like old books.

Jason turned a page. He had never shared it with his mom, but he did have an interest in history. Somewhere between the angst of youth and the responsibilities of adulthood, a curiosity about the past had piqued and he had read everything he could get his hands regarding Western Canadian history. Who were the *coureur de bois*, the early unlicensed French traders who ventured far and wide, including up the upper Missouri—and likely Alberta—long before the Treaty of Paris was signed and centuries before the forty-ninth parallel became a thing? Or the brutal fur trade wars that only halted post-amalgamation. That a business merger could stop that much violence spoke volumes about what people were fighting for.

The Indigenous Peoples had their own trade and business partnerships, their own enemies and allies long before contact with any non-Indigenous trader. Yet the cultural and geographical landscapes of North America were gripped in an ever-shifting wave of adapt or die as the fur trade pressed farther west. Then there was confederation, which Jason had always felt patriotic about until he started reading history. When unpacked, the celebrated shift carried the stink of yet another business venture. The theme was consistent: wealthy white men from the east—on either side of the Atlantic—had ambitions to convert natural resources into their own bulging bankroll.

As Canada and the United States solidified the once fluid border on the western frontier, American whiskey forts and wolfers moved into southern Alberta with fire water and fire power, with hard men hardened by the American Civil War. After the Cypress Hills Massacre, Canada created the North-West Mounted Police, the precursor to the RCMP.

The U.S. Cavalry and NWMP shared an uneasy relationship as the federal policies on western expansion from their respective countries made the border a contested finish line. The systematic annihilation of the great bison herds and the building of the railroads sealed what had started centuries ago. The post-contact history of Canada shook out as privileged white men living east taking what they wanted of the west.

Little had changed. Instead of men in London, men in Ottawa now made the rules for their western hinterland. Any student of history knew western alienation wasn't a new concept. Just ask Riel.

Jason had never understood why Canadians thought their history was boring. It was layered, painful, and poignant. Pain was never boring. Neither was humanity.

Jason let his fingers slide across the first page. The journal was written in French. He knew French was the language of the fur trade even after France lost the Seven Years War. He struggled to read the unfamiliar words scratched in a concise yet not exactly flowing hand. His distant grandfather's hand.

Jason picked up his pen and notebook and started to translate the journal. Sometimes the entries read almost like poetry, other times they were succinct, choppy even. Jason could tell when his grandfather respected or enjoyed the company of his contemporaries, as well as when he did not.

Armand also had an eye for detail and described the land and daily workings with acute clarity. Hand drawn sketches sometimes accompanied locational descriptions and appeared reasonable facsimiles of reality. His commentary was dry with an occasional bite.

Jason eased another page over. At first the image drawn appeared like the others he had seen so far. The same penned lines, the same cross-hatch shading style. But there was something familiar to the curve of the stream, the peaks in the background. Goose bumps appeared on his arms. He read the caption. *Fort Roche Cachée, sixteen leagues southwest of Fort La Jonquière.* He reached across the table and retrieved the printed report Lillian had compiled. He flipped until he found the page he was looking for. *Fort La Jonquière is generally accepted as the earliest western most fort. Its whereabouts are unconfirmed but from what I can surmise, the likely location is where the Bow and Elbow Rivers meet in the present day city of Calgary, Alberta.*

Jason got up and retrieved his laptop. A few keystrokes later and he was reasonably certain an historic French league was about forty miles. He pulled up an online map and pinned Fort Calgary. Then he eyeballed another pin and checked the distance. Forty miles.

He picked up the journal again and scrutinized the sketch. It predated Fort La Jonquière by ten years.

It was also a scene from his childhood.

# Chapter Forty

Tucker was exhausted. He got off the elevator on the eighteenth floor and unlocked his front door. Feminine laughter sounded from his kitchen. His sister wasn't alone. Tucker frowned and kicked out of his boots before he made his way down the hall. The long bank of living room windows were dark except the muted light of the downtown skyline. It was a foggy night and the skyline looked surreal, otherworldly.

So did his kitchen. Tucker rubbed his eyes. Becca and Meredith sat at his kitchen table, laughing, an empty pizza box and nearly empty bottle of wine between them. What alternate reality had he stepped into? None of them hung out with Meredith, least of all Becca. She had been pretty clear she wanted nothing to do with the woman their dad left their mom for.

"Tucker! We saved the second pizza for you." They both irrupted in giggles.

"Are you guys high?" Cannabis was legal in Canada now. Maybe Becca took up smoking. He wouldn't blame her; she was wound pretty tight.

"*Tuck-er.*" Becca drew out his name, exasperated.

Tucker looked between the two women trying to gauge what in the world had changed in the few hours since he last saw Becca. "What are you guys doing?"

Becca looked over the rim of her wine glass, her eyes twinkling. "Don't you mean why is Meredith here?"

Tucker eyed the older woman sipping her own glass of wine. "Maybe."

"Oh, it's alright dear. We must have given you a start." She set her glass down and straightened her spine. "I left your father."

"And that means you came to my house?" Tucker winced. Just because he wasn't surprised the marriage hadn't lasted didn't mean he had to be an ass about it.

His sister scowled. "Tucker, god, don't be a boob. We're both having a shit-ass day. Meredith helped me write my emails canceling my opening weekend and I offered her your spare bedroom here. With us."

"Damn. I know how much your opening meant to you." He turned to Meredith. "Thanks for helping my sister."

Meredith smile was hesitant. "Anytime. I mean it. Anytime."

Becca picked up the nearly empty bottle of wine. "Bring the other bottle when you bring the pizza over."

Tucker found the second pizza box in the oven. He retrieved it and a wine glass for himself. He set both on the table before going back to pull a small container out of the freezer and pop it in the microwave. He punched a couple numbers before picking up the second bottle of red on the counter. "You guys want me to open this one now?"

Becca tilted her empty wine glass upside-down in answer.

The microwave pinged and Tucker retrieved the container he had thawed and set it in front of them. He refilled Becca's glass and topped-up Meredith's before pouring one for himself. He sat down and took a healthy swig of his wine. The weight of the last few weeks was heavy.

"Is that what I think it is?" Becca pointed at the container.

"Brownies."

Her whole face lit up. "I forgive you for being a boob." She launched herself out of her chair and wrapped her arms around him. His chair tilted precariously back, and he just barely caught them before spilling his wine. "You're welcome."

Becca stilled and held on to him. He closed his eyes and held back.

Becca straightened and rubbed her nose, reaching for a brownie. "Glad you're home bro. And not just because I wouldn't have looked in your freezer for these puppies." She took a bite. "*Goddamn*, that's heaven. Meredith, you have to try one. Tucker is a true and proper wizard in the kitchen."

Meredith accepted a desert and took a bite. "Oh my."

"Positively carnal, aren't they?"

Tucker plucked the container back. "Don't use words like that. They're just brownies."

Becca tore off another piece and popped it into her mouth. "Those brownies are going to get you a wife."

Tucker choked on his wine. "I am so not looking for a wife. Seriously, how much wine have you two had?"

Meredith tilted her head, assessing him. "Why aren't you married already? You're handsome and you bake."

Tucker let Becca pry the container out of his hands. She said, "I know, right? He cooks, too. I asked him ten times if he would be my chef. You know what kind of reviews I could score with him in my kitchen, let alone the souvenir calendars?"

"Ew, don't be gross."

"Money is not gross. You'd be my little cash cow." Becca leaned over and pinched Tucker's cheeks.

He swatted her hands away. He was way too sober for these two. "I'm a police officer, not a chef."

"You're a chef with a badge and the highest charity calendar sales record." Becca retorted and popped another bite of brownie into her mouth. "Seriously, these are so good. Why do you catch bad guys, again?"

Tucker opened the second pizza box before looking up. "Saved me a pizza, did you?"

Becca looked sheepish. When Meredith smiled, she looked ten years younger. Tucker looked again. He barely knew Meredith, but he knew victims. Meredith was scared under the smile.

Tucker ate the half of pizza they had left him and listened. When Meredith spoke of Bruce, she was careful when she described the verbal altercation. He could tell she was either playing down the event, or it wasn't the first time she had considered leaving. Tucker also wondered if his father was violent with his wife.

The conversation turned lighter when Becca shared the latest email from Anna, Gabe's partner.

Tucker smiled as Becca recounted the story of Gabe falling for Savannah, or Anna as he had known her by. Gabe had always been rather self-contained. He had opened up a lot since meeting Anna. Becca was looking rather relaxed and happy at the moment, too, especially considering the week she had had. Tucker would wait and tell her about the Fischer shooting in the morning. A night of peace would do a world of good for her. She was safe here; the news could wait until morning.

# Chapter Forty-One

Becca woke up disoriented, her head pounding and with blankets wrapped around her in disarray. She pushed the blankets away and sat up. The events of last night came flooding back.

She had cancelled her opening weekend.

Becca knew it was the right thing to do; it just didn't make it any easier. All she had wanted was to build a sustainable home, one for herself and something she could share with guests looking for respite and renewal. She could nurture them and try to learn how to nurture herself, too.

It felt like her heart was breaking; she needed to get out of here. It was still dark outside, but Becca knew she wouldn't be able to get back to sleep. As quiet as she could she slipped out of bed and got ready. Meredith was in Tucker's guest bedroom and Tucker was softly snoring on the couch. They would wonder why she left without a word. She'd apologize later. Closing the front door with a soft click, Becca fled back to the country.

The morning rush-hour traffic hadn't helped. As the sun rose, it crawled at a snail's pace and Becca had felt the walls of her truck closing in around her. She hadn't realized just how close to the edge she had swayed.

She needed to ride. Just her and Pixie and the sound of Pixie's hoofbeats playing with the wind. There were a million other things she should be doing. Safer, more productive things.

Becca saddled Pixie in the wide hallway of her barn. Deep angled light from shoulder-high windows highlighted shafts of dust. Her mare was gentle, but a few sidesteps gave away Pixie's impatience to be out, too. Becca hurried, eager to run away if only for a few brief kilometers. She packed a water bottle, apple, and a ham and cheese croissant before checking her jacket pocket for flares and hip holster for her bear spray.

Becca jumped when she heard the sound of a vehicle pulling in and reached for the curry pick. She really had to invest in actual weapons. She slid over to the window, afraid of what she would find. A now familiar RCMP truck slowed to a stop in her driveway.

Jason.

Conflicted, Becca hesitated. Part of her wanted to run straight into his arms, press her lips against his and pick up where they had left off in the cave yesterday. But what if he didn't feel the same about her? She was precariously close to breaking. Her resilience could only stretch so thin.

Becca led Pixie out the back barn door. With more speed than grace, she mounted the large horse. She heard loud knocking from her front porch.

*"Becca, it's Jason. Can I come in?"*

Her heart squeezed. Jason had come. Again. She had waited so long to be with him, longer than she had dreamed of opening her own inn. She had already lost one dream indefinitely. She wasn't ready to lose another, if that was his decision. Tightening her legs, Becca silently urged Pixie forward. Several strides later she cleared the small rise on her side pasture and gave Pixie free rein. Her mare responded with a spring and steady speed. The rhythmic thumping of Pixie's hooves felt like both a lullaby and battle cry. The wind whipped at her face, snatching her tears before they could fall, and she turned to her back lease for sanctuary.

# Chapter Forty-Two

Jason had woken early, restless. He couldn't stop thinking about yesterday in the cave. About how everything had changed. He had to clear the past behind them, had to understand. The crumbled, folded letter was in his pocket. It would blow up his future or finally make peace with the past.

Jason knocked harder on Becca's front door.

*"Becca, it's Jason. Can I come in?"*

She wasn't answering her door or his text messages, but her truck was in the drive, so she wasn't still at her brother's. Jason made his way to the barn. No Becca. He checked Pixie's stall. Empty. He was about to turn when he heard beeping. Becca's cell phone was vibrating on an exposed wall beam next to Pixie's empty stall.

Jason picked it up. "Hi Tucker, it's Jason."

There was a pregnant pause. "I'd be asking why you're answering Becca's phone at this hour of the morning, but she slept at my condo last night."

"Did you tell her what happened to Clint? She's not here. Neither is that big mare of hers."

Tucker swore. "She was here with Meredith when I got home, I figured we'd talk in the morning. She left before I even woke up. Why are you there?"

*I had to see her.* "Know where she would be headed?" Jason ran to the tack room.

"No idea. *Fuck.* We can't even track her if she left her cell phone."

"I'll find her. Keep your phone close." He hung up, pocketing Becca's phone. With sure, quick motions, he saddled her gray gelding and headed out the back at a trot. The animal seemed to sense Jason's mood and was eager to take off.

The bracing, cold air was a blessing. Pixie's hooves had left a trail in the frosted earth to track, but he would have to follow fast before the morning sun melted all the signs taking him to Becca.

That same sun hit the golden aspen leaves low. They were posted light sentinels, a line of fluttering torches pulling Jason deeper into the backcountry.

The trail stopped at a shallow, fast-moving creek. He led his horse in, splashing through the glacial water, and paced the shoreline until he picked her trail back up several meters downstream. A breeze swelled and dry leaves fell like confetti all around him. It was getting harder to follow her trail. Another twenty minutes and the frost would be gone, leaving Jason with only a whisper of a trail and what he hoped wasn't time running out.

# Chapter Forty-Three

Bruce Tanner used the brass door knocker in the upscale neighborhood south of downtown. He held an oversized bouquet of flowers in one hand and an expensive jewelry box in the other. With his first wife, Samantha, expensive jewelry could right any wrong, any indiscretion. Meredith would no doubt fall in line, too. Women were predictable and tedious like that. Easily distracted by baubles. He knocked, again. Impatient.

"Bruce, hello." Ruth answered the door. She held a water bottle in one hand and the door with the other. She was in a lavender track suit. She looked like she had been working out, even managing a light sweat at her temples. He had to stop himself from snorting. Sweat never looked good on women, not even if they were exerting themselves pleasing him.

Bruce pitched his voice to a seductive octave. "Good morning, Ruth my dear, you're looking rather fetching today."

His wife's friend raised an eyebrow. She kept her hand on the door.

"Sorry to show up unannounced. I was hoping to surprise my wife," he said smoothly, trying to see past the older woman. Meredith was no doubt listening. She was hopelessly in love with him. He had been with her, too.

At the start. But now he needed his passport; she was always reorganizing their house with the latest trend. And he needed to know if she suspected anything.

Ruth eyed the contents in his hands. "Aren't you a charmer?" Her voice didn't match her words. "She's unavailable. Maybe she's trying that new Pilates class. Pilates is such a wonderful form of exercise, you should try—"

Bruce spoke over her, "Yes, yes, Ruth, thank you." He couldn't stand his wife's ridiculous friends. He pressed the bouquet and box into her hands, nearly upending her water bottle. "Please tell my wife to call me." He was sure she would call before dinner.

A truck pulled into the large drive, blocking his Jaguar. A well-built young man got out, carrying a large duffle bag.

"Bruce, you'll have to excuse me. I have an appointment." To the younger man she said, "I do love a man on time."

The younger man gave Ruth a sensuous look. "I couldn't leave you waiting, Ms. Ruth." He completely ignored Bruce.

Instead of correcting the slight, Ruth gave the young man a once-over. "Or wanting. Come in, darling." The man pressed close, trailing a hand across Ruth's breasts as he went through the door. Ruth smiled, slapping him on his ass before turning. She held up the flowers and elegantly wrapped gift. "I'll see that your wife gets these."

She went to close the door. Bruce stuck out his foot, catching the door before it could close any farther. "Your boy toy blocked me in."

"That man is nobody's toy. Though he does know how to play." Ruth peered past Bruce and scoffed. "If you can't get around his truck you shouldn't have a license old man." She closed the door firmly enough to dislodge his foot.

Bruce turned, indignant, and finally noticed his wife's car wasn't there. He pulled out his phone and made a call. "I need you to locate someone. My wife."

# Chapter Forty-Four

Meredith dialed her friend's number. Ruth answered on the first ring. Not waiting for small talk, she said, "Your husband stopped by with an indecently large bouquet of flowers and a box with a large bow and an expensive jeweler's name embossed on it."

"Oh Ruth, I'm sorry."

"Relax, this is not the first time a husband came around with an *I'm sorry* bribe, although usually its chocolates and flowers, not jewelry. They always us that same dumb voice."

"What did you tell him?"

"Not much. I mentioned Pilates but Anthony arrived."

Meredith gasped. "That could not have gone over well." Bruce did not take aging gracefully.

"Yes, your husband was visibly insecure."

"He thinks you're doing a detox, that I'm staying with you to help out."

"Well that partially explains why he showed up here. Want to tell me what this is all about?"

"Does lunch work?"

"Only if we pick a place that serves, I'm going to need a cocktail after round two with Anthony."

Meredith blushed at Ruth's openness. "Of course. I could use a drink, too. I stayed at Tucker's place last night."

"Bruce's son Tucker? Finally! He's half your age, right?"

"Oh, stop! I called Becca and she was staying at his condo. Seems there is a threat out by her place."

"Is she okay?" Ruth asked in a rush.

"Yes, she's fine. A bit unsettled, poor dear. Tucker and Officer Chasseur think she'll be safer in town. I was just happy she answered my call."

"Officer Chasseur you say? He's a tall drink of water I'd like to sip on."

"Ruth! What has gotten into you?"

"Two words. Hormone. Therapy. I had no idea meno-pause could be this delicious. If you're not interested in Tucker, mind if I try my luck? Some young men prefer a classic."

"Please no. There's already so much tension with me and this family. Maybe just sit this one out."

Ruth snorted. "Not a chance. You just said he was tense. I have learned so many new things that can help him release in so many different ways."

"Ruth, you know I love you, but I beg you, please do not try to sleep with Tucker."

"Fine. Then I think you should, you are wound rather tight. Let me know if you need anything. Now, I have a young man in my back room I should be getting back to."

"I expect you'll share all the gory details at lunch."

"Juicy details, no gore involved."

"Your juicy is my gory. Want to meet at the Canoe House? Does noon work?"

"Make it 12:45."

Meredith ended the call. It was unlike Bruce to check in on her. Of course, she had always gone along with what he wanted, deferring to his judgement. That letter from the pipeline company and how he treated Becca had sparked something within her to finally say something. She knew she wasn't Becca's mom, but Meredith cared for all the Tanner kids deeply.

In fact, it was Bruce's treatment of his children, particularly the past several months, that had alerted her to the change in him.

He had spoken with increasing criticalness of his oldest son Gabe's time with CSIS, going so far as to call his patriotic son a trained killer. He had belittled Tucker when the young man had made detective, taunting his son's support of Truth and Reconciliation, and the BLM, LGTBQ+ and #MeToo movements, saying the young man was a liability to any police force. Bruce had sneered at Colt's new fiancé, an incredibly accomplished and kind-hearted women, while at the same time reminding Colt that someone who rides bulls for a living does not deserve a piece of ass like that. And Becca, my goodness, Bruce had joked she would be better off peddling drugs than her silly eco-crusade.

At first, Meredith had thought he was joking, albeit horribly inappropriately. Now she wasn't so sure. Bruce had always been ambitious and driven, cocky even, but lately he was also ruthless and needlessly cruel, base even.

A troubling thought arose. Bruce had always put her above his children. That had never sat right but she had never known how to bring it up without starting a fight. If he treated her better than his kids and she was afraid of him, should his kids be worried about what he might do to them, too?

# Chapter Forty-Five

Becca brought Pixie to a stop and looked around her in awe. She was in a narrow, forested valley. Through the dappled canopy she had peek-a-boo views of mountain peaks. Golden poplars rubbed shoulders with the odd white spruce and lodgepole pine. The ground cover was shades of reds and browns, and Becca could see rose hips dotting the bush.

Frost no longer covered the ground. The spot was secluded, even for the backcountry, and warmer. Typically, there were some signs of human activity. A cattle gate, pipeline right-of-way, hiking trail markers, something to indicate that people had tried to run a comb through the wilderness.

This spot felt more hidden, further away somehow. Different. It was also hard to shake an uneasy feeling that had been building the deeper she got in the backcountry. The last few days had robbed her of the feeling of safety she had always taken for granted. They had changed the angle of her repose.

Cell reception was spotty out here, but she should try to call her brother. No doubt he would be worried after finding her note this morning. She slid her hand into her left jacket pocket and found flares. At her right hip was her holstered bear spray. Her right jacket pocket was—empty.

She checked her backpack. It held her lunch, water bottle, small first aid kit and a pocketknife. Her cell phone and backup satellite phone were glaringly absent. "Well, that was stupid."

Riding alone always came with a certain degree of risk but she was breaking her own rule right now: take your frickin' cell phone. She dismounted and led Pixie over to the small stream running through the unusual valley. She loosely held Pixie's reins as the mare dipped her head and drank from the steam. Becca stroked Pixie's long neck, taking comfort in the corded warmth. Strong and soft at the same time.

She should head back. She'd had her ride. Found that moment of hushed tranquility she'd been looking for.

A swath of white caught her attention downstream. Curious, she tied Pixie's reins around a nearby tree and made her way towards it. The stream widened and she dropped from the raised bank to hop across small boulders and gravel bars. She noticed a sign indicating a local university's research site. She crossed the watercourse at a shallow point, hopscotching across rocks, and barely got her boots wet.

The swaths of white were actually tarps. She hadn't noticed earlier, but there were black ones, too. The tarps covered two-inch-thick wooden frames. Some were four-sided, others opened towards the creek. When she got closer, she froze. Inside each were cannabis plants. Marijuana's been legal in Canada since 2018, and a handful of States, but this outfit certainly went beyond the rules of growing for personal use. She eyed the university sign and frowned. These were makeshift greenhouses and what looked like test plots on Crown Land. Becca was enough of a gardener to know the foothills was a harsh zone to cultivate anything but the hardiest of plants. She was not a cannabis expert, but it seemed like a weird place to run marijuana test plots, even a university one.

The sound of a snapping branch scared her, and she immediately crouched, scanning for danger. Becca had bear spray and flares. It would have to be enough.

# Chapter Forty-Six

Jason had lost Becca's trail with the warming sun and was spending precious time trying to pick it back up. He couldn't believe his luck when he heard a horse nicker and his gray gelding answered. His relief was short lived.

Pixie was alone.

Fear spiked in his gut. Jason scanned the surroundings and squinted. In the distance he saw what looked like white and black banners dotting a curve in the glacial fed stream. He dismounted, leading his horse down the short bank and across the stream before walking towards the peculiar setting. He kept close to his horse, one side at least shielded by the large animal. No sounds disturbed his progression.

As he got closer, he saw the banners were actually tarps. Tidy rows of framed tarps, three deep, lined the shoreline. Jason recognized the iconic jagged, star-leafed weeds in various stages of growth. It looked like a test grow op but in the most inconceivable place imaginable. A university plaque announced it as a research area. He didn't buy that for a second.

He sensed the danger before a high-pitched shriek sounded. A blur of movement launched itself at him and a cloud materialized in front of him. Piercing pain hit his eyes, nose and lungs. His eyes burned and each breath felt like fire. His horse reared. Blindly, Jason tried to keep his hold on the reins. His horse bolted and a hand locked on his arm.

Jason tried desperately to open his burning eyes while simultaneously trying to figure out where to land a punch.

"Jason, it's me, it's me."

He registered Becca's voice the same time her hand grabbed his other arm. She said in a commanding, clear voice, "It's bear spray, we need to get you to the water." A half second later he stopped struggling, his brain processing what she said.

Becca was safe, at least for now.

He let her lead him the short distance to the stream. He still couldn't open his eyes but if he was going to be of any use getting them out of here, he had to get the cayenne out of his eyes and face.

Becca was holding one hand and had the other on his shoulder. "We're at the bank, there's a small step down to the gravel...there you go."

Jason felt the gravel give under his boots and dropped to his knees. He cupped the frigid water and repeatedly rinsed out his eyes and nose. The cold water soaked through the knees of his pants and dripped down his forearms, wetting the arms of his jacket. It had a bracing effect.

Becca stood a foot away, hovering. "I'm so sorry, I didn't know it was you, I was hiding behind—"

He sat back on his heels, trying to blink. His throat was raw but he managed to ask her, "Are you hurt?"

Becca squatted and put a hand on his back. She sounded confused, "I'm fine, you're—"

Jason held up a finger and still blind, shook his head. He gave his eyes and face another soaking, letting the sharpness of the frigid water wash away more of the stinging spray. He flipped his head back, blinked and rubbed his sore eyes. It still hurt like hell, but at least he was able to open then.

She had water droplets on her. He squinted at dark circles on her pants and shirt. He asked again, "You're not hurt?"

"No."

"We need to move. Now." He rose to his feet and held out his hand to her.

She took it and stood. He dropped her hand as soon as she was standing. His whole head hurt. Jason turned to go and called behind him, "I need to snap a few pictures, meet me at the horses—" He stopped. "Shit, my horse bolted. I mean your horse, that I borrowed, bolted."

She whistled twice. A few moments later the gray gelding reappeared next to Pixie.

"You rode Stürmisch?"

"If you say so."

"He doesn't accept male riders."

Jason pulled out his phone and started snapping a few pictures of the test plots and plants. "He accepted me fine."

Becca held up a hand. "Truce. Please, I have zero headspace left to fight with you."

"I don't want to fight, either," he said quietly.

"Why did you come?"

"Please, just stand by your horse. I'll just be a sec."

He quickly snapped off a few more photos. The plants that were left were slightly different sizes and each set up was different, from the tarp color to the angle it was positioned to the stream. A cannabis test plot in the mountains didn't make sense. Everything he knew about grow operations was to maximize certainty. Namely indoor operations with strictly controlled growing variables. Dynamic weather and pressure patterns of a montane environment didn't make sense. He pulled out an evidence bag from his jacket and snapped off a discreet bud from the bottom of one of the plant stalks. As an afterthought he clipped another whole plant. He looked closer and saw some of the plants had been grafted onto sturdier root stock. The lab should be able to tell him what was so special about these plants.

Jason scanned the area. There were too many plants to fall under the new Canadian regulations that allowed growing marijuana for personal use. The limited aerial cover did nothing to conceal the enterprise from overhead surveillance, either. Maybe it actually was a university test plot on Crown Land. It would explain why the hell this place wasn't booby-trapped.

Jason tucked everything back in his pockets and crossed the frigid stream to Becca. She held both Pixie's and the Stürmisch's reins when he reached them. He cupped his hands. Becca stepped into them and pushed off, swinging her other leg over Pixie's back. She settled in the saddle, and he took the gray's reins, skip-mounting into his own saddle.

Long minutes passed as they put more distance between them and the test plots. They rode in silence as Jason kept up a steady scan of their surroundings. Finally, he pulled in their pace.

Becca took the opening. "Why did you track me out here?"

The letter was still burning whole in his pocket. He went with practical. "Clint showed up last night right after you left. He had been fencing out at Chimney Creek when he heard shots fired. One of the Fischer brothers got shot up pretty bad. Clint helped them get to the hospital. We don't know who did the shooting."

Becca made a startled sound and her horse shied. She regained control and Pixie fell back into a walk, more alert than usual. Jason tucked his mount in close. When Becca held out her hand, he took it. "Tell me Clint is safe."

Her hand was cool to the touch. He wished he had gloves for her. "Clint wasn't hurt. If that Fischer kid is still alive, it's because Clint saved his life."

"Did he see the shooting?"

Jason hesitated, unsure how much to tell her. "No. Christopher, the other Fischer brother, pulled a gun on Clint before he realized Austin would bleed out if he did."

Jason rubbed his thumb across Becca's hand.

"Chimney Creek has nearly the same conditions as that plot we just left does. Do you think it's a coincidence, or maybe there are more test plots there?"

Jason had wondered the same thing. "That would explain the shootout."

She looked behind her. "I was in danger there, wasn't I?"

His hand instinctively tightened around hers. "Maybe. We don't know all the players."

She squeezed his hand back before pulling it away. "The cameras Tucker and Colt put up yesterday, will they work?"

He nodded. "The software is designed to trigger a notification if the cameras spot a human form."

"You'll see me?" Becca asked, her voice a whisper.

"I don't have the live feed. I just get a notification."

"Oh." She considered that a minute before saying, "I saw you this morning. I'm sorry I put you in danger, again."

"When I saw your truck and you didn't answer the door..." He broke off, unwilling to voice his greatest fear. "Why'd you leave, if you saw me?"

"After sending those emails last night cancelling my opening weekend, I couldn't handle another failure, not if it meant failing you."

He stilled. "What are you saying?"

"Nothing right now." She faced forward, refusing his question, but her earlier words gave him hope.

She was quiet a moment before she whispered his name.

"Yeah?"

"Thanks for coming after me." She finally looked at him, worried. "How do your eyes feel?"

"Like they had cayenne pepper injected into them," he teased.

"*Jason.*"

"What? My sinuses will never be the same." When her frown deepened, he relented, "Becca, I'm kidding."

"Is it always like that? My brain only saw danger. I didn't recognize you as you, I just felt scared and sprayed."

"You protected yourself in a hostile environment. You did good." Jason was damn proud of her, actually. Too many didn't defend themselves.

"I hurt you."

"You protected yourself. I know the difference. Will you stay at your brother's in town until this blows over?"

Becca snorted. "Our relationship would never survive it."

"I need you to survive this, period."

"Don't say stuff like that, it scares me."

"It's meant to. Becca, these guys are dangerous."

"You and Tucker are on it. I trust you guys."

Before he could unpack that she asked, "How's the file?"

He kept his voice even when he said, "What file?"

Becca slanted him a look. "*The* file. The one Officer Cooper oh-so-indirectly asked if I had given you."

"What did you tell him?"

"You mean did I tell him that I handcuffed you and then to keep you quiet I made out with you, and by my math we're now even?"

Jason had to readjust in his saddle.

Becca smiled. "Because I didn't. I did insinuate I shared what Lillian and Colt had turned up. He seemed relieved."

"I put him in a shitty spot; that wasn't cool."

Becca shrugged. "So you read what appeared in your inbox when you shouldn't have. You know I would have given you access to it."

Jason gave her a look. "No, I didn't know that."

She shrugged. "I handcuffed you, you accessed a restricted file. Sounds like we've both been naughty."

His breath caught at the word *naughty* coming from her lips.

"I would have shared it with you, but someone stormed off before I had a chance to."

"You really would have?"

"You're the one with the actual connection to the land. All I have is a piece of paper that my dad dangles whenever he wants me to come to heel."

"That's cold." Jason knew Bruce was ruthless with others, he just didn't realize that extended to his family.

"You know my dad's frost more than others. I think he had something to do with why we started fighting all those years ago?"

Jason pulled out the crumbled folded note from his pocket. He handed it to Becca. "This about sums everything up. I don't know why I even kept it."

Becca accepted the yellowed piece of paper and read it. It was a letter in a feminine hand, dated from when they were in high school. It was terse and severe, and deeply unkind.

"You thought I wrote this?" She stared at him. "This is why you asked Shelly Robins to Winter formal, isn't it? I thought you were going to ask me."

Jason's chest tightened. "I did ask you. I wrote you a letter, first."

Becca pulled her horse up short. "What letter?"

Jason stopped his horse. "*The* letter. How many letters do you think a sixteen-year-old boy writes? The one was hard enough."

Becca looked confused. "I never got a letter."

"I left it in your car, at your house."

Becca swore a blue streak. "How much you want to bet my dad intercepted it?"

"You really never got my letter?"

"No, I really didn't." Becca waved the piece of paper in her hand. "This is awful. And not me. Why didn't you just confront me?"

Good question. "I was a teenager who had just been rejected by the girl I was crazy about. I did what any self-respecting guy did. I got mad and stayed that way."

Becca's shoulders sank. "The entire basis of me hating you since high school was from a miscommunication orchestrated by my jackass father."

"Huh,"' Jason said, thoughtful.

"What?"

He turned in his saddle to face her. "This is the first time you actually said you hated me. It kinda stings."

"You've hated me for years."

"I've never hated you Becca," he said quietly. Not even close.

She handed the note back to Jason. "I didn't write that."

Jason tucked it back in his pocket. "I know that, now."

An uncomfortable silence descended.

"I don't like letting myself feel." Her voice was whisper soft and he wondered if he heard her correctly.

"Huh? You're one of the most," he searched for the right word, "*emotive* people I know."

She raised an eyebrow and smiled at that. "You don't have to feel anything to be expressive. Being expressive is just hiding in plain sight."

Jason watched her, shoulders hunched, tense. "I don't get it, what are you hiding from?" He waited for her to answer. "Becca?"

"Don't say my name like that."

"Like what?"

"Like you care."

"Of course I care."

"I'm your assignment, even if I want—" She broke off.

"What if you're more than that?"

An eerie, high-pitched scream stopped them both. She spun around, eyes wide. His own gaze panned the surrounding bush looking for a victim.

"Tell me that is not a woman being attacked," Becca whispered, peering through the bush.

Jason had already unholstered his sidearm. It had seemed prudent to bring it under the circumstances. The horses were agitated, shuffling and snorting. Their unease amplified his sense of dread.

The bush surrounding them was thick and Jason had the dark thought that they wouldn't see what was attacking them until it was too late. The unsettling scream sounded again, although it sounded farther away. Nothing moved in his line of sight until he saw Becca's shoulder shake. He stared incredulously as he realized she was trying to hold in a laugh.

"What is so funny?"

"We're fine. I mean we should be fine."

"I'm going to need more to go on."

Becca blushed. "I think it was a cougar."

"Still striking terror here, Becs."

"Pretty sure that's the sound of cougars mating."

Jason paused. Finally, he holstered his gun. "How do you know what that sounds like?"

Becca shrugged. "I dated a wildlife biologist. Once. A long time ago—"

"Don't need to hear details."

"Wasn't going to offer any."

They stared at each other. Jason's brain tripped on Becca with a wildlife biologist. He was no doubt outdoorsy. And probably really smart. Well, he couldn't have been that smart if he let Becca go.

Jason had let her go, too. Stupid.

She was the first to break eye contact. "The horses are settling down. We should be fine."

They were quiet the rest of the way back. When they were just coming up on her back pasture Becca asked, "Please don't read into this, but will you stay with me tonight?"

Jason's brain tripped on her words and his imagination created a rapid-fire series of visual images.

She added, "I know Tucker and Colt put up the cameras. I should feel safe. But I feel safer with you here."

He coughed. Cleared his mind. Reminded himself she was looking for security, not sex. "Yes, of course. I need to drop off the plant samples at the lab first, is that okay? You could come with me if you don't want to be alone." He would do anything to help her feel safe.

Becca smiled. "Lillian and Colt invited me over for a family dinner. I can hang out there early." Becca paused. "Will you come join us?"

"Sure." The words were out of his mouth before he realized how stupid they were.

"I'll text you the address and time."

"Sounds great." No, it didn't, it sounded like a trap. Becca's family was a minefield.

A notification pinged on Jason's phone.

Del Fiennes had been located. He was at Bruce Tanner's house.

# Chapter Forty-Seven

**M**eredith paced the large hotel suite, unsure what to do. She had checked in under her maiden name and although it was clean and nice enough, it was nowhere near the luxury she was accustomed to when she traveled. But she wasn't traveling. She was a woman unsure if she should be scared of her husband.

She replayed the phone conversation she had overheard again. Who had her husband been talking to and why would he be interested in purchasing information about the Fischer brothers from Bruce? Her husband was a hedge fund manager. What could he possibly know about gun and drug runners?

There was a knock on the door and Meredith froze.

Had Bruce found her?

*Bang, bang, bang.*

A stern voice called through the door, *"Meredith?"*

That sure wasn't Bruce.

She hesitated, unsure what to do.

In the end the decision was made for her. She heard a soft click and the door opened. A man she had never seen stood before her. He closed the door behind him. The click of the latch seemed so...final.

She edged away from the door. "Who are you?" She tried to keep her voice as normal as possible. Inside she was terrified.

The man had walked into the room and stopped on the far side, as far away from her as possible in the space. It had the odd effect of reminding her of a time she had been out for an early morning walk. It had been still dark, and a man had crossed the street *away from her*, so as not to frighten her on the lonely, dark sidewalk.

He was tall, and his eyes were lifeless—no, that wasn't true. *Haunted* was a better description. He looked familiar, though for the life of her she couldn't place from where. Strength and danger emanated from him. She felt more curious than afraid, and she dared ask, "Why are you here?"

The man kept his distance from her. "How well do you know your husband?"

"Not as well as I should, why?"

"You're not safe with him."

Meredith's mouth opened in surprise. "You came to warn me?"

A small smile teased on the corner of his mouth. It transformed him and Meredith's fear eased another fraction. "I came to suggest you distance yourself from him. I have reason to believe it would be in your best interest."

"Why do you think I'm here," Meredith muttered before she could catch herself. Now was not the time for sarcasm.

His smile faded. "It's harder to see the shots coming from family."

"How do you know Bruce?" Meredith looked closer at him. "Do I know you?"

The man simply shook his head but stopped suddenly. "Are you wearing vanilla?"

"No." What an odd question. "Will you at least tell me who you are?"

He shook his head again but that small smile was back. "I didn't think so. Do take care Meredith. Keep your distance from your husband." The man turned to go but stopped. "How's Becca?"

His question started Meredith and fear spiked. "She has nothing to do with Bruce, please, she's innocent to anything he's doing."

The man said, "I know."

"Then why are you asking about her?"

"I have my concerns about her well-being, too."

Meredith stepped forward and grabbed his hand. "What do you know?"

The man looked down at where their hands were touching and Meredith immediately let go. Stunned, she said, "You don't want to hurt me."

"No. Advise her to keep her distance from him, too."

"Please, who are you?"

"Lady, I ask myself that a hundred times a day." At that cryptic remark, he left as quickly as he entered, leaving Meredith alone and more troubled than ever. She rushed to the door after him. "Wait, can I at least get a contact for you?"

The man hesitated. When finally he reached into his open jacket, movie scenes flashed through her mind. So it really did look like this; the stranger pulling the gun out of his coat.

"Meredith?" The man was calling her name. He hadn't shot her. He was trying to hand her a card, not a bullet.

She took the small card stock. A phone number was printed on it. She looked up at him.

"That number can reach me."

What an odd way of saying it.

"Thank you." *For not killing me.*

He turned to go, and recognition crystalized. *"You're Christopher Fischer."*

The picture of him on the true-crime book was hopelessly out of date. The man in front of her must have been at least a decade older. He was harder, still, those haunted eyes made her want to make him a sandwich instead of run for cover.

She had completely lost her mind.

He brought his index finger up to his lips. *Shhhh.*

Then he was gone. Meredith ran back to her room door. It was locked. She patted her slacks until her fingers found the rectangular piece of plastic. It took her three tries to get into her room. Once inside she set the deadbolt and latched the swing bar door lock. Then she checked the deadbolt again. If he had found her, Bruce could, too.

Now what? How could she help Becca when she had no idea what to warn her about?

Meredith retrieved her laptop and connected to the hotel's Wi-Fi. In a few minutes and three password tries later, she was accessing her husband's email. She didn't take the breach lightly. Even with her and Bruce's less than honorable start, she valued trust in relationships.

She opened an email folder labeled *Business*. Graphic pictures of him with a bouncy looking brunette stared back at her. Another one showed him with a well-endowed blonde whose assets seemed to defy gravity. Through the anger, Meredith cocked her head in wonder: how was that position even possible? Others still showed him with multiple women, all in various states of undress and arousal.

Humiliation wrapped around her heart. He had been married when they had gotten together. That had never sat right with her, but she had convinced herself it was forgivable because she was in love with him. How foolish she had been. Swiping at her eyes, she started scrolling through the other folders. If Becca was in danger, she had to find out why and how, and warn her.

Twenty minutes later Meredith gasped. She had found an email of a marijuana patent application—in Austin and Christopher Fischer's names! She scrolled. The email had been forwarded to a coded nickname. Attached were spreadsheets that looked like production estimates, distribution plans and map coordinates. Meredith rolled her eyes when she saw the non-coded memo included, *Del, these are the latest projections. Bruce.*

The laptop pinged; a new email had come in from a local hardware chain. Odd, Bruce had never been inclined towards using his hands. Meredith only hesitated a moment before clicking it open. It was a receipt. The list was short. Four large jerry cans and a barbecue lighter.

Oh dear.

Meredith picked up her phone but paused. Surely she was blowing this out of proportion. This was her husband for goodness sakes. He couldn't actually be dangerous. This sort of thing happened to other people. Besides, Bruce was always telling her she over-reacted to things. Did she really want to blow up her marriage if this was all nothing? Bruce was not the forgiving type, but she was. Maybe they could work through his infidelities. Meredith closed her eyes. Or she could pretend she didn't know.

Her hand hovered over the phone. She wanted to do the right thing, problem was, she had no idea what that was.

# Chapter Forty-Eight

Jason pulled into his mom's gravel driveway and got out of the truck. His phone pinged with a status notification. Del Fiennes had left Bruce Tanner's house and gone straight to his hotel room at The Balmoral. He hadn't left since. Where the fuck did this Del guy fit in and what was Becca's dad into? A storm was brewing, he just didn't know where it would break.

His mom came around the side of the house. She had gardening gloves on and held an empty flower bulb package. "Jason, what a lovely surprise. What are you doing here, honey?"

Most of the time he could roll with his job. The last few days had taken a toll. He pulled her into a hug.

She squeezed him back, her petit frame hiding pure steel. "What's wrong?"

He pulled back, embarrassed. "I'm fine, just wanted to stop in."

She really looked at him. "My goodness, what's happened to your eyes? They're all red."

Jason's hand went up to his face. "Oh, yeah. Becca got me with bear spray."

"Why on earth would she do that?" She poked him in the chest. "What did you do?"

"Really mom?"

She gave him a measured look. "Well, come in, then. I'll make a pot of tea and you can tell me all about it."

"I can't stay long. I just wanted to pop in." Jason followed his mom inside.

In the kitchen she put on the kettle. "There's fresh cranberry muffins in the tin on the table."

"I'm just on my way to dinner with Becca." He winced. His mom would pounce on that.

"She sprays you with bear spray and then invites you to dinner? I don't understand you kids. Have a seat."

Jason dutifully sat at the kitchen table. "She sprayed me before she realized it was me. I'm proud of her, actually. It's the ones who don't fight back that I'm more worried about." Jason trailed off, unsure how to explain. "Doesn't matter, she's safe. For now."

"You still care about her."

Jason looked up, unwilling to go there. "So, you're good? I just wanted to check in on you."

"Thanks. What are you going to do about you and Becca?"

"Nothing. We don't work. Besides, she's using us, using our history to try to reroute the pipeline. How could I possibly overlook that?" Even if they both wanted something more, Jason would do well to remember it just wasn't possible. A man could only slam his heart in the same door so many times before finally learning to walk away.

The kettle whistled. His mom turned off the burner and poured the boiling water into the tea pot. Her eyes

were haunted when she turned back to him. "Do you remember what I told you about your father, him joining
up and being sent to Vietnam?"

"Yeah."

She leaned against the kitchen counter, her hands resting on the counter on either side of her. "You don't know
how many times I've asked myself what could have been
if we both would have shared how we really felt before
he was half a world away, and in a damn war to boot. He
needed a ticket out, but enlisting? We could have run
away together; we could have figured out a way out of
this place together. But we didn't. We kept quiet until it
was too late and then what we had wasn't what it could
have been. Your dad came back a broken, angry, hurting
man. No one talked about such things back then, let alone
know how to help men heal. Pride kept us quiet. Let me
tell you something about pride—it takes, it doesn't give
back. You can't embrace it at night. It doesn't love you
back. It doesn't help you build a life with someone. We
lost so much, it just makes me sick thinking you and that
dear Becca are going down the same path."

"It's apples and oranges, mom. Becca and I aren't the
same as you and dad. I'm not dying to get out."

"She got out of here. Sure, she waited until after she
was all done with her schooling, but she left. Why do you
think that is?"

"I don't know, the job market?"

"Think so? She had to go all the way to *Germany* because there was absolutely nothing in her field closer?"

Why *had* Becca gone all the way to Europe?

"And what did you do? You waited for her." His mom folded her arms like it was a fact.

"Woah! Absolutely not. Check the record. I have *not* been waiting for her."

"Really? How many women have you dated over the years?"

"I've dated, there just hasn't been anyone serious enough to bring home to you."

"And why haven't any of these women worked out?"

"I don't know, they just haven't." Jason started running through a tally in his head. He was typically the one to head for the door in a relationship but the few who had beat him to it had said he was emotionally unavailable. But that was just something women said, wasn't it? It wasn't like he had been pining after Becca all these years.

"Don't look so horrified. I just might get grandkids while I'm still young enough to spoil them proper."

"*Mom.*"

She sat a mug in front of him. "Drink your tea. Then go to your dinner and figure out how you and that nice Becca are going to work things out this time."

# Chapter Forty-Nine

Fading evening sunlight filtered into the third story room brightening Lillian and Colt's kitchen table. Lillian held open a cabinet door open and asked, "Tea, espresso or scotch?"

"Tea, please," Becca answered. Jason and Colt were watching a pre-season hockey game in the living room while Becca and Lillian had stayed in the kitchen after dinner.

The condo in the mountain town was a comfortable blend of soft white walls, modern furniture with clean lines, and the occasional splash of color. Lillian's tasteful decor made the space warm and inviting, while also giving away nothing about its mistress. Colt had technically moved in last week, but they were only staying long enough to find a place out of town that appealed and had space for Colt to train horses.

Lillian sat a glass in front of Becca.

Becca pointed at the tumbler. "That's not tea."

"Tea will be ready in a couple minutes. That's your pre-tea."

Becca took a small sip of the smooth amber fire. "Thanks for dinner. Sorry I sprung both of us on you."

The kettle whistled. Lillian flipped open the spout, silencing the sharp sound. She crossed her arms, waiting for a hard boil. "We're happy to have you both, just a bit surprised."

Becca eyed the doorway that led to the living room. The women could hear the hockey game going. Becca leaned forward.

"Wait," Lillian said. "I want to hear everything." She flicked off the burner and sloshed the boiling water into the tea pot before setting the decked-out tea tray on the kitchen table. Becca stared. Even in a rush Lillian managed impeccable presentation.

Becca waved at the tray. "How do you do that?"

Lillian looked down, confused. "It's tea."

"Your tea is art."

"Aren't you a dear." Lillian sat down and leaned forward. "Now I'm ready."

Becca whispered, "I've decided to sell the land to Jason."

Lillian's eyes were kind but concerned. "I thought that land was pivotal to your business plan?"

"It is, but it's not right what my dad did, and it was a mistake partnering with him on anything legally binding. I know better. I'll make what I've got work. Besides, you're always saying that business is telling people what they want, right?"

Lillian gave a hushed laugh. "Good point. How are you going to get your dad to agree?"

Becca tapped her fingers on the table. "I haven't figured that part out yet. He's so, volatile. The past year it seems to be getting worse. And then the intel your spy-people found suspected him of having something to do with Gabe's ambush. He's always been arrogant, but everything just feels escalated somehow. Before he just irritated the crap out of me. Now he actually makes me nervous."

Lillian eyed Becca. "Colt doesn't say much about Bruce."

Becca shook her head. "He wouldn't. After Gabe left, Colt tried to fill in as family peacekeeper. It got ugly when my parents split and stayed that way. Gabe was always the mediator. When my dad married Meredith, he wasn't even speaking to Tucker or I, so we didn't go to the wedding."

"I'm so sorry Becca, that sounds upsetting."

Becca laughed at Lillian's diplomacy. "I appreciate that. You know, you helped get us through that. If you hadn't found out about our half-brother Tanner, Gabe would still be holding that awful secret to himself. Poor guy. My dad should have never put that responsibility on him, let alone when Gabe was so young."

Lillian looked uncomfortable and Becca hurried to reassure her. "Seriously, you helped us. I know you had reasons for running that INCEPT check on Colt. It freaked the shit out of Gabe and Tucker, but they don't understand. They don't get it's always in the back of our mind that the guy we just agreed to go to dinner with might be a rapist, ax murderer, or," Becca leaned closer, "a double agent selling state secrets. They don't understand, but I do."

Lillian blinked back tears. "You don't know how much that means to me. I just couldn't take the chance that I could be duped like I was with Fernando."

Becca reached over and squeezed her hand. "See, it worked out. I still think the guys should have applauded your ingenuity instead of acting all affronted. Boys can be so unaware. Colt understood and that's what matters."

Lillian chuckled. "You've never had someone do an unsolicited deep dive into your past. It's disconcerting even if it is for a greater good. That's why your law enforcement brothers blew a gasket."

"You lived such a wild life." Becca lowered her voice even more. "Don't take this the wrong way but how are you doing? I mean, everything has been so sudden. Do you want to settle down now?"

Lillian's face took on a dreamy quality. "I'm happier than I have ever been. I wouldn't have chosen a surprise pregnancy, or your brother before I got to know him, for that matter." Lillian laughed. "I mean, a bull rider? But I wake up next to him and am just so *delighted*. I love him. And I love the life we're building together. I never thought I would want to put down roots. With him I do. Completely."

"Good. Well that settles it then. The land I built the ranch on hasn't been in my family for generations but it's where I want to start the rest of my life, put down my own roots. Maybe it'll even end up being generational."

"I never thought of it like that, choosing where you want to set down roots," Lillian mused.

"That's why it's so important I extract myself from being legally associated with my dad and whatever scheme he's cooking up. I can't build something meaningful if I stomped on others to get it. That's just not how I want to build something lasting."

"So you're dropping the land because you don't want to be linked financially to your dad, not because it's important to Jason?" Lillian asked, keeping her voice low.

Becca scrunched her face and whispered back. "Ooh, you *are* a journalist."

Lillian snickered. "I was one of the best."

Becca eyes the doorway again, confident the guys were still distracted with the hockey game. "With Jason I can't help thinking what if the roles were reversed? The additional parcel of land would make my life easier and the business stronger. But at what cost? I can't face him thinking I might be hurting him, even unintentionally. I'll figure something out without the extra parcel."

"Or you and Jason could work something out."

"Doubtful."

"More like probable. You two are totally hot for each other. Remember when Sophie and Craig got their truck stuck in the mud? The fireworks between you two were spectacular."

Becca remembered the day. "We were yelling at each other the whole time. How is that hot?"

"That was unfulfilled passion, my dear. You two would be perfect together."

"That's not what I would call perfect for each other."

"You're right. It's called foreplay."

"It wasn't foreplay," Becca grumbled.

"You sound disappointed instead of indignant."

Becca pointedly changed the subject. "Speaking of *land*, the pipeline is for hydrogen." She knew that would get Lillian's attention. "Another oil or gas pipeline is just more noise in the energy conversation. A hydrogen pipeline, that's a dialogue we're long overdue for."

"Green or blue?"

Becca was impressed with Lillian's understanding. "Green. The pipeline will be from the Lefebvre Wind Farm to the Banff townsite."

"So the pipeline that a criminal element wants you to stop represents a historic shift to our renewable energy future?"

"Yes."

"Bloody hell."

Becca agreed. "I tried to tell them when they called."

"You gave the caller a lecture on energy sustainability?"

"It wasn't a lecture," Becca grumbled again.

"Any idea who would want you to stop a green hydrogen pipeline?"

"Besides the usual suspects? No."

"Who are the usual suspects?"

"Sometimes I forget you're new to here. We're known as a died-in-the-wool conservative province anchored to the idea of the good ol' days of fossil fuels and waiting for the next oil boom to save us. We are thought to be incapable of change."

"By whom? I'm so far left I don't even look right, but even I know your non-renewable energy sector has been crapped on hard. People need to team up instead of beak off. The technology is there to rapidly shift to a low carbon economy. Honestly, the only hard part of the equation is empowering people to dare work with those they perceive as the *other side*. Like I said, the technology is there."

Becca studied Lillian. "You make it sound easy, kind of."

Lillian shrugged. "It is. Imagine how swift, and painless change would be if we all focused on cooperation instead of fighting?" Lillian paused. "Sorry, now I'm the one lecturing."

Becca laughed. "You're passionate. There's a difference."

"This province's conservatism isn't as carved in stone as everyone assumes."

"You're the first person I've ever heard say that."

"My perspective hasn't had time to form a groove and fall in."

Becca started laughing. Lillian began to laugh, too. Soon both women's eyes were watering from laughing so hard.

Colt popped his head in. "You guys okay?"

"Of course, dear," Lillian sniffled to cover another laugh.

Jason stood next to Colt, his gaze on Becca.

"Do you want to stay here tonight?" Colt asked her. "I know the cameras are up, but you're welcome to crash here if you like."

"Do stay," Lillian added.

"That's sweet of you guys but I'll be okay. Jason's staying with me."

Lillian widened her eyes at Colt suggestively.

"As an *officer*," she clarified.

"Suuurre," Colt replied, not having it. "Officers always stay with the public. That's a new service the RCMP is offering."

Lillian bit her bottom lip to keep from laughing out loud.

Jason stood behind Becca as she unlocked her front door. The night air was cold, and she could see her breath in the porch light. She keyed in the lock code. The lights flashed red. She tried again, distracted by the scent of Jason behind her. He smelled of soap and man and sex. Okay, the last one was her mind imagining. The lights beeped red again. Her phone pinged in her pocket, followed by Jason's.

"Can I help?" Jason moved to stand next to her. Embarrassed by his closeness, she turned again and retried the keypad. This time green lights blinked, and she let them in. Inside, she pulled out her phone. It was a weak avoidance tactic, but she didn't know how to be alone with him anymore. With Jason. In her house. At night.

# Chapter Fifty

"Here's your room." Becca motioned for Jason to enter ahead of her. He looked around. The room was spacious, roomy even with the four-poster queen size bed and pair of reading chairs. The outside wall was made of thick logs, the other three were painted a soft earthy brown. A tasteful selection of framed pictures adorned the walls. He set his overnight bag on the delicately embroidered duvet. Jason was pretty sure the room was larger than his first apartment.

"Will this do?" Becca sounded nervous.

"Of course. Honestly, Becca, I would be fine sleeping on the couch."

"You're my first guest."

"Oh." *Smooth.* He looked for something to say. Being in one of her guest bedrooms was a new intimacy he wasn't sure what to do with. She looked as uncomfortable as he felt, like neither was sure where they stood.

One of the framed photos caught his attention. Mountains loomed in the background; the foreground was rolling foothills with a dirt track streaking across the landscape. "Did you take this?"

Becca's cheeks pinked. "I wanted local scenery for the guest rooms."

"Isn't this where Lillian's niece and Craig got stuck?"

Becca gave a vague shrug. "Maybe?"

Jason leaned forward. "I'm sure that's where the police chase, such as it was, ended." He turned towards her. "Do you remember that day?" He did. It had been one of their more fiery encounters. Not his finest hour.

"I remember you yelling at me."

Jason cocked his head. "You gave as good as you got."

Becca smiled. "I did, didn't I?" And just like that the uncomfortable tension dissolved. "How are your eyes?"

"Better." They still hurt like hell, but he knew she still felt bad about spraying him and didn't want to worry her.

"That's a relief. Make yourself comfortable. There are towels in the ensuite. I need to get some work done in my office."

"Mind if I camp out there, too?" Jason asked.

Becca looked relieved. "Yes, please. It's still all a bit much that someone broke in here."

"That's why I'm here."

Becca phone rang and he turned to give her privacy.

"It's for you." She held out her phone to him. She looked confused. "It's my dad's wife, Meredith."

Jason took the phone with more than a little trepidation. "Hello, this is Officer Chasseur."

*"Jason, thank goodness. It's Meredith, Becca's, um, stepmother."*

Becca was watching him, and Jason shrugged back. He had no idea why Becca's stepmom would be calling him. "Meredith, what can I do for you?"

"Well that's just it, I'm not sure." Meredith explained how she recently had felt physically in danger around her husband, how she had overheard a cryptic phone call and what she had found in his email to Del Fiennes. "Officer Chasseur, please understand, I'm not a paranoid woman. I don't snoop in other people's lives, my husband's included. But something feels very off."

Jason agreed. "Is there anything else?"

Meredith continued, "A man came to the hotel I'm staying at warning me to distance myself from Bruce, and that Becca might be in danger. I-I think it was Christopher Fischer."

Jason looked at Becca, she was twisting her hands together. "Are you sure?"

"No. I thought I recognized him from a true-crime book, but it is quite dated, and he didn't confirm when I asked him."

Jason tried not to blanche. "What exactly did he say?"

Meredith sniffled and Jason softened his voice. "You're doing great, ma'am. Do you remember what he said?"

"He warned me that Bruce might not have my best interests in mind. He also asked after Becca and suggested I let her know to distance herself from him, too. I'm worried for her. We don't have a strong relationship; I wasn't sure she would welcome me trying to help."

Jason digested what Meredith had said.

"You've been most helpful. Thank you, Meredith."

"He also said *it's harder to see the shots coming from family.* He gave me his phone number when I asked him for it." Meredith read the number off to Jason.

"Do you feel safe where you're staying? Does Bruce know where you are?"

"He doesn't. Officer Chasseur, there's something else you should know. When I was snooping in Bruce's email a receipt came in for four large jerry cans and a barbecue lighter."

Jason held the phone tighter. Becca was safe and whole in front of him. But for how long? Could Christopher Fischer actually be helping Becca or was this just part of some darker plan?

Perhaps more concerning, though, was what, or who, Bruce Tanner was planning to set fire to.

# Chapter Fifty-One

"What was it? What did she say?"

Jason handed Becca back her phone and briefed her on what Meredith had disclosed before asking, "Do you know why your dad would purchase several jerry cans and a lighter?"

Becca frowned. "My dad barely knows how to use the barbecue and hires out all physical labor required around the house."

"Any idea what he knows about marijuana patents, or why he's partnering with internationally recognized arms and drug dealers on them?"

Becca shook her head. "He's a *hedge fund* manager. I figured the only criminals he knew were the white-collar captains-of-industry variety."

"Your stepmom—"

"Meredith." Becca interrupted.

"Sorry." Jason started over, "Meredith overheard Bruce speaking to a Del Fiennes about selling out Christopher and Austin Fischer. Your dad might be in bed with some very dangerous players."

A twinge of fear flickered for her dad's safety. Still, she had to ask, "Do you think *my dad* knows whoever's been harassing me?"

"I don't know. We shouldn't rule the possibility out."

"Do you think it is the Fischer brothers or this Del Fiennes?"

"I don't know."

"This sucks."

Jason reached for her hand. "We'll figure it out."

"What now?"

"I need to keep Tucker in the loop and run the number Meredith gave. How about you?"

"I'm going to pour myself a glass of wine and then design the maps for the posts you put in. God, was that just yesterday?"

"Jumping right back on that horse, I like it." Jason's word choice was teasing. He was trying to lighten the dark mood.

They worked in Becca's office until Jason tried calling Tucker. Then he spoke quietly in the hall.

Becca looked up from her laptop when Jason came back in the room. "He's not picking up. Twenty-eight OD's so far tonight, though. There's a tainted batch of something out there. I'm guessing he's busy with that."

"It hit him hard doing undercover work on the street. He hasn't been the same since."

"Watching people continue to make choices that destroy their lives is not easy."

"Why do people take drugs that can kill them in the first place?" Becca asked, truly curious.

"Because facing hell, every day all day, is really fucking hard." Jason swore again. "Sorry. Sometimes I hate my job. Too many people live in hell. Drugs are an escape, a coping mechanism, but addiction just creates more hell. It's a vicious, awful cycle."

"Is there anything I can do to help?"

"Stay alive?—sorry, that was insensitive."

"I'll do my best." Her phone pinged with a notification. Three seconds later Jason's phone did the same.

"There's someone pulling up the drive."

"You expecting anyone?"

She shook her head.

He turned, deep worry etched on his face before making his way to the front of her house in the dark. Becca trailed after him. She had the irrational thought to hide under her desk. If her uninvited company was dangerous, she didn't want to be cornered. How did people live with fear every day?

Her phone pinged again with a new image. Relief flooded her. "Jason, it's my mom." Louder: "It's my mom," she repeated, holding up the phone.

His face softened but not before she saw how bleak it had been. Without thinking she walked forward and wrapped her arms around him. They held each other for several moments. The doorbell rang, breaking the fragile spell.

"I should get that." Becca whispered, reluctantly letting him go. Jason nodded, silent. She stared at him, the realization hitting her like a bucket of ice water.

She was in love with him.

The doorbell rang again.

"Becca, you okay?" Jason asked. "Do you want me to get the door?"

She stared at him. He was such a good man. He was kind. Principled. Protective. Gorgeous with those strong arms and soulful eyes.

"Becca?"

She smiled at him. "I'll get it."

Becca knew he was nearby, ready if she needed him.

She flicked on the foyer light and opened her front door. "Hi Mom."

Samantha walked in, a take-out bag from a local deli in her hand. "I met someone."

Becca blinked. Her mom often made dramatic declarations. This one was new. She closed her front door. "Mom, do come in."

Becca saw Jason watching discreetly from the darkened hall and she felt a rush of warmth. She shook her head once. He retreated silently. Becca was certain her mom hadn't noticed.

"I'm freaking out." Samantha said in a rush. "I brought dinner."

Becca opened the bag her mom thrust at her. "You brought desserts."

"Same thing." Samantha's eyes were a bit wild.

Becca used the voice she took when dealing with a wayward equine. "Take off your boots, give me your coat and we'll sort this out."

Her mom obliged, looking distracted and a bit lost. In moments the two were sitting curled up on the plush living room sofa facing each other in the soft light. Becca said, "Tell me what happened."

"Gerry."

Becca drew back. "The rig mechanic Gerry?" Not her mom's typical target.

Samantha buried her face in her manicured hands, wailing. *"Yes."*

Becca smiled. "What's the problem, he doesn't feel the same way?"

Samantha dropped her hands and sat up. "Of course he does, he's crazy about me."

Becca ignored her mom's bravado. "So what's the problem? You're clearly into him and he's a really nice guy. You could do way worse than Gerry."

"I should be doing way better," she wailed. "He's a *mechanic.*"

"I'm not following," Becca said, deliberately obtuse.

"Becca, he comes home from work with grease under his fingernails." If they had been standing Becca was certain her mom would have stomped her foot.

"Some women would call that hot," Becca quipped. "Can the man use his hands?"

Samantha's scowl transformed into a saucy smile. "That man can."

"Again, I'm not seeing the problem."

"Your father will have a field day with this. He's always called me white trash. I can't date a mechanic." Samantha fanned her face, no doubt to scare away the tears that were threatening to fall. Her mom hated it when her mascara ran.

"First of all, you're being as snobby as Bruce, so knock it off. Second, you like Gerry?"

Her mom nodded.

"Then who the fuck cares what your ex-husband thinks?"

"Becca, language! Besides, it's not that simple."

Becca shrugged. "I think you're using dad as an excuse. Are you really hung up on Gerry's profession or are you afraid of getting hurt?"

Samantha sat up straight. "I hadn't thought of that. I've never dated a man that happy. Or kind. It isn't easy to admit it but I'm a better person with him. And he's so cute in his work coveralls. Oh Becca, do you really think so?"

Jason walked in carrying a heavily laden tray. "I wasn't sure if you guys would want tea or something stronger. I've brought a selection."

Samantha eyed Jason. "Why Officer Chasseur, I didn't realize you were here. My daughter didn't mention it." Samantha pivoted her gaze to Becca. "Dear, why is Officer Chasseur here?"

"Funny story, mom. My house was bugged, I keep getting threatening phone calls and random packages, and I have been precariously close to gunfire recently." Becca looked up at Jason. "Officer Chasseur is keeping me company while all of this gets sorted."

Samantha's face turned white. "Becca, why didn't you tell me? Are you alright?"

It never dawned on Becca that her mom would be worried for her. They just didn't have that sort of relationship. "I'm sorry I didn't tell you. It's all been a bit much." Becca didn't add she was barely keeping it together herself.

Her mom stood, smoothing her slacks. "Geez, and here I went on and on."

Jason set the tray on the large coffee table and started backing away. "Don't leave on my account. I didn't mean to interrupt, I wanted to help."

Samantha eyed Jason. "Is he helping get you all sorted for opening weekend?"

Becca took a deep breath. "I had to cancel opening weekend."

Jason walked closer to her, not touching. His solid presence soothed her.

"But I thought it was important to you."

Becca blinked. "It is. But keeping everyone safe is more important."

Samantha gave a small smile. "You always did look out for everyone else. I always wondered who you got that from, it certainly wasn't from your father or me."

Becca stared at her mom, surprised at the rare admission. "Thanks, mom, that means a lot." She didn't add a fruitless objection to how she was parented; everyone in the room knew the truth anyway.

Samantha stood. "If you don't need me, I'm going to get out of your hair and go find Gerry."

Becca gave her mom a hug. Samantha looked at Jason. "Take care of my little girl."

He nodded. Samantha left in the same rush as she arrived, leaving Becca and Jason alone again.

He stood in front of her, silent and strong. Becca had never wanted a man as much as she wanted Jason in that moment. Which was why she couldn't act on it; she had taken too much from him already. It was going to be one of the longest nights of her life.

She plastered a friendly smile on her face. "Want to hang out a bit?"

"Sure." Jason's answer was swift, almost automatic. He sat in one of the oversized chairs. Away from her. An uncomfortable silence grew in the dim light. Finally, Jason stood. "Actually, I should head to bed."

"Oh! But—I'm selling the land back to you."

She watched as he dropped back into the oversized chair he had been sitting in, almost like his knees had buckled.

"I'm selling the land back to you," she repeated.

"I heard you." He looked dazed.

"I can't afford to just give it to you, although I wish I could."

"Why?"

"I don't have enough money to."

"No, I mean why are you letting me buy it?"

"Because it's important to you." Becca ducked her head. Before she lost her nerve she added, "And you are important to me."

"I am?"

"More than you know," Becca admitted.

"You're important to me, too," he said in a low voice, nearly a whisper.

Becca smiled weakly. "Yes, you've mentioned that. The task of protecting me is certainly drawing out longer than I imagined. I hope you're getting overtime at least."

Jason looked at her. "What if I was here as a man, not as an officer?"

Becca's breath hitched. "What are you saying?"

He stood, and slowly closed the distance between them. With each of his steps, her head spun with hope. He held out his hand and she allowed him to pull her up. She stood, so very near him. He smelled good, masculine, an earthy spiciness that made her a little bit high.

Jason leaned forward slightly. "We need to get something clear. You're not selling the land back to me."

Becca opened her mouth to protest but Jason gently placed his finger over her lips. "What's between us has nothing to do with land."

Before she could protest, he kissed her, his lips ignited hers like firecrackers. Explosive and hot. Breathless, she grabbed at him, pulling him as close as she could. She felt his strong back through his shirt, felt his heart beating in his chest, felt his desire. He wrapped his arms around her and lifted. Instinctively she wrapped her legs around his waist while their mouths sought each other's heat.

Jason broke away, panting. He gently sat her down on the couch, before kneeling in front of her. His arms stayed cradled around her.

"What are you doing?" Becca leaned down, kissing his temples, stroking his cheeks. The stubble there. "Why did you stop?"

"You asked me to not read into you asking me to stay here, that you feel safer with me here. You've been through a lot the last few weeks." He looked down. "I don't want to be an ass, or a passing distraction. It hurts too much when you drop me."

Becca's heart stopped. No, no, no. All those years ago, she had promised herself she would never let anyone close enough to hurt her like that again. It had been a defining moment in her life. As hurt as she had been by him, so had he by her. Knowing she had caused this beautiful man pain wrecked her. She held out her hand to him.

"I need to show you something."

# Chapter Fifty-Two

Becca led Jason to the foyer. She pointed at a black and white mountain lake photo framed on the wall. "Do you know where this is?"

Jason had noticed it the first time he'd walked into her house. "That looks like the same place as our class senior trip."

"I took that photo that day. You waited for me."

Jason backed up. "You weren't supposed to know that."

Becca was looking at the framed image, not him. "I know. I fell behind, I was having so much fun talking pictures. You were the only one who noticed." She spun on her heel. "Next."

She led the way back to the living room and pointed to something hanging in front of the dark front windows. "That prism is from the day we went to that hippie gem shop."

Jason smiled. "Summer before junior year."

Becca nodded before heading down the hall. She pointed at more framed landscape photos as she passed them. "You'll know all of these. You were there for each one." Jason stared. The carefully constructed truths he'd told himself for years were imploding before his eyes.

In the kitchen she grabbed a potted herb on one of the large box windowsills. "Recognize this?"

Jason's hands started sweating. "I gave you that pot freshman year. It had tulips in it then, not—" Jason ran his hands through the small fragrant leaves. "Oregano."

Becca nodded. She put the plant back. He followed her as she made her way to her study. She pulled a couple of photography books off a shelf.

Jason accepted them as she handed them to him. The inscriptions he had written still inside. "You kept them."

"I did. Almost done."

This time he followed her upstairs into his guest bedroom. She stopped in front of the photo he had asked her about, the day his police cruiser had gotten stuck in the mud. "I took this photo that day."

"Why?"

Becca was hugging her arms across her body. "Are you going to make me say it?"

Jason's whole body was tense. He wanted to go to her, wrap his arms around her but he didn't want her to stop talking. He had to know. "Please, Becca, why did you take that picture?"

Becca gave a half-hearted smile. "Because I've never gotten over you. You've always been this—this undercurrent in my life, pulling at me." She brushed a tear away. "Seems I've filled my house with memories of you."

Jason stepped close, daring to hope. She leaned in, bunching his shirt in her fist. They stood like that for long moments. "One more." She dropped her hand to his and led him down the hall into her private area, away from the guest rooms. Once in her own room, she bent down, picking something up off the floor. It was a large river stone. She held it out to him.

His eyes widened. It was the banded river rock he had found in the quad trailer when he was putting away their gear.

"I picked this up two days ago. The day with you. You are many things, but you most certainly are not a passing distraction."

Jason took the large stone from her and put it back on the floor. When he came back up, his hands were already finding her hair, already caressing her throat. He kissed her mouth, parted her lips with his tongue. Stroked her. Becca's breath came hot and fast. She grabbed each side of his face, her possessive grip igniting him. She whispered between kisses, *"Please."*

Her words split him in two. They backed up towards her bed, and he only took his hands off her long enough to pull off his shirt. He tore at her clothes, discarding them in clumsy haste. She landed on top of him, her hands on his bare chest. He reached up and kissed her lips, her neck, each breast as she held them over him.

"Jason?" She panted, pulling a stray stand of hair from her lips.

"Mm?"

"Mind driving?" Her eyes flashed and she bit her lip. "I've thought of you so many times—above me."

It was the hottest moment of his life. He flipped them over, pinning her to the mattress. He tried to take his time kissing her everywhere, but her whole body was tight, frantic, thrumming with electricity. She gasped and writhed each time he put his mouth on her skin but kept holding him tight. The friction was building between them, and he wasn't even inside her yet.

"*Jason, please.*"

Jason held her still. "Hang on, I have a condom in my wallet." Jason looked over his shoulder. "Where the hell did I leave my pants?"

"Nightstand." Becca panted, pointing.

He pulled a silver packet from her nightstand and sheathed himself. He cradled her face between his hands, and she turned her head, kissing his wrist. She let her hand trail down the side of his body before finding him. She guided him to her, and he thought he'd break right then. Slowly, they started to move together, finding their rhythm, undulating like waves. Suddenly, Becca's eyes widened, and she gasped. Deep inside he felt her pulse around him.

His whole world stopped. He had never made a woman come so hard or so fast.

She smiled and stretched sinuously with him still inside her. "I wasn't kidding, I was ready for you." She shifted her hips, rolling him over. "Your turn." She straddled him. When she slid over and onto him his world stopped. His whole body felt like it was floating. Then she started to move, and he fell harder, if that was possible. He hung on as she rode him. She toyed with him, until he was panting and sweating, taking him nearly to the point a few times, only to slow down when he got too close. Again and again, she led in a sensual push and pull until finally he couldn't hold on. He grabbed her arms, clinging to her as his back arched and he exploded inside her.

It was the hottest, rawest, most powerful sex of his life. He was slow to come back down to earth, slow to move. Becca slid off and curled into him, her eyes closed. He kissed her shoulder, still grappling with what had just happened. Sex didn't feel like that.

He pulled off the condom, disposing of it before tucking himself around Becca. She wiggled closer and kissed his hand. Within moments he heard her breath even out.

She slept like a baby while he felt like his skin was inside out. Like he was raw.

She loved him. It scared the shit out of him.

# Chapter Fifty-Three

José Martinez waited until the cowboy left. It would be easier that way.

With a stealth that he hadn't had to use in a long time, he silently let himself into the third-floor condo. She was in the kitchen. He saw the moment she realized she wasn't alone. With a speed that nearly killed him, Lillian Kensington grabbed a knife from the butcher block and hurled it at him. He turned his head aside just in time.

The blade buried itself into the wall behind him.

She reloaded, so to speak, and fired another one at him. Her aim was off but true. The knife missed his face but plunged into his shoulder. José grunted before he could stop himself. He hated making crude noises.

"My dear, do stop. I will not harm you or your man. You have my word."

He sighed, assessing the damage to his haberdashery. He had dressed for the severity of the occasion. The jacket he was wearing was new and had set him back several thousand euros. It wasn't the expense but the waste he hated. His tailor was skilled, a true artisan, and José was bleeding all over his masterpiece. "Lillian Kensington, may I presume?"

The woman watched him. Another knife in her hand, ready. Was she to throw the whole block at him?

He held up a hand. "My name is José Martinez. I believe you were acquainted with my younger brother, Fernando." Her eyes flashed and she raised her arm, ready to hurl another sharp projectile. "Hush, my dear, before we both regret your next throw. I have recently been made aware that my brother came here to kill you, and that you, in fact, had the good fortune of outwitting him. My dear, I know my brother. He was—tenacious. He had made up his mind up to kill you, and he would not have stopped until he succeeded. You wouldn't have had a moment's peace, I swear it."

Her eyes never left his. "I didn't kill him."

"You didn't?"

She shook her head.

José assessed the woman. She was intelligent and beautiful. Fernando had been a fool to misuse her.

"Who did?"

"I'm guessing one of his crew." She closed her eyes briefly. "When I ran into the room, Fernando was dead and Colt," she swallowed, "was badly beaten and bound on the floor. He doesn't remember much from that night."

Her pain was palpable.

"May I sit?"

She hesitated, then nodded.

He edged his way around the prim divan but thought better of it. "Perhaps a kitchen chair. I don't wish to soil your fabric."

"Do you need a doctor?" Her voice was stiff, proper. He had watched her and knew she rarely spoke in such a manner. She was still wary of him.

José looked down. As long as he took care to not move his arm, the jacket should hold the knife, and excessive blood loss, in place. "It'll keep."

José was unsure what to say. How do you apologize to the woman your brother tried to murder? "What I know is that my brother acted in a foul manner indeed. I beg your pardon, but I know he seduced you, exploited you, destroyed your career and nearly your life. He used your kindness and trust in him against you. If that wasn't vile enough, he escaped from prison with the sole purpose of tracking you down here, to Canada. His intent was to murder you. But I swear, I had no idea he meant you harm." José sat straighter. "In fact, I am here to apologize for his actions."

Lillian grabbed the counter.

José pressed on; he wasn't done. "My apology doesn't change what my brother did, but I am hoping it will start to make amends between our families. Family honor matters to me and my brother betrayed you, as well as our family."

Slow tears started to stream down her face.

"My dear, please don't cry. I did not mean to upset you. I thought apologizing was the right thing to do. I'll go at once." He rose to leave.

Lillian shook her head; her eyes were haunted. "You don't understand. No one has ever said what you just said. During the arrest, my trial, the not guilty verdict, no one ever said that."

Her declaration twisted his insides. "Hear me. My brother betrayed you, he betrayed *you*. He used your dear sweet heart against you."

She was crying openly now, swiping at her tears.

José's voice was firm when he said, "That's on him. Not you."

"You don't know how much that means to me. I thought I was over it. That I had moved on." She motioned towards her tear-stained face. "Clearly not."

José could have killed his brother all over again. Some things were sacred. Some things you simply did not desecrate. A woman's trust was one of them. "You will."

Lillian swiped at her face. She stood taller. "Thank you."

"Anytime, my dear." José gave a small smile. "Although, I do apologize for entering your premises without permission. I was afraid you wouldn't accept an audience. Please forgive me for forcing one."

"See that you don't ever do that again." She smiled. "And you're right, I never would have let you in."

He turned to leave.

"José?"

"Yes, my dear?"

She pointed to his shoulder. "Do you need me to attend to your shoulder?"

"I would very much appreciate a ride to the closest medical facility, thank you. Although I understand if you're not comfortable."

"Are you sure about that? You've got a knife in your shoulder because you broke into my condo. Medical staff have a duty to report."

"That is true, my dear, but I enjoy something my brother never had; diplomatic immunity."

"What do you do, again?" Lillian asked.

José smiled. "Few know and fewer still understand. Suffice it to say I am honorable, and covered."

Lillian held up her phone. "I'm going to text Colt, then we can go."

"I'll make a few calls, too, just to make sure you don't suffer any backlash."

Lillian smiled. "It's been a long time since I heard something like that."

José perked up. "Do you want back in the game? You need only say the word."

"*Goodness no!*"

"Excellent, you'll think about it."

Once they were in her car, she asked him, "It was you who came to Becca's inn, wasn't it? Why did you wait so long to make contact?"

"Yes. I waited to make contact as there was a man who impersonated me to enter Canada moments before I arrived. I needed to figure out where he fit in the picture."

"And you know now?"

He smiled, appreciating her quick mind. "I think he's here to hijack a pharmaceutical patent."

"What kind of patent?" Lillian turned on her blinker and waited for her turn to make a left-hand turn.

"I suspect a game-changer in the opioid crisis. I believe this man to be one of Fernando's former drug connections. In the right hands, this patent could save a lot of people. I'm in the business of helping — not hurting — people." Unless they were bad.

The light turned red. Lillian tapped the steering wheel.

"What is it?"

She glanced at him. "I was just wondering if the guy impersonating you has anything to do with the unwanted attention Becca has attracted."

"I hope to know more soon and am happy to keep you in the loop."

If José's suspicions were right, Del Fiennes would exploit and abuse this incredible innovation if given the chance. José, on the other hand, wanted to legitimately sponsor the widespread production of the patent product. A breakthrough like this could save so many lives. Maybe offset some of the lives his brother took, both directly and indirectly.

Lillian made the turn and frowned. "Sorry, I still can't believe I fell for Fernando. It's embarrassing."

"Darling, he was a professional liar, cut yourself some slack. I would have tried to stop him, had I known."

Lillian pulled into the emergency room parking lot, finding a spot close to the doors. "Fernando never did take orders."

A wave of grief passed over José. "I keep asking myself if I could have done anything differently, somehow point my brother on a different path."

Lillian turned off the car. "For a long time I thought it my fault. I was taking responsibility for a grown man's actions." She looked at José. "That's bullshit. It wasn't my fault, and it wasn't yours. Fernando made all of those decisions by himself. No one held a gun to his head"

José admired her spark. "My brother was a fool. Your Colt is a lucky man."

Lillian smiled. Her whole face glowed. "We're both pretty lucky."

José blinked, a bit dazzled. He could only dream of a woman smiling like that over him.

"Come on, then, let's get you sorted."

They both got out of the car. He held out his good arm to usher her inside. "My shoulder really is starting to throb."

A helicopter was quickly approaching. José looked up. "Perfect timing."

Lillian ducked her head at the rotor wash. "Friends of yours?"

"Yours, too, my dear."

# Chapter Fifty-Four

Becca woke up happy. It was the first time in weeks. Her good mood vanished when she opened her eyes. Jason was laying on his back, staring at the ceiling. Did he regret what they had done?

Time to rip off the band-aid. "Morning," she said.

He turned his head, smiling. "I want to show you something." Jason leapt out of bed and started getting dressed.

Becca propped herself up. "Now?"

"Yeah." His smile slipped. "Is that okay? We'll need to go on horseback."

Becca sat up, holding the blankets to her naked body. She wasn't sure what she had expected but it wasn't this. "Where are we going?"

The grin was back. He leaned over and kissed her. "You'll see. I'll go make breakfast. You get ready." He headed out the door.

Becca spoke to an empty room. "I guess that's a no to talking about last night."

A half hour later, Becca worked on Pixie as Jason led her gray gelding, Stürmisch, out of his stall several feet away. She cast sidelong glances at him, afraid she would blink, and he would be gone. He was there, in the flesh, tethering her horse in place and picking up a curry comb. And as far away as he'd always been.

Jason swept Stürmisch's coat in long, smooth stokes and Becca felt a tingle move across her body. She had never dreamed sex could be as hot as it had been last night with Jason. "If my horse presses against your hand any more you're both going to topple over."

Jason agreed. "He does look pretty blissed out."

"*I can relate,*" Becca muttered. Last night with Jason had been explosive, followed by complete and utter relaxation. A few times. Now she wasn't sure what they were.

"You say something?"

Becca blushed and focused on Pixie. "Just that I still can't believe Stürmisch let you ride him yesterday. I wasn't kidding. As a rule, he doesn't accept male riders."

"Are you saying I'm not *masculine* enough?"

Becca threw the comb at him. He easily caught it and walked over to her.

Becca accepted the comb and put it away. "I know better than to touch that one. Besides, the obvious, I have three brothers." She stopped. "Four, actually."

Jason followed her into the tack room. "Who's the forth?"

She handed him tack and took down her own. "Tanner Stone. We found out a couple months ago my dad had a kid with one of his side projects. Tanner is Gabe's age."

"Holy shit—sorry. That was harsh. Finding out you have another brother must have been a shock."

"You have no idea." Becca put a bitless bridle on Pixie. She looked up. Jason was gone. "Hello?"

Jason appeared, saddle in hand, walking out of the tack room. "Have you met him yet?"

"No. Not yet. He hasn't returned any of our messages. I can't blame him. Our dad never publicly acknowledged him. I don't blame him for not wanting anything to do with us."

"But you want to meet him?" Jason saddled Stürmisch.

"Hell yes. I love my brothers. To think I have another one is amazing." Her smile slipped. "And awful at the same time. How could my dad keep one of his kids a secret?" It was a rhetorical question. No one except Bruce knew the answer to that one.

Jason squeezed her shoulder. "Let me go get your saddle."

"Thank you." Her emotions were churning all over the place and she could use a minute to compose herself.

Jason returned and fitted Becca's saddle on Pixie.

Becca took over, cinching it. "Maybe someday Tanner will change his mind. If he does, I'll be here."

She had built a home big enough for all of her siblings to be able to come together. To come home.

Someday.

# Chapter Fifty-Five

Jason watched a storm of emotions cross Becca's features. "We don't have to go out today." He should have done more than drop a simple quick kiss on her this morning. He should have reassured her. Now the tension was back between them.

"I want to go. Besides, you want to show me something. Where did you say we were going again?"

"I didn't. Patience, good woman. Wait, is it sexist to call you woman?"

"Anyone else, yes. With you I haven't decided yet."

"You know I don't mean it in a derogatory way."

"I know. That's why I haven't decided yet. Let me just grab sandwiches in the bar fridge in the barn office and fill a couple of water bottles."

"You keep sandwiches in your barn?"

"Yeah, I make a bunch every few days and keep them in the barn office. That way I can work longer without having to stop to make a meal in the house."

"Drip coffee is a no go, but you'll eat days-old sandwiches?"

Becca shrugged. "I'm complicated. Don't worry, I haven't figured me out, either. Just ask my parents."

Jason didn't like how she so easily dismissed herself. "I like your kind of complicated."

She flushed at his words and ducked her head. "You just earned yourself some of my secret chocolate stash."

The morning sun was still low in the sky, but a dark blanket of clouds rolled itself out over the back country. The effect was stunning. Sunlight lit everything under the dark canopy. Jason smiled to himself. He couldn't imagine living anywhere else.

They had been riding for nearly two hours and following the winding mountain river for the last kilometer. They had gained enough elevation to find a few areas dusted with snow. Years had passed since he had last been here, but it held the kind of memories that only strong emotions could forge. Without siblings and with adults grumbling at home, he was left to make his own fun and had created grand adventures to keep him company as he explored every inch of this land.

He had never told anyone about what he had found. Then, before he knew it, his dad had sold the land, not before brush-ins with the law and Becca's father. Jason figured it was hurt that made his dad sell—he had had an explosive relationship with Jason's grandpa. But maybe it was simple economics. The land was valuable, and they never had a lot of money growing up. Maybe it was both. He'd never know now.

When they came upon a partially treed area with lighter groundcover, he stopped. "I think this is it."

Jason dismounted and Becca did the same. She tied her horse's lead to a sturdy tree branch and Jason followed suit. The mountain stream was visible through the trees and Jason knew from experience it was glacial.

She walked a few steps through the low underbrush before she turned to face him. "What am I looking at besides an Upper Foothill-Montane transition zone?"

Jason looked over, smiling. "This is your Hail Mary, if you still want one." He stepped over deadfall and held a low hanging branch out of the way.

She looked around with renewed interest before following him. "I'm listening."

"I'm fairly certain it's Fort Roche Cachée."

"Sounds cool. But I have no idea what that means."

Jason gave her a brief summary of the mystery of Fort La Jonquière, the oldest known western fur trade fort in Canada.

Becca asked, "I thought you said this was Fort Roche Cachée. What does this have to do with Fort La Jonquière?"

"Fort Roche Cachée predates Fort La Jonquière by a decade. That in and of itself is a big deal. Up until now, Fort La Jonquière had that claim. It also supports the theory that Fort La Jonquière was where Fort Calgary is in present day Calgary. That has been argued by historians for decades. This should help shed light on the conversation."

She eyed him. "What do you know that historians don't?"

"I used to play here when I was a kid. One day I tripped over a metal lock box and discovered this." Jason spread his arms wide.

"Your parents let you play here by yourself?"

"I don't think my parents realized how far afield I'd wander."

He was always home for dinner and never required medical attention beyond a band-aid. So why would they wonder?

"Hey, what's that?" Becca pointed.

"An old chimney. Come on, there's more."

Becca followed him, excited. "That looks like a foundation."

"There should be three." Jason smiled, pleased at her enthusiasm. He walked around what was left of the foundation and chimney, stepping over what could be rotting logs. Its outline was barely visible through the thick carpet of vegetation and leaf litter. He paced and found the second foundation. Its chimney was completely crumbled. He angled again and paced off until the shadow of an outline for the third foundation became visible. Its chimney was mostly obscured from sharing space with a plucky tree still holding tight to most of its leaves.

"There should also be metal debris around if it hasn't all disintegrated."

Becca bent over and picked something out of the back dirt of a small animal den. "This looks like it could be a nail." She studied it. "It's square, that's important, right?"

Jason walked over. "Yes, round nails were a later technology."

She toed the pile of dirt at her feet. "A button!"

Jason smiled. He remembered having the same feeling of discovery here.

Becca looked around, her eyes filled with wonder. "Jason, this is incredible. You found a fur trade fort. Wait, how do you know this is Fort Roche Cachée?"

"My mom gave me my great grandfather's grandfather's fur trade journal. This fort was discussed by name and mapped."

"That sounds old like Lillian's fur trade journal."

"Lillian has an historic journal, too?"

"She has several of them, actually. She brought them over from her family's estate library in England. One was written by a woman."

Jason's eyebrows rose. "That's a really big deal."

"I know, she was pretty excited. She donated them to one of our archives, but I can't remember which one."

"I'm assuming they were personal journals?"

"Aren't all journals personal?"

"There were company journals, too, but those were most likely turned in. A lot of the company men also kept personal journals to record where they were going and what they were seeing. The information they recorded would be incredibly useful to a lot of people."

"That makes sense. When is your grandfather's from?"

"From what I can tell it is from 1747."

Becca's eyebrows rose. "I know I wasn't a keener in history class, but that sounds earlier than anything I remember."

Jason shrugged. "When Henday came through in 1754 he mentioned French traders on the Battle River."

"Who's he?"

"A trader and explorer for the Hudson's Bay Company. He was tasked with convincing Indigenous trappers to make the trek to Hudson's Bay and trade with the HBC instead of trading with the French inland."

"His bosses wanted him to convince people to make the trip from what is now Alberta to Hudson's Bay when there were French traders here at the time? That must have been a hard sell."

"Yes, I imagine so."

"I didn't know you were so into history."

Jason shrugged. "I've got a French last name and I'm from western Canada. I read a few books on the subject."

Becca looked around. "We should have been taught this stuff."

Jason smiled. He couldn't agree more.

They walked around the area, exploring what was left of the outpost. The area was overgrown but they found several cut logs. Their ends could have been notched, though it was hard to tell with the aged wood. They found more metal debris and what might have been an old bit of leather.

Becca was still looking around, her eyes filled with awe. "It's so beautiful here. Imagine living here, at the fort."

"Ooh, that's the romance of history talking. The fur trade era was a violent time, not to mention the starvation, constant uncertainty, and questionable hygiene practices."

"Right." Becca frowned. "Don't forget culturally mandated misogyny."

"That, too."

Becca looked around. "This seems pretty important. Regardless of the pipeline, we need to report this."

Jason's childhood held a mix of memories he always thought better left to the past. Now he wasn't so sure. Talking to his mom had opened up the vault where he stored the memories of his father. It had the curious effect of making him feel lighter. "I think Clint knows a few archaeologists. They'll know the process."

Becca pulled out her phone. "Mind if I take a waypoint?"

"Good idea."

"I'll cross reference this with the proposed hydrogen pipeline map I have. I'm pretty sure this is not on the proposed right-of-way."

Jason was surprised. "Hydrogen pipeline? I assumed it was oil or gas."

"It's a hydrogen pipeline from the Lefebvre Wind Farm down south to Banff. It's part of their decarbonization plan."

"Isn't the hydrogen used in Alberta produced from natural gas?"

"Blue hydrogen is. Green hydrogen is from wind or solar."

"What did you do in Germany again?"

Becca smiled. "Not pipelines. I was in regenerative agriculture."

Jason shook his head. "I don't know what that is."

"Current industrial agricultural practices are no more sustainable than burning fossil fuels. There was a time and place for both, now it's time to shift. I helped producers shift to regenerative agriculture practices that create and support healthy soil chemistry and structure, which includes a natural carbon drawdown. It's a pretty big deal. And retaining topsoil—besides obvious growing implications—means it isn't blowing elsewhere and choking surface water systems. Improving soil chemistry means the nutrients are already in the soil and eliminates the need for damaging pesticides and fertilizers, and includes drawing down carbon dioxide from the atmosphere where it belongs: in the ground supporting soil and food health. Rotating crops, not ripping out the old stalks, stuff like that. It's working with nature to achieve industrial-sized results instead of sticking with our previous short-sighted and damaging methods."

"Wow, Becca, I had no idea." He could kick himself for how bad he had fucked it up with her. "Why did you move back?"

"A few reasons. I was homesick. I also was sick of the unnecessary uphill battle."

"What do you mean?"

"Most people are hesitant to change. I get that. Adapting to sustainable practices means rocking a big scary boat. But the backlash just got too much. It's worse here. I imagine it's not so different to what you and Tucker see. People making damaging choices, over and over, literally on a crazy train headed straight towards Wrecksville, yet have very personal, very anchoring reasons why they are unwilling to contemplate there is an easier, better way."

"Is there?"

"Yes!" Becca said emphatically. "We have been conditioned to think nature must be conquered or subdued when it is nature's ingenious designs that can navigate us out of the very real mess we've made. We don't need dominance and more force; we need fucking cooperation. We need to open our hardened minds and our fucking eyes. Sorry, this means a lot to me and I get so angry people dismiss this as frivolous hippy talk. I get called a hippie a lot."

Jason contemplated that for a moment. "In policing, shit gets dark when people try to dominate others. The harder anyone tries to force another, the greater the likelihood of violence and damage. It makes sense there would be some compelling parallels to our relationship with the natural world."

Becca stepped forward and grabbed his face between her hands. "That is the hottest thing I have ever heard you say." She tugged his head down and kissed him.

He kissed her back with as much passion.

When they broke apart, they both were breathing heavy. He felt inside-out. He couldn't keep doing this. God, she was so beautiful. "Becca, I—"

His phone pinged.

Jason ignored it. "I'm sorry, I should have kissed you the second you woke up this morning."

Becca's eyes widened.

His phone pinged again. He didn't want to answer it. He wanted to wrap his arms around Becca and kiss her for the rest of their lives.

Becca smiled. "Answer your phone. I'm not going anywhere."

"It's your brother." Jason answered the call. "Chasseur here."

*"You sprint to answer the phone?"*

Jason eyed Becca. "Something like that. What can I do for you, Tucker?"

*"The lab report is in from the bud sample you took. The CBD levels rival opioid potency."*

Jason straightened. "I didn't think that was possible."

*"I did, too. The lab checked three times. It matches the Fischer brothers' patent. They have grown a marijuana plant with a CBD potency equal to an opioid without the lethal side effects. The implications are huge. I'm at the hospital now to try and talk to the brothers, though I expect only one will be talking. This could be a game changer in the fentanyl crisis."*

"Keep us posted." Jason hung up and briefed Becca.

Becca started pacing. "Oh my god, what is Tuck doing?" She started wringing her hands. "It wasn't bad enough Gabe took a fucking bullet in the head. Colt has had god knows how many bull wrecks. Now Tuck is hitting up violent criminals to help with the fucking opioid crisis? Again? I can't take this." Becca grabbed at her hair, her eyes as wild as they were wide. "I couldn't breathe when Tuck was doing undercover work. I couldn't breathe when Gabe was with CSIS or when Colt was riding bulls or fucking kidnapped." She unzipped her jacket and started pulling at her sweater. "Jason, I can't breathe now." Tears pooled in her eyes as she fought with her layers of clothing.

Jason opened his arms to help, and she melted into them.

As she held him tight, she whispered, "What if he doesn't come back? What if he gets hurt? Gabe got hurt."

"Tucker knows what he's doing." Jason hoped it was true.

"I feel like I keep breaking," she whispered.

He held her several moments before saying, "My mom told me how strong you are."

Becca pulled back and looked at him.

Jason tucked a strand of hair behind her ear. "She did. She also gave me hell for not helping you. She is so proud of you, Becca."

"Is that why you're helping me? Is that why you brought me here?"

Jason kept playing with her hair. "No. Although it's pretty bad to get called out by your mom at my age."

Becca giggled. It was a welcome shift.

"Don't laugh. Do you know how intimidating it is being surrounded by women who can run circles around me? I brought you here because this morning I realized I don't want anything between us. Never again."

"Me, either," she whispered.

"I was so excited to get you out here I completely bungled this morning. I'm sorry for that."

Becca raised her face, pressing her lips to his. The kiss turned hot. He broke away. "Sorry, I have to stop kissing you like that when you're upset."

Becca pressed her index finger against his lips. "Don't even think it. And I'd say we actually run circles around each other." She lowered her finger from his lips. "Thanks for helping me weather that storm."

"Always."

"I appreciate you showing me this."

"You want to head home?"

Becca nodded. "I'm worried for Tucker."

"Let's get you home."

The closer they got to Becca's place, the more agitated Jason felt. Something was wrong. He felt like he did before a storm broke, when you could feel the energy building.

A feeling of fucking impending doom.

# Chapter Fifty-Six

Christopher Fischer sat in the stark hospital room chair while his brother clung to life in the bed next to him. The uniformed officer had moved and stood outside the door.

Austin hadn't woken up yet. Machines beeped, fluid dripped, and Christopher waited. He knew better than to believe life was fair, but did every family member have to be violently ripped from him?

The doctor who had first taken him to see Austin walked into the room. "How are you holding up?"

Christopher stared, angry. She must have heard him puke earlier. "You don't need to check in on me."

"I wasn't." She lifted the digital tablet she was holding and moved to the beeping machines on the other side of Austin's inert body.

"Oh." Christopher watched as she tapped against the tablet's screen and reading the numbers on the machine. He asked, "Why hasn't he woken up yet?"

"Because his body is healing." She didn't look at him, just kept typing into her tablet.

"Oh. You don't like me very much, do you?"

Finally, the doctor slid her tablet into the large pocket in her white coat and looked at him. "I'm attending to your brother, that's what you need to know."

"Whatever." Christopher looked down, breaking eye contact. As far as getting the last word in, it was weak.

The doctor stood a moment before exiting the room and Christopher swore to himself. Why did he have to be such an asshole? The woman was simply doing her job, keeping Austin alive.

His phone vibrated. Christopher pulled it out and punched in a code. He keyed in the record command and held the phone up to his ear to listen to Bruce Tanner's conversation.

He barely registered the soft knock on the door.

Detective Tuck Tanner stood in the doorway. Christopher held up his hand, the universal signal to wait your fucking turn. Only when Bruce had ended his call did Christopher put his phone away and turn to the detective. "What the fuck do you want?"

The detective walked into the room. He must have been near Austin's age. His hands were in the jacket pockets, and he spread his arms wide, showing the inside of the jacket. No gun. "I just want to talk."

"I'm not feeling chatty, so get the fuck out of here."

"Found your test site. Did you guys develop a CBD to rival opioids?"

"What's it to you?"

The cop faced Christopher in his chair and Austin still unconscious in his hospital bed. "I pulled your patent application information. You guys are going to save lives."

"No, we're going to make a lot of money." Christopher smelled a trap. No way was this cop praising their illegal grow op.

The detective took a step forward. "Have you ever seen people die overdosing on opioids?"

Christopher glared at the guy. "As a matter of fact, I have."

That stopped the cop. "So you've seen that pain and you seriously don't fucking care?"

"Get the fuck out of here! I don't need to take your shit."

"You peddle poison, and you don't need to take my shit?"

"You've got a lot of balls coming in here."

The doctor came back in. She looked between Christopher and the annoying cop. "Detective Tanner, always a pleasure to see you."

Christopher watched as the detective smiled at the woman. "Doctor Williams." The way he said it implied familiarity, maybe even intimacy. The cop got a woman like that? Unfuckingbelievable.

"Forgive the interruption, I just needed one more reading." She bent over Austin and recorded what she needed and left the room.

Once she was gone, the cop started in again. "I'm serious. If you guys can actually produce CBD that provides comparable pain killers to opioids without the addictions and overdoses, you guys should win the goddamn Nobel Peace Prize."

Christopher wanted to punch the guy. He just didn't get it. "What, so—hypothetically—big Pharma can cash in? So bored housewives and junkie executives don't die in the gutter like the rest of us little people? Fuck you. You don't give a fuck about street junkies dying."

Something flashed in the detective's eyes then and Christopher knew he had misjudged him.

But the only thing the cop said was, "This will save lives. That matters."

A clatter in the hallway made Christopher glance over the cop's shoulder, uncomfortable. Why wasn't the uniformed officer there?

A masked man charged into the room, gun drawn. A silencer capped the weapon. He aimed at Austin's prone body. The detective leapt forward at the same time Christopher sprawled across his brother's form on the bed.

*Pop, pop, pop.*

Christopher saw the detective's body convulse before he dropped to the ground. Christopher grabbed the knife he always wore strapped to his ankle and hurled it with all his might. The gunman's grunt came out like a gurgle around the blade buried to the hilt in his throat. He staggered once before dropping to the ground on top of the downed detective.

Christopher bounded off the bed. He dragged the gunman off the detective, dumping him in a heap out of the way and turned to the cop who lay in a widening pool of blood from the bullets in his back. Christopher bellowed for a doctor and dropped to the ground. He turned the detective over and cradled him in his arms. "Stay with me man, stay with me."

The detective's eyes were wide. Doctors and more uniformed officers rushed in while Austin's heart monitor ticked in the background, unchanging.

 Why had the cop taken the bullets meant for his brother? Everything was going fuzzy. Christopher's vision darkened around the edges, and he couldn't make out distinct sounds. Over and over, he said, *"He saved my brother's life, he saved my brother's life."*

Doctor Williams appeared in his field of vision, holding out her hand. He latched onto it like a lifeline.

"Your brother is safe. Come with me."

She didn't say anything about the cop with the bullets in his back.

# Chapter Fifty-Seven

Rose opened her front door just enough to look out, unimpressed. "What do you want, Mr. Tanner."

Bruce Tanner stood on her stoop. "Come now, Rose, my dear, we're closer than that."

"No, we're not and we both know you don't hold anyone dear." She held her rifle behind the door. She had learned a long time ago not to trust this man.

"Are you still mad? That was decades ago." Why did his eyes look so red and…hollow? He didn't look drunk, but he certainly wasn't sober.

"You tried to take what wasn't yours." Rose tightened her grip on the gun.

"Everything's mine. Besides, Jason needs you. He's in danger. You need to come with me."

Fear spiked within her. What had happened? She kept her face impassive when she asked, "Whatever do you mean?"

"The task force he's been working on."

Rose knew if Jason was working on a task force, he sure as shit wouldn't have told the likes of Bruce Tanner.

"What task force?"

"The one with my son, Tucker. He's a detective now, you know."

"Yes, you must be very proud. About Jason?"

Bruce snorted. "Right. Becca has had a spot of trouble with the new foolish eco-inn she's trying to open. Hare-brained bullshit is what it is. Never going to work…I'm seeing to that."

Rose tried again. "Yes, but why are you here?"

That focused him. He grabbed at her arm through the narrow opening. "I need you to come with me. You, and Becca, and Meredith. If only I could get Samantha there, too."

Rose deflected his grip, angering him. He raised his hand to strike her, but she moved fast, shoving the barrel of her rifle into his chest. "Time to go."

Bruce staggered back. "You haven't seen the last of me, old woman. You're next."

Rose held the rifle higher. Bruce ran to his car, spraying gravel as he peeled out of her driveway.

She waited until he had cleared the end of her drive before calling her son. He didn't pick up. She tried Becca's number. Nothing. She called nine-one-one. Impatient, she paced, waiting for an officer to arrive. She hated this feeling of helplessness. It reminded her of too many nights waiting for her husband to come home, and later, waiting for help to arrive when her boyfriend got violent. Terrified it would be too late this time.

She could call Detective Tanner. Maybe he would know what to do about his father. She looked up Tuck's number. A different officer picked up. "Detective Tanner's phone."

"I need to speak to Tucker, it's Rose Chasseur."

"He is unavailable ma'am. How can I help you?"

Rose listened carefully; she knew that background noise. "You're in a hospital. Which one? What happened?"

"Ma'am, you need to calm down."

Rose suddenly realized where Bruce was going. She barked orders to the officer before hanging up. She got into her car and headed after Bruce.

# Chapter Fifty-Eight

Christopher Fischer stood in fresh visitor scrubs just beyond the emergency room doors. He stared through the leaded window. Detective Tanner was being prepped for surgery. The prick who had fired on them hadn't made it. Good.

Doctor Williams approached. She stood next to him and looked through the window, too. "Now I am checking in on you. You okay?"

"No. Detective Tanner took the bullets meant for us."

"Sounds like Tuck."

The doctor's voice had caught and again Christopher wondered about their relationship. He shouldn't care. "I had just reamed him out for trying to talk to me."

"That wouldn't have phased Detective Tanner."

Christopher stared through the window, his arms crossed. "I said he cared that bored housewives and junkie executives didn't die in the gutter but that he didn't give a fuck about street junkies dying."

"He's not like that."

"I know that. Now." Christopher rarely misjudged people, but he had misjudged the cop. "Will he make it?"

"We'll know more when he's through surgery." Again, that catch in her voice.

Christopher wanted to throw something. "I hate my job."

The doctor frowned. "Then stop talking and do something about it."

With that, the doctor swiped her ID and went into the surgery ward, leaving Christopher standing alone.

The haunting scent of vanilla flittered briefly, and Christopher spun around, catching the barest flicker of a spectral form. "Mom?"

But the hallway was empty, and he didn't believe in ghosts.

A notification pinged on his phone. Bruce Tanner was on the move and Christopher was pretty sure he knew where. Christopher sprinted out of the hospital. He had to get there before it was too late.

# Chapter Fifty-Nine

"Dad? What the hell are you doing here?" Becca had nearly collided with her dad. The pail of water she was carrying splashed, soaking her legs.

"Must you be so crass?"

Becca rolled her eyes and set the water bucket down. "Whatever. Actually, I'm glad you're here. I want to talk to you about us selling the land to Jason Chasseur." She finally looked at her dad. "What's wrong with your mouth?"

It looked like her dad had foam or something frothing at the corner of his mouth.

"Nothing. Don't be ridiculous." Bruce swiped at hip lips. He wasn't looking at her when he answered, he was eyeing the barn's support beams.

She looked up, too, but didn't see anything that could have captured her dad's attention. "What are we looking at?"

Bruce snapped his gaze back down. "Don't be a smart ass. I didn't like it when your mother sassed me, and I don't like it when you do either."

Becca bit a nasty retort. She glanced over her shoulder making sure Jason wasn't back yet. He'd offered to drive a bale of hay out to the pasture where the horses were grazing. She didn't want him to have to deal with her temperamental father. Her dad would no doubt say something ugly.

"I want us to sell the land to Jason Chasseur. It's the right thing to do. I'm not comfortable how you blocked him. I mean, it is a valuable piece of property, but you put in a bid only after Jason made an offer. You did it on purpose, didn't you?"

Bruce snorted. "You were always such a naive do-gooder." He shook his head. "That doesn't matter now, I have plans for that land that have nothing to do with you."

"What are you talking about?"

"None of your business. You know, you're just like Meredith. Nosy."

Becca instinctively stepped back. "Dad, you're scaring me."

Bruce's smile was more a jeer. "Good. I always like that more."

"What are you talking about?" Becca stepped back again, and her foot caught on the bucket handle. She started to stumble and reached out to him to stead herself. Instead, her dad pushed her. She fell hard on the concrete floor, blinking away the pain, dazed. She tried to pull herself up on a nearby stall, but a form caught her eye. There was a body in one of the empty stalls. It wasn't moving.

She risked a glance back at her dad. He wasn't looking at her, he was dousing the barn's wooden support beams with accelerant.

She took the opening and rolled into the stall. The prone form was Meredith. She lay unmoving on the floor, blood drying on her temple.

"What did he do to you?" Becca whispered. She checked for a pulse. Meredith groaned softly. Becca pressed the emergency dial before hiding her phone in the empty trough. She stood, grabbing the pitchfork leaning against the wall, and peered out of the stall.

Bruce held a gun to her head. "I told you I don't like sass."

She couldn't believe her eyes. The gas fumes were making her feel lightheaded. How was she going to protect Jason? He'd be here any minute. "I don't understand, what's going on?"

Bruce laughed. "I know. You understand so little."

"The dropped weight, the pallor of your skin, we know it wasn't cancer—oh my god, you use. You're fucking stoned out of your mind right now. You're frothing at the mouth."

Bruce swiped the back of his hand across his lips. "Fuck you, you guys saw what you wanted to see. You kids are ungrateful, stupid, selfish disappointments."

Becca's mind was reeling. "Was Meredith in on it? That desperate grab for sympathy?"

Bruce rolled his eyes. "The old bitty laying on the floor? I think not."

"What about Del Fiennes? Did you lie to him, too?"

Bruce roared. "What do you know?"

Before she could answer he pistol-whipped her. The force knocked her to the ground. Her father raised a large jerrycan over her and started pouring gasoline on her.

She screamed, trying to scramble away.

"I've been working for months to cultivate this deal. You idiots are not going to ruin everything. You kids and your hard-on for law-enforcement nearly broke the deal. Gabe was with fucking CSIS and Tucker made detective. Colt started banging that MI6 courier and you're fucking that piece of shit Mountie." Bruce snorted. "You all are so naive. You fell for that cancer shit. Boo hoo." Bruce laughed. "Lucky for Gabe, he moved across the country. And now Tucker won't be a problem anymore, either."

His tone chilled Becca. "What did you do?"

Bruce waved his phone. "Tucker, that's such a stupid name. I can't believe I let your mother name you kids."

"Dad, please, what happened to Tucker?"

"He just took three bullets meant for the Fischer boys. Saves me from staging an accident. I have ears everywhere."

Becca's knees buckled. *Tucker.*

"He's always been too much of a do-gooder. Not like you, though. Cozying up with the Fischer boys. Don't worry, they'll be dead soon, too."

A commotion sounded from the far side of the barn before Becca could parse what the hell her father was talking about. She looked up to see Jason walking forward, hands up. The side of his head was bleeding. A man Becca had never seen before walked behind him, holding a large gun at Jason's back. "I found him outside. Doors are all locked, boss."

"Becca, are you okay?" Jason's voice sounded off and she wondered how hard he had hit his head. The man slammed the butt of his gun against Jason's temple. Becca watched in horror as Jason crumpled to the floor unconscious.

*"Stop."* She started to run to Jason, but her dad grabbed her. She tried to shrug him off and he slapped her. "Why the locked doors, dad?" Becca needed information. She needed to get Jason and Meredith out of here.

"A fire, my dear. I'm tying up loose ends." Bruce looked around the barn. "It's really too bad. You had the start of something good here. I'm kind of surprised actually. Didn't know you had it in you."

"This won't look like an accident."

"This doesn't have to. I've already framed the Chasseur kid. Murder-suicide."

Bruce fired his gun at Jason, and turned and fired at Becca. She was spun around from the force before dropping to the ground from the pain in her arm.

"You shot me!" Becca stared in macabre fascination as warm blood spread across the fabric of her long sleeve shirt. When she looked up, Bruce and his henchman were emptying jerrycans of gas on the support beams of her barn. She reached in her pocket to pull out her phone and remembered she had already called nine-one-one. Her phone was in the trough, several feet away. She started to crawl towards it.

Bruce called to his hired muscle. "Knock her out, I only want one bullet hole in her. Let's go."

The man stepped forward, then everything went black.

# Chapter Sixty

Christopher drove like a bat out of hell. Becca Tanner's rural inn was an hour from the city, but he made it in thirty-five minutes. While running out of the hospital he had called for fire, police and ambulance. How the hell weren't they here yet?

The scent of vanilla was strong in the truck. "Mom, if that's really you, I need your help."

He was too late. Christopher could see bright orange flames licking over the roof of Becca's barn, a grotesque light in the dark night. He sprinted from his truck, crouching as he ran.

He expected gunfire but he heard nothing over the roar of the fire consuming Becca's barn.

Bruce had hired muscle. Christopher was certain he would find Becca and Officer Chasseur in the barn, but he didn't know if Bruce or his man would have killed them first. He made it to the large barn doors where a large chain was looped through and linked with a padlock, locking him out. He heard the sound of splintering wood and a loud crash and ducked instinctively. The sound was muted only by the steadily growing fire crackling inside.

Christopher shouted Becca's name and pounded on the wooden door. It was warm. He spun around. Becca's tidy yard gave away nothing, no tools were left out, no handy pickaxe.

Squinting from the smoke, Christopher thought he saw an old woman running towards him, shouting. Was he hallucinating? Finally, he made out what she was trying to say.

*The gnomes.*

What the fuck? Christopher looked down. Three garden gnomes stood in the garden bed that flanked the far side of the barn door, staring at him in the eerie orange light. They held a large antique plough blade that rested against a watering can. Christopher grabbed the plough and swung, bringing it down hard on the barn door handles. Wood splintered and gave. He tossed the plough blade aside and ran inside. The backdraft he created hit him and knocked him back on his ass, hard. Heavy smoke billowed out over him. The enormity of what he was about to do hit him harder than the backdraft. Sommelier's needed their nose and he was about to destroy his sense of smell. He grabbed the watering can. It was full, thank god, so he drenched himself.

This time crawling on the ground with his soaked shirt covering his nose and mouth, he made his way back inside. In a minute or two, he crawled into two bodies. They were unmoving, but still breathing. He dragged the smaller one out first. It was Becca Tanner. She moaned. She was alive. Relieved, he turned back towards the barn.

The old woman was there, about to charge into the burning barn. He grabbed her. Christ, she was half his size. Christopher grabbed her shoulders and yelled in her ear, "I'll get him."

She shouted something back, pointing. Before he understood what she wanted, she had upended another large pail of water over him. Pulling his wet shirt back over his nose and mouth he ran back inside. This time, the wall of heat and smoke dropped him to his knees. On all fours, he crawled as fast as he could to the second figure. It had to be Officer Chasseur; the body had a tall frame with a muscular build. He grabbed two fistfuls of jacket and heaved with all his might. The body didn't budge. With his lungs screaming, Christopher took as large a breath as he dared before rising into a crouch. He bent and grabbed the man under his arms and heaved.

Six inches. He had moved the body six whole inches.

Christopher changed his hold and started dragging. After what felt like an eternity, he got the body out. In the eerie flicker of light, soot colored blood ran down both of the man's temples.

The old woman had been at Becca's side and now launched herself at the prone man, calling his name over and over. It was Chasseur.

Christopher collapsed onto his back. His lungs burned. Sirens wailed in the distance. He heaved himself up and crawled over to check on Becca and Chasseur. He couldn't tell if they were breathing.

The old woman was kneeling between the two, crying.

"They're breathing," he repeated, trying to comfort her and hoping like hell he was right.

A voice croaked. Becca was trying to talk. She was alive. He hadn't been too late.

He held her hand. "It's okay, it's okay. Jason's here, right next to you. The ambulance is on its way."

She made a garbled sound again. It was awful. The unholy sound sliced through him.

In that moment he vowed to kill Bruce Tanner with his bare hands.

"The paramedics are on their way. It'll be okay."

Becca weakly grabbed his collar and croaked out, *"Meredtih, my stepmom…second stall…left."*

Fuck.

This good guy crap was going to get him killed.

Christopher pulled up his shirt again and crawled back in. The smoke was even thicker now, and his throat and lungs screamed with pain. Everything was hot, the air, the concrete floor, the flaming timbers dropping around him. His hands were raw and starting to blister from crawling. He hugged the left, counting stalls. He crawled into the second one and bumped into another body.

With strength he didn't know he had left, he dragged Meredith out of the burning barn. Two fire crews were on the scene and starting to fight the blaze while paramedics knelt next to Becca and Chasseur, fitting them with oxygen masks. Two more jogged toward him. They took Meredith from him just as he collapsed.

An explosion sounded and he looked up as a fireball roared over his head. He stared at it, mesmerized. So this was it, hell really was a fireball. The stars and air were gone, replaced by eerie, glowing orange smoke.

Christopher's last thought was he wasn't going to be able to kill Bruce Tanner with his bare hands.

Damn.

Maybe the devil would.

# Chapter Sixty-One

Becca woke up screaming for Jason. Her throat felt like it was on fire and she started clawing at it. She had to get to Jason, she had to save him.

A clear voice rang. "Becca, it's Lillian. You're in the hospital. Jason is getting some tests run. You can see him soon. Don't try to talk."

Becca blinked. Jason was alive. Lillian was here, sitting in a chair next to her bed.

Becca tried to sit up, but everything hurt. Colt ran into the room wild-eyed and Lillian held up a hand. "You heard your sister wake up. She's okay. She's safe."

Colt brought his hands together in front of his face. Becca had never seen that look in his eyes. He took a breath. Then a second one. "You two have got to stop scaring the shit out of me." He strode to the other side of her bed and picked up her hand. "You would have been in so much trouble if you had died."

Becca started to laugh but pain exploded inside of her. "Ow, it hurts to laugh." Her voice came out like a croak. "Jason?"

"You can see him soon."

Becca blinked before tears started streaming. "Meredith was there. Dad hurt her."

Colt and Lillian looked hesitant. Becca pressed. "What? Tell me."

"What do you remember?" Lillian asked.

Becca closed her eyes and whispered, "Dad came. I told him I wanted to sell the land to Jason. He laughed at me. I tripped, then I asked him about Del Fiennes, and he doused me with gas."

Colt swore violently and Lillian hushed him.

"It's okay. I grabbed a pitchfork. But Jason was bleeding." Becca started crying full on. Swallowing was agony. "A guy hit him on the side of his head with his gun. I saw it. Wait, where's Meredith?" Suddenly Becca remembered what her dad had said. "Ohmygod Tucker. Is Tuck okay? Dad hurt him, too."

Colt squeezed her hand. "Tuck's banged up pretty good but he came through surgery."

A doctor walked in before Becca could ask Colt for details. "Ms. Tanner, you're awake. I'd ask how you're feeling but I imagine you feel," the doctor glanced at Becca's bandages, "like hell, actually."

Becca liked her on the spot. "Sorry about the screaming. I hope I didn't scare everyone."

The doctor looked at the tablet in her hand. "Screaming means you've got air in your lungs. It was music to my ears." She tucked the tablet away. "Mind if I check your vitals?"

Becca nodded. The doctor finished assessing her. "You're in surprisingly good shape for someone who went through what you did. How's the arm?"

Becca looked at her arm. She hadn't noticed the thick bandage. "What happened to my arm? Oh shit." She tilted her head back and closed her eyes. "I remember.

My dad fucking shot me after dousing me with gas." Becca closed her eyes and brought her hand up to her temple. "This is going to take years of therapy, isn't it?"

The doctor winked at Lillian and Colt. "Oh, I like this one. She's a survivor. I'll come back later and check in on you. We need to keep you overnight for observation. We don't mess around when it comes to smoke inhalation."

After the doctor left, Becca asked, "How did we get out?"

Colt and Lillian looked at each other. Lillian nodded at him. Colt said, "Christopher Fischer pulled you all out of the barn to safety."

Becca couldn't have heard correctly. Confused, she asked, "I thought he was one of the bad guys."

Colt shrugged. "After Tucker was shot protecting Austin Fischer, Christopher flew out of here. He was the one who smashed open your locked barn door and dragged you, Jason and Meredith out of the burning barn. Jason's mom Rose was there, too. Seems dad made a stop at her house first and she got suspicious. Fischer wouldn't let her go inside the burning barn. She was there, saw the whole thing. He saved you guys."

Becca blinked, trying to absorb what Colt was telling her. "Where is he now?"

Lillian clasped her hands together. "Christopher Fischer is in a compression chamber getting oxygen for carbon monoxide poisoning."

"He'll be okay, though, right?" Becca didn't want to think about the man who had saved so many lives dying for his heroic efforts. That shit wasn't right.

"He inhaled a lot of smoke, Becca."

In that moment Becca hated Lillian's composure. Why wasn't she flipping out over all this?

Lillian gave Becca a knowing smile. "I'll flip out later."

Becca loved her for that and felt disloyal. Becca knew Lillian's composure was hard-earned. "I'm glad you can read my mind, saves me having to put my foot too far into my mouth." Becca's eyelids were starting to droop. She looked at Lillian and smiled. "You're the best sister-in-law ever."

"You need to rest. We'll be back," Colt said.

Becca's eyes were closed when she asked, "Wait, why would I be in trouble if I died?"

"Because you're hosting Thanksgiving," Colt answered.

Becca heard her voice from far away. "I am?" She sighed, her eyes sill closed. "I always wanted to host holidays for all of us. Tucker needs to cook, though, he's so good at it. Colt, why did dad go crazy?"

There was a long pause and Becca wondered if Colt had heard her but opening her eyes felt like too much work. Finally, Colt answered quietly, "I don't know, sis. I don't know. Get some rest. We'll get to the bottom of it."

Sleep took her then.

She dreamed of Jason.

# Chapter Sixty-Two

Moving hurt. Breathing hurt. Hearing Becca call out for him hurt more.

He had to see her. Jason waited until the nurse left him to rest, happy with his test results, to gently unhook the intravenous line, taking care as he slid the needle out, before pulling the oxygen tubing from his nose. He forgot to mind his stitches. Jason checked under his hospital gown to make sure he wasn't bleeding again. He wasn't. His lungs were still in rough shape, and he had a wicked concussion, but his gunshot wound could have been a lot worse, and he had escaped the fire with only minor burns.

He found a camouflage robe and brown slippers in the bathroom. The odd pair would have to do. He had no idea where his clothes were; they had to have been trashed. As he shrugged into the robe, he saw an over-sized rodeo logo on the back with a sexually inappropriate tagline. Either the hospital had teamed up with the rodeo for a questionable marketing campaign, or Becca's brother had left it for him. As he toed into the slippers, he realized they were made to look like cow patties.

*Who thinks of this shit?*

Mindful of his condition and ridiculous outfit, Jason did his best to blend in and look like just another patient making his way around the halls on his rounds. It was hard not to wince with every step. He saw one of his nurses coming towards him, head bent to the tablet in his hands. The man would be on him in seconds.

Jason opened the closest door and slipped in.

It was a dark supply closet. He waited, expecting the nurse's footfalls to pass at any second.

"Jason, what are you doing?"

At the sound of his name, he stilled. The room was in total darkness. The man must have recognized him when he opened the door.

"I could ask you the same thing," Jason rasped. He was eighty percent certain it was Becca's brother Colt.

A cell phone light came on. Colt's features were cast in eerie shadow.

Jason took a step towards him. "You look like hell."

Colt held up the phone and started laughing. "Says the guy croaking instead of talking. I see you found the robe and slippers."

Jason pulled the robe tighter around his body. "Who the hell wears shit like this?"

"It was free swag and the only thing I had in my truck. You're welcome, by the way."

"Sorry, you're right. Thanks for letting me borrow it."

Colt held up his hands. "Oh, that's a gift, bro. No take backs."

Jason snorted, in spite of himself. "You okay? Seriously, you look like hell."

Colt shook his head. "Women."

Jason raised an eyebrow.

"Between worrying about Lillian and the double agent trying to kill her a couple months ago, and now this shit show, I'm a mess. I'm hiding in a fucking closet in the dark so if I lose my shit even I won't see it."

Jason didn't know what to say. That Colt opened up that much spoke volumes. Shit had to be on fire for men to share like that. "If you're going to be awhile, can I borrow your real clothes?"

Colt laughed. "Not a chance. What are you doing here, anyway?"

"Hiding from a nurse. I need to find your sister. She was calling for me..." He let the sentence hang.

Colt nodded, his face serious and Jason knew the other man understood. Colt said, "Come on, I'll take you to her." He led the way, motioning for Jason to follow when the coast was clear.

Becca's room was the first one around the corner.

When Jason saw her, he almost dropped to his knees. Her right eye was swollen with a violent bruise, and a raw red welt slashed across her cheek and brow.

But her face lit up when she saw him. *"Jason,"* she breathed. Her voice sounded as rough as his.

He hobbled as fast as his battered body would take him. *"Becca."*

Lillian stood, then, excusing herself and pulling Colt along with her out the door, leaving Becca and him alone.

A million things were going through Jason's head. "I'm sorry I wasn't there when you called for me."

Becca's eyes widened. "You heard that? I'm sorry, I didn't mean to alarm anyone, I just—"

He stepped closer and picked up her hand, needing to touch her. "Me, too."

Becca scooted over, making room for him on her bed and nearly pulling him down. "Will you stay?"

"You asked me that before." Before the fire.

Becca held his gaze. "I meant it then, too."

"Me, too." Jason gently settled himself next to her and she curled into him. It felt so right, and he was so tired. He let himself close his eyes, just for a bit. *I love you so much.*

He felt her hold him tighter. "I love you, too."

The last thing he remembered before sleep claimed his healing body was Becca's whispered declaration in his ear.

He didn't want to wait any more. He wanted to ask her the question that was burning a hole in his heart.

# Chapter Sixty-Three

Officer Cooper wheeled Officer Chasseur back to his hospital room. "I don't think you're supposed to sleep with other patients."

"Becca asked me to. She sleeps better when I'm there." Chasseur's voice was grumpy.

"Hmm, mmm," Cooper said, noncommittal. He helped Officer Chasseur into his own hospital bed. "Since you're still healing from a bullet wound, a severe concussion, burns, and smoke inhalation—"

"And your point is," Chasseur interrupted, slowly lowering himself back onto the pillow

"Not a damn thing sir." Cooper switched gears. "I do have good news, though. Detective Tanner is in stable condition."

Jason swallowed hard. "That is good news."

Tucker had made it through surgery, but just barely. It had been touch and go.

"And I have a confidential informant for this case."

*"You have a what?"*

Cooper tried not to shift under Officer Chasseur's scrutiny. Even from a hospital bed, his training officer was intimidating. "I filled out all of the appropriate paperwork."

Chasseur closed his eyes. "I'm not worried about your paperwork, Coop. What information do you have?"

Cooper stood taller, relieved, and pleased to have done a good job. "My informant turned over several recorded conversations between Bruce Tanner and a man named Del Fiennes. They're not admissible in court, of course, but we're running down each lead they've provided. Do you remember Fiennes? He was the gunman who broke into Austin Fischer's hospital room and shot Detective Tanner before Christopher Fischer killed him."

"Yes, Coop, I remember," Chasseur's eyes were still closed.

"Fiennes and Bruce Tanner were the ones trying to steal the propriety CBD information from the Fischers."

"Anything else?"

"Bruce Tanner is still at large." Officer Cooper really didn't want to say the rest.

Officer Chasseur opened his eyes. "Coop, what is it? Tell me the rest."

Cooper swore his training officer was psychic when he did stuff like that. "You're really not going to like this. Maybe I should tell you another time? Yes, when you're feeling better."

"I'm fine. Tell me."

"Sir, you're in a hospital bed. With all due respect, how fine can you be?"

"*Coop.*"

He hated when Chasseur used that tone with him. It was the same tone his mom used when she was cross. Cooper took a deep breath. "Bruce Tanner framed you for the arson and shooting Ms. Becca Tanner and Mrs.

Meredith Tanner. My informant turned over detailed recordings of Bruce Tanner planning the arson and frame job." Cooper sucked in a breath. "Thank god he sucks at details or you guys would be dead. 'Er, I mean might not have made it."

Chasseur looked a little green and Cooper mentally chastised himself.

"How did you find this informant?" Jason asked.

"A José Martinez brokered the information exchange. That's in the regular file. I'm allowed to share that part."

The corners of Chasseur's mouth shifted. It was the closest thing to a smile Cooper had ever seen on him. "I'll be damned."

"You know who that is, sir?"

"A high-ranking Spanish diplomat."

"Sir, I don't know what that means. I mean, I understand the words, I just don't know how he's involved in this. Should I have filled out different paperwork? A diplomat sounds fancy."

"No Coop, you did a good job."

"Thank you, sir," Cooper said, pleased.

"Did you meet the confidential informant?"

"Yes, sir," Cooper was hesitant when he answered. It was important he kept the confidence part of the confidential informant.

Jason shook his head. "Don't worry, I'm not asking you to break protocol. What did you think of him?"

"You want my opinion?" Cooper asked. When Officer Chasseur nodded Cooper continued, "Pissed, sir."

"Excuse me?"

"Pissed, as in angry. He had some choice words for a father who would try to murder his own kids. He didn't go into detail, I suspect he's way too smart for that, but I think he would do Bruce Tanner harm if given the chance. I actually kind of like the guy." He didn't add the man was in this hospital, barely off death's doorstep. Cooper got the impression that as soon as the man had regained consciousness, he had contacted Martinez to help. The doctors hadn't even known if the guy was going to make it and he was protecting them all from his deathbed.

"Coop, we need to find Bruce Tanner first. We need to protect Becca and her family. And your informant from doing something on the other side of the law."

"Yes, sir."

Cooper had an idea.

# Chapter Sixty-Four

Jason and Becca were snuggled under a blanket in her living room, watching the soft autumn snow fall outside. It was a surreal experience; Jason didn't know he could feel this happy. He hadn't left Becca's side in the two weeks since they were released from the hospital. Tuck had arrived a week later, after his doctors had cleared him for release.

Physically, the younger officer was healing from his gunshot wounds. Jason was worried about the rest of him. Gone was his lightheartedness; in its place was somber seriousness. Jason missed the old Tuck, ridiculous jokes and all.

Meredith was there, too, although she had taken more convincing to settle into a guest room. She hadn't wanted to upset Samantha. There was still a Canada-wide arrest warrant out for Bruce, and it was finally Samantha who had mentioned to Meredith the kids would be less worried, and heal quicker, if they weren't worrying about their father murdering his current wife. Meredith had immediately conceded the point and had moved in to recover under the watchful eye of their extended families and friends. The four of them had been enveloped in a healing cocoon at Becca's inn, which had more than enough room so each could have their own space when they needed to.

Becca gently readjusted the blanket, careful of her mug of coffee. Over the last two weeks Jason had perfected her coffee-making technique. What he hadn't figured out was the right time to ask her if she would let him make her coffee every morning for the rest of their lives.

Becca traced two of her fingers up and down his arm wrapped around her. "Do you think we can pull off hosting Thanksgiving dinner for everyone?"

"If you want a traditional Thanksgiving, let's do it."

Becca smiled. "Everyone has been so kind. I want to say thank you. What better time than Thanksgiving? I'm talking the whole thing, all the fixings."

That sounded pretty good to Jason, too. He had thought quiet holidays with his mom were enough. Watching her drink tea with Samantha, Meredith or Ruth, or fuss over Becca and her siblings had cracked open another layer Jason hadn't realized was inside of him. Family mattered, however those people came into your life, by birth or otherwise. Becca's family had welcomed Jason and Rose whole heartedly. In fact, his mom was the only one Tucker sounded like his old self with.

"I've been laid up for two weeks and my to-do list is now done." Becca was quiet a moment. "It never occurred to me it was okay to ask for help. I wanted to prove to everyone I was finally taking life seriously, that I could do it all on my own. I wasn't running away to Europe as my parents lamented, I was building a home and a life."

Jason kissed the top of her head and Becca snuggled closer. "Now it just sounds like I was being stubborn instead of inspired."

"You, stubborn? No way."

Becca turned and pinched him. He tickled her in retaliation, and she stopped him with a long kiss.

"Are you going to kiss me every time you want me to do something?"

"Maybe."

"Works for me."

Jason dropped his head, letting his lips linger over hers.

The moment was perfect.

He stopped, remembering the ring in his pocket. He moved to retrieve it as Becca spoke, "If the Fischers hadn't bugged my house or wanted me to stop the pipeline, we wouldn't be here together, would we?"

Jason shifted, reaching for her mug instead of his pocket, the moment over. He took a generous swig of her coffee. "You mean shot and burned up?"

"Ha ha, not funny. Anyway, that was my dad not the Fischers. I still can't believe Christopher Fischer pulled us out of a burning building. Or that my dad tried to—"

"I remember." Jason said softly. He still didn't know what to make of that. Except drug addiction turned people into husks, capable of monstrous things. A shiver raced down his spine and made his burns stretch uncomfortably.

Becca snuggled closer. "I meant here. I wouldn't be here in your arms. Every time I was scared, I ran straight to you."

Jason closed his eyes. Sometimes he still woke in a cold sweat and reached for her. He didn't know if he'd ever get over almost losing her. "Say it again?"

Becca's smile reached all the way to her eyes. "I love you."

Curled up together in her hospital bed, they had whispered their love for each other. It had been strong medicine.

He threaded his fingers through hers. "I love you, too."

"Do you trust me?"

"Completely."

"And you know I trust you, right?"

Jason's mind thundered with dark possibilities. "Yes."

"I want your advice. I'm thinking of hiring Christopher as my sommelier."

In a hundred guesses Jason would not have come up with that one. "Don't you need fancy training for that? And you know, not to be a drug dealer?"

"Yeah, he's actually a properly trained sommelier. Can you believe it? Austin uploaded Christopher's sommelier résumé using their mom's maiden name as his surname to a job site a month ago. I reached out before I knew who it was. Austin emailed me this morning, telling me what he had done."

An uneasy feeling iced Jason's stomach. "Are you sure hiring that Fischer is a good idea?"

"Hell no, that's why I'm asking you. It's either brilliant or suicidal. I just don't know which. What do you think?" She sniffed. "Do you smell vanilla?"

"Yeah. I thought that was you."

Becca shook her head. "Nope. So, what do you think about Christopher as my sommelier?"

"Interview him."

"Seriously? I honestly thought you'd be hell bent against it."

"You need more information. The guy nearly died pulling us out of a burning building, ask him why. Interview him. Feel him out." Jason laughed. "Fuck that. That came out wrong. Do not feel him. Do not collect $200 and do not pass Go."

Becca pressed her lips to his. The kiss, gentle and teasing at first, turned hot, consuming. When she finally lifted her head, she was breathless. "My hands are too busy touching you." She slid her hand down between their bodies and found him.

Jason's breath hitched.

He put his hands on her shoulders. "Before I ask you to keep going with this train of thought, one quick thing. I trust you, I trust your judgement, but would you be offended if I spoke with Christopher, too?"

Becca shifted, bringing her hand to a more innocent position. "I was hoping you'd say that. I figure between the two of us, we can figure out anything."

Jason smiled. God, he loved her.

Becca cocked her head. "Now, do you mind if we stop talking about work?" She moved her hand again and coherent thought became impossible.

Later, they would figure out everything.

Later and together.

# Chapter Sixty-Five

Becca stood in the hospital doorway, nervous. How did you thank the guy who saved your life?

"Mr. Fischer? It's Becca Tanner."

He turned his head toward her, his face brightening. "You made it." He was in a hospital gown and covered in several bandages. He had an IV drip and an oxygen tube under his nose.

"I'm sorry I didn't visit sooner."

"No, I meant you made it, you're still alive. I'm sorry I didn't get there sooner." His eyes widened. "How about the others?"

Becca stepped forward. "Jason and Meredith are doing well, thanks to you."

He nodded once, unsmiling, yet still looked pleased.

Becca took a steadying breath. She just had to blurt it out.

"Why did you save us?"

Christopher jerked his head to look at her. "That's a complicated question."

Becca remembered Clint's universal advice. "So uncomplicate it."

"Your brother took bullets meant for *my* brother. A man doesn't forget that."

"That explains why you stopped Fiennes with your knife in Austin's hospital room. But why did you run into a burning building, three times no less, to save Jason, Meredith and I? You even protected Jason's mom, Rose, by making her stay outside. I want to know why."

Christopher broke eye contact to look at the ceiling. "Chasseur and I each have a hundred pounds on her. There's no way she could have dragged him out. She would have died trying."

Becca swallowed the lump in her throat. "I know. That still doesn't explain why you did it."

"Why does it matter? It's over."

Becca hesitated. "Because I need a sommelier."

"What?"

"You heard me. I need a sommelier and your résumé looks good, the wine part, anyway. I don't think I want to see your full CV."

Christopher looked incredulous. "You're offering me a job?"

"I'm not sure. I need to know I can trust you. I can tell that you're not using, but I need to know that you're not going to murder me or anyone else for that matter."

He looked her square in the eyes. "You need to stop believing everything you hear about me. I will never hurt you; you have my word."

His eyes were so bleak.

She believed him. Still, she persisted. "Why?"

"I'm no saint, but your dad was acting like one evil motherfucker. I've seen it before—" He broke off abruptly. "You wouldn't believe it if I told you the truth."

Becca shrugged. "Try me."

Christopher held her gaze. "I saw my mom."

"I'm confused, I thought she passed away years ago?"

Christopher angled his head. "She did."

Becca's eyes widened. *"Oh."*

"Look, I don't believe in ghosts, but I've been smelling vanilla for weeks. That's the scent she wore. And I *saw* her. Clear as fucking day." Christopher looked at his hands. "She didn't look proud of me, of what I've become."

Becca crossed her arms, holding herself. The room suddenly felt colder. "Did you say vanilla?"

"Yeah. Look, I don't believe in ghosts, but there was no way I was letting you guys die, especially if my mom is watching." Christopher cleared his throat. "Your dad is a fucking monster."

Preaching to the choir.

"What was she like?"

"My mom?" Christopher gave a small smile. "Kind. Nurturing. She was everything good in the world; our heart and soul."

"What was your dad like?"

"He was hard where she was soft. They loved us and each other. We were lucky. Until we weren't."

It was Becca's turn to look down. "My dad doused me in gasoline. He shot me, too, then fired on Jason." Becca clenched her fingers. "I can't forgive him for trying to murder Jason. We're here because of you."

"You love him."

Becca didn't answer.

"He's a good man, you know, for a cop."

Becca did smile at that. She gently squeezed Christopher's hand once. "Thank you for saving us, for giving us a chance."

Christopher looked uncomfortable. "I've never regretted my past; Austin and I survived, that's how I see it. But I would have regretted not trying to help you guys. Your father doesn't deserve you."

She swiped at the tears forming. "You know, I think you're right about that." Quieter, she added, "There's a warrant out for his arrest."

"Good."

Becca hesitated. She wasn't sure she wanted to know the answer to her next question. "Is he in danger from you?"

Christopher pinned her in place with his gaze. "You mean will I kill him with my bare hands, slowly, for what he did to you and your family? Probably not. But will I kill him for the attempt on Austin's life that he cooked up with Del Fiennes? I can't make any promises."

A chill ran down Becca's spine. She had a lot of unsorted feelings about her father.

Christopher cocked his head. "I've alarmed you. I am sorry for that."

She shook her head. "No, I'm worried about you—he's not worth going to jail for." Becca made a decision. "I can't afford to pay you what you're worth."

"You're seriously offering me a job? After everything, including what I just said? Are you fucking nuts, lady?"

On paper, it was beyond crazy. In real life, it felt like the right thing to do. "I am."

Christopher brought his hands together in front of his nose. "You have no idea what that means to me."

Becca sighed, relieved. "Wonderful."

"I can't accept."

"Why? Your brother said this was your dream job."

Christopher tapped his nose. "A sommelier is his nose. Mine is wrecked."

Becca felt like her heart had dropped out of her chest. "The fire."

Christopher nodded, silent.

"By saving us you destroyed your chance at the career you actually wanted, oh my god, I am so sorry." Tears blurred Becca's vision.

Christopher shook his head. "Woah, no. Don't cry. That's some hippy-dippy bullshit right there."

Becca laughed through her tears. "Why are people always saying that about me?"

A doctor entered Christopher's hospital room. "Ms. Tanner, what a lovely surprise. How're you feeling?" She stopped, noticing Becca's tears.

Becca swiped at her eyes. "Doctor Williams, hello. I was just visiting Mr. Fischer." Becca turned and saw the way Christopher was looking at the pretty doctor. It was the same look of longing Becca wore when she looked at Jason. The doctor's face was impassive. Becca said, "We were just discussing Mr. Fischer's nose."

"His nose?"

"Yes, I want to hire him as my sommelier, but he seems to think that's impossible. Is it?"

"Becca, what are you doing?" Christopher did not sound pleased.

Becca held up her hand to him, and asked Doctor Williams again. "Is it possible? Hypothetically I mean, I'm not asking for his specifics, just if it's possible."

The doctor looked a bit taken aback. "Yes, I suppose it is possible. After a trauma like this, some make a full recovery, others don't. We have no way of knowing which, each body heals in its own way."

Becca turned to Christopher, beaming. "See? It's possible. I expect to see you when you're out of here. If nothing else, I'll need help selecting vintages for my wine cellar. The extent of my wisdom is red wine with red meat and white wine with fish."

Christopher visibly blanched.

"Hey, don't judge me. I'm a beer girl." Becca clapped her hands. "Okay, it's settled."

Austin Fischer peeked his head in the doorway. "What's going on?"

Becca smiled at him. "I'll let your brother tell you. Good to see you on your feet." She nodded to the doctor as Austin shuffled toward his brother's bedside with the help of a walker. "Thanksgiving, my place, noon, you're invited. I think you guys already know where it is?"

The Fischer brothers turned to stare at her like she had grown a second head. She smiled. "Bring desert." She pointed at both of them. "And don't let me down."

# Chapter Sixty-Six

Thanksgiving weekend was one of Becca's favorite times. The last golden poplar leaves had blown away and dark clouds scuttled across the sky. While many lamented the shorter days and cooler weather, Becca savored them. Especially this year. Her whole family was here under her roof.

Everyone except her father. He was still out there. Somewhere.

Becca turned from the window in her bedroom, rubbing her arms through her long-sleeved shirt. She should join everyone downstairs. Jason and his mom were here. Gabe and Anna had flown in yesterday. Anna's parents, including Meredith's sister, would be coming later today. Colt and Lillian were staying for the weekend, too. Tucker had wanted to get back to his condo last week and she had promptly called bullshit. She could hear his laughter downstairs. It was a brief but beautiful sound. She hadn't heard it much since he'd almost died.

Becca sat on her bed and just listened, smiling. She had built a home and her family had come.

There was a soft knock on her open door. Meredith stood, holding a small envelope.

Becca jumped up, running her hands through her hair. "Hi, I was just coming. Everything should be ready to eat in about an hour."

The older woman smiled. "Oh, take your time dear, I wasn't worried about anything, I just wanted to give you this."

Becca accepted the envelope. "What is it?"

"Open it, you'll see."

Becca peaked into the envelope and gasped. There were a lot of zeroes. And the words *thank you* were in the memo.

"I don't understand."

"I'm a rich old woman. What else am I going to spend my money on?"

Becca tried to push the envelope back at Meredith. "It's too much. I can't accept this."

Meredith slid her hands behind her back, refusing the envelope. "My dear, you opened your home and heart to me when I needed a friend. There are not enough checks in the world to repay your kindness. You had to push back your opening. You have to rebuild your barn. You're still healing, for godssakes. It would make me incredibly happy if you'd accept this small gesture to help you when you could use a wee boost."

Becca held up the cheque. "This isn't a wee boost. This much could buy a small island."

Meredith shrugged. "What can I say? Being rich has its perks. If it makes you feel any better, this is my money, not your father's. I'm way wealthier than him with a rock solid pre-nup. Please, I would be honored if you would accept it."

Becca hedged. It was a lot of money and would help make the first few years as she grew her business more feasible, not to mention comfortable.

"Please. Let me help."

Emotion washed over Becca. "Thank you. This will help a lot."

Meredith stepped forward. It was the first time Becca had hugged Meredith. Both women held on.

"I'm glad we're here," Becca said softly.

Meredith understood. "We survived. Fuck him. Now, we thrive."

"I wish I had half of your strength."

Meredith cradled Becca's face in her hands. "My dear, if you could only see what I see. You are principled and kind, a woman of unshakable character and strength, as smart as you are beautiful. You *are* strength."

Becca glowed under the praise. "Wow. I never thought of myself like that."

Meredith smiled. "We never do, luv. That's why we have to have it pointed out to us. There's a mojito with my name on it downstairs, you coming?"

Becca nodded. A knock on the front door interrupted them. They hurried downstairs to the foyer.

"Hey kiddo, happy Thanksgiving," Clint said, coming in.

Christopher and Austin held back on the front porch. They each were holding a large white bag from a popular bakery.

"Is your invitation still open?" Christopher asked, hesitant.

Becca smiled and opened the door wider. "Of course, everyone's in the back. Follow Clint."

Jason walked into the foyer and wrapped a protective arm around Becca. Christopher and Jason eyed each other. Austin looked between the two men, before calling, "Hold up, Clint."

Austin followed Clint inside the house and down the hall.

Becca looked between the two of them. "I need a drink. Don't kill each other."

# Chapter Sixty-Seven

Christopher stood in the foyer, arms crossed and unsure what to do.

Officer Chasseur's stance was no less tense. "Porch?"

Christopher nodded and followed the officer out. They passed the porch swing without a word and settled uneasily in the Adirondack chairs looking out over Becca's ranch inn yard.

Chasseur asked, "Your brother okay?"

"He's got a lot of physical therapy ahead of him, but he'll be good." Better than he had been for a long time.

"You okay?"

Christopher nodded.

"Good." Chasseur got straight to the point. "I've tracked you for a long time."

Christopher nodded. There was no point denying it.

"Convicted or not, there are a lot of dead people in your wake," Chasseur said.

"My past is complicated. And now it's over."

"You've mentioned that a few times." Chasseur's face was impassive.

"And I still mean it. Look, are you here to arrest me?"

"Not today." He paused. "I've seen a lot of people say they're going to change. Few do. What makes you think you can?"

The officer had a point. "Look man, all I want to do is move forward."

"And how exactly do you plan on doing that? What's changed?"

Christopher met Chasseur's hard gaze. "My life changed when a cop took three bullets that were meant for my brother, and a father tried to torch his own family." He looked out across the yard. "That role reversal shit screwed me up until I realized I could change too."

"So? What does that mean exactly?"

"You wouldn't understand."

"Try me."

"Look, Detective Tanner thought Austin mattered enough to take bullets for him. No one's ever done anything like that for us before. Let alone a pi—I mean a cop." Christopher didn't mention no one had cared that much since his parents. Others had pushed them down further, including their foster family when five scared boys needed a home and direction. "The only thing you need to know is that Becca is safe around my brother and I. So are you. So is everyone she gives a damn about. I'm here to pair wine, that's it. I give you my word."

"And her dad?"

"What about him?"

"Is he safe around you?"

Christopher eyed the officer sitting next to him. "I doubt he's safe around anyone who cares about the Tanner siblings. Everyone has a line. Bruce Tanner crossed mine when he doused his daughter with gasoline and lit up her barn. You don't fuck with family. I'm guessing I'm not the only one who would celebrate his demise."

It was Chasseur's turn to stare across the yard. "You forgot he also shot her. And his wife. He left them both to die."

The cop hadn't mentioned himself, Christopher noticed. A man didn't when the woman he loved was all that mattered.

Christopher held out his hand. "Truce?"

Chasseur pointed at it. "Did that hand ever carve anyone up?"

"Turkey count?" He wasn't about to incriminate himself.

Chasseur slowly shook Christopher's hand.

Christopher said, "I won't give you cause to regret that."

Chasseur answered, "Neither will I."

Christopher believed him.

The officer broke contact first. He coughed, uneasily. "What does your mom look like?"

Christopher stilled. "Where did you see her?"

"I'm not saying—"

*"Be straight with me."* Christopher's voice bled emotion.

Chasseur gave him a long look before finally admitting, "I saw *something,* in the burning barn when you pulled me out. And I smelled vanilla, in a fucking inferno."

Something he thought long dead started to beat inside Christopher.

Emotion clogged his throat and he had to try twice before he got out, "Thank you for telling me that."

The men sat on the porch, looking out across the yard for long moments.

"So, about Becca," Christopher started.

Chasseur's tone iced. "What about her?"

"You need to get on that."

Chasseur's eyes went dark and he looked like he was going to take a swing at him. Christopher held up his hands in surrender. "I mean 'get on that' as in 'lock that shit down' or 'put a ring on it.' I'd kill to have a woman look at me the way she looks at you—shit, that was not the right choice of words."

Chasseur visibly relaxed, cracking the world's smallest smile for like a second.

Christopher took it as a start. For the first time in his adult life he felt like he might be right where he was supposed to be. He was being given a second chance. He wouldn't let Becca down. He would prove himself to Detective Tanner and Officer Chasseur, too.

He just had one more thing to do.

# Chapter Sixty-Eight

Becca stood in the doorway between her kitchen and formal dining room. It was a bittersweet moment. Austin and Clint were in the kitchen mixing drinks, laughing. Her mom, Samantha, and her mom's boyfriend, Gerry, of all people, were playing cards with Meredith and Ruth on the far end of the table: a Thanksgiving miracle. Closer to the dining room doorway, Gabe and Anna were laughing at a story Colt and Lillian were telling. Probably about international assassins.

Tucker looked on, quiet and pale.

Just as Becca was about to go to him, Jason's mom Rose passed her, pausing long enough to squeeze Becca's shoulder before making a beeline for Tucker. She held a plate in her hand.

Rose placed the plate in front of Tucker. It had a brownie on it.

He looked up, eyebrows raised.

Rose smiled. "I heard you're the brownie king."

Tucker merely shrugged. It was painful to watch. The old Tucker would have said something charming back, setting the whole table laughing. A lump grew in Becca's throat.

Rose sat down next to Tucker. "Well, I'm the queen. And I'm challenging you to a bake off."

Everyone at the table stopped talking. Tucker wasn't serious about many things, but he was as serious as a heart attack when it came to baking.

Tucker eyed the brownie. "With that?" He pulled the plate closer, turning it first one way, then the other.

Rose's eyes twinkled. "Playing the head game, nice."

The corners of Tucker's mouth lifted a fraction.

Rose leaned forward. "My brownies are magical. You'll see."

Tucker turned his head sharply. "Are you talking weed brownies?" The moment hung and the air felt charged.

Rose laughed. "You are a little stinker."

"You didn't say yes or no."

"For our purposes, how about no ingredients you need an ID to buy? That is, if you're not worried about being upstaged by an old woman?"

"I'm pretty sure you're a firecracker. And you're on."

Rose stood. "Let's go then, I'm not getting any younger."

"Oh, you mean now?" Tucker jumped up out of his chair. It was brief but Becca caught the glimmer of her brother's spark ignite.

Tucker and Rose headed to the kitchen. Gabe caught Becca's eye and smiled.

"I need to go check on the horses." Becca fled.

It was all too much. And perfect. Her family was home and safe. For now, at least.

She hadn't realized where she was headed until she stood in the charred remains of her barn. Her horses were fine in the pasture. It was she who was a mess. She hugged her arms around herself and let her gaze travel across the burned-out shell. She had built as much of the barn with her bare hands as she could. It had been a labor of love. Her love and hopes and dreams. And now it was ashes, stirred by the autumn wind.

Becca turned, sensing Jason. He stood a few feet away, hesitant. "Do you want to be alone?"

Becca shook her head. "No, I want you." She held out her hand.

Jason slid his hand around hers. "Do you mean that?"

Something in his tone made her heart skip. She held her breath and said, "I do. Always."

Still holding her hand, Jason reached into his pocket and pulled out a small box. He bent down on one knee in the ashes of her barn.

Becca tried to remember to breathe.

"Becca, I love you. I want to spend the rest of my life making you happy. Will you please be my wife?"

She launched herself at him. He wrapped his arms around her and rolled to the ground under the force of her hug. He smiled up at her as she captured his lips in a deep lingering kiss.

Finally, she broke away, answering, "Yes. Um, yes. That's a yes."

Laughing, Jason retrieved the box and teased, "Do you want to see the ring?"

Becca raised her eyebrows suggestively. "I don't know, the handcuffs will be pretty hard to beat."

Jason opened the box and Becca gasped. Two round-cut diamonds and a marquee cut emerald were offset to a large round-cut sapphire on a platinum band. It was the most stunning ring she had ever seen. Jason slipped it on her finger. She stared at her hand. "It's so pretty."

"So are you."

"You don't understand, I've never seen anything like it. This is incredible."

A wind gusted, scattering the last low-lying clouds long enough to let a beam of sunlight warm them and glance off the ring. Sparkles of light danced around them.

"That was the point, Becca. It's one of a kind, like you."

# Epilogue

Bruce pushed the plunger of the needle in. Soon relief would return. He let out a breath. He'd had this studio apartment for years with no one the wiser. He had actually committed his first murder in the apartment. He was safe here. He just had to figure out what he was going to do next.

Bruce had torched Becca's barn, but the little bitch had lived. So had Meredith. And that piece of trash Chasseur. It had been a disaster, but he'd correct everything. He would find a way to cash in on the land and the Fischers' patent. Bruce Tanner always landed on his feet.

The door at the far end opened and he spun around. Bruce pulled the needle out and tossed it to the side. A man he had never met stood just inside the studio apartment. The door closed behind him, echoing in the sparse open space.

He watched Bruce a moment. "Hello, Bruce."

"What? Who are you?" Bruce's heart had kicked up and it was hard to hear anything above its pounding.

The man laughed. "Cute." He walked across the room, hands in his pockets and looking around. "Don't stop what you're doing on my account. Take your time."

Bruce eyed the man. "Are you looking for money? I don't have money if that's what you're looking for." He did, loads of it, not that he'd give a dime to this clown.

"I don't want your money," the man said, continuing to circle the room.

"What do you want?" Bruce pulled at the collar of his shirt, needing to get more air in his lungs.

The man's lips moved but Bruce didn't hear his response. He popped his ears and sound flowed in again. "What did you say?"

The man ignored him. "You know, I'm surprised. I was expecting your lair to be, I don't know, bigger? You have extravagant tastes."

"How do you know what I like?" Bruce could feel his heartbeat in his lungs. It was a good high.

"I know a lot about you. I know you tried to kill my sister, and that you would have killed my brothers too."

Bruce's buzz dipped before racing back. The room began to shift. He pulled at his collar again before yelling, "You're not making sense, and I'm not giving you any fucking money. Get out of here." He stumbled, trying to herd the man out the door.

The man watched him. "Disoriented, loss of motor skills. Right on track."

Bruce was on the ground. How did he get here? He started to crawl. Bruce tried to form words. Sounds gurgled up. Finally he managed, "How...find...me."

"I always know where to find you, dad."

A wave a clarity rolled over Bruce's brain. "Whose dad?"

The man was now in front of Bruce. He crouched down. "Aw, that hurts, *dad*." He held something in his hand.

"That…what." Bruce forgot what he was trying to say, his throat felt like it was missing.

"This? It's a Naloxone kit. You're going to need it soon."

Bruce watched the man smile. It was as cold as fuck. "Tanner?"

"What, are there more of us?"

Bruce shook his head. Foam flew from his mouth. He tried to work his mouth. "Good boy."

His son didn't like that. His eyes darkened. "You haven't been a very good boy, have you, dad?"

Bruce couldn't speak. He clawed for the kit.

Tanner held it out of reach. "You tried to kill my siblings." He shook his head. "You shouldn't have done that."

Bruce's whole body spasmed. He tried to make his limbs work but they wouldn't. He flailed, helpless.

Bruce tried to blink, to make the image of his son clearer. Doris had always said Tanner was such a good boy, his son would help him.

Tanner whispered, "Dad?"

Bruce was beyond speech and could only grunt, willing his son to understand, to use the kit. He tried to nod.

Tanner crouched lower before whispering, "Go to hell."

# DON'T MISS: LOYAL TO YOU

Book 4 in the *Hearthstone* series

## Shocking Family Secrets Exposed
## Lives Threatened – Loyalties Tested

The quaint eco-inn nestled in the foothills of the Canadian Rockies seems the perfect place for Her Royal Highness Grace Furulund to hide while she figures out how to thwart those who would see her dead or muzzled in a forced marriage. She is, after all, more humanitarian than proper royal heir. Her conservative family sees her social and environmental sensibilities as a threat to tradition, even revolutionary.

When newly minted homicide detective Tuck Tanner, who took three bullets meant for a brilliant young criminal is postponed from returning to work, he fills in for his sister's eco-inn's head chef. He can handle his sister's snobby European clientele and hunt down their treacherous father who was the gunman responsible.

Neither Grace, nor Tuck expected the immediate attraction, or the mounting danger as new and old threats target them. The two run headlong into untangling conspiracies that threaten both of their families. As their family secrets start to unravel, Grace and Tuck must work together and stay ahead of a dangerous plot to their lives.

Will they be able to keep each other and their families safe, and will their loyalty to each other turn into love?

# Author's Note

I'm fascinated with fur trade history. Several years ago, I came across references to Fort La Jonquière, the oldest known French fur trade fort in western Canada. Get this—no one knows where it actually was. In a day and age when a few keystrokes can pull up information on *anything*, I couldn't find anything that conclusively stated where Fort La Jonquière was on a map. Excellent, I love nerdy mysteries. Fort Roche Cachée is imaginary, though. I was inspired by all of the posts and forts lost to time, their stories long forgotten.

The *coureur de bois*—those entrepreneurial (i.e. unlicensed) traders, typically considered to be from New France, who crisscrossed the continent and went about their "illegal" business under the radar, have also sparked my attention. I swear sometimes, when the wind is playful, we can hear their laughter.

The Upper Missouri and Saskatchewan River trades were hopping at the turn of the nineteenth century, and the 49th parallel was not a thing until the second half of that century. I wonder about *before* that? That's what inspired me to place the fictional Fort Roche Cachée in the mid-eighteenth century, north of the American-Canada border and south of Edmonton House, Canada. History is a curious thing; what gets passed down isn't necessarily how things went down. Giving a fresh look at what we think are our "truths" is a worthwhile exercise.

Like hydrogen, solar or wind energy—or even the gentle energy technologies as-yet undreamed of. The truth of our energy futures simply can not be the truth of our energy past, the math doesn't work. Change can be unsettling, or even rather scary. That's why I write the stories I do. Tapping into characters navigating their own changes and challenges helps me process our communities and planet pivoting, too.

With that being said, happy pivoting! And while we're at it, may these shifts be gentler and more cooperative and beautiful than we ever dreamed of. That might sound hopelessly naive, but just imagine if that were possible? I am.

Bright blessings, dear reader.

Sarah Kades
Calgary, Canada
16 March 2022

# Acknowledgements

I am surrounded by the kindness, love and support of a lot of remarkable people. I would especially like to thank Stark Publishing and the intrepid Mark Leslie Lefebvre, my editor of awesome Adrienne Kerr, beta readers extraordinaire Liz Anderson and Deb Drape. Dr. Scott Hamilton for the decades of mentorship and geeky Canadian fur trade chats, Craig Fandel and Paul Sargent for years of sharing outdoor expertise and happy, Maggie Hanna and Energy Futures Lab for introducing me to Alberta's hydrogen energy sector, as well as Kathy and Bill Graham, Tania Therien, Dawn van de Schoot, Loraine Paton, Jessica L. Jackson, Susan Forest, Allison Gorner, Shelley Kassian, Dave Sweet, Joan Johnson, and the late Harold Johnson—Harold, I treasure the wisdom and grace you shared with me. I miss you, friend.

Finding new normals in such shifting times has been a tumultuous ride for many, and art helps so many of us get through incredibly challenging times. I love writing books for readers to enjoy, to have their own adventures in the pages. I am humbled to share the Calgary Arts Development and the City of Calgary awarded me my first individual artist project grant from to write *Not an Easy Truce*. I can not overstate how this support—and being valued by my community as an artist—has changed my life. Art matters. My sincere *Thank You*.

Finally, to my dear family—I love every adventure with you.

# About the Author

Sarah Kades writes eco-thrillers, and narrative non-fiction as Sarah Graham. Her writing is largely inspired by her previous careers as an archaeologist and Indigenous Knowledge study facilitator, where she routinely lived in tents, caught rides in helicopters and gaped at the awesomeness of the landscapes around her.

Sarah is a two-time Energy Futures Lab Banff Summit storyteller, a recipient of the Calgary Arts Development individual artist grant, and has presented at the British Society of Criminology conference on the application of using arts-based approaches.

When she's not writing you can find her running, bumping into her next adventure, or trying to figure out where in the garden to put the makeshift wood fired pizza oven.

Learn more about Sarah online at:

sarahkadesgraham.com

# Book Club Availability & Questions

Sarah is available for virtual book club meetings and is happy to connect with readers. If you are interested in having her as a guest for your book club, or if you are curious about purchasing bulk copies of **Not an Easy Truce** in print or eBook edition, please contact mark@starkpublishing.ca.

Below are potential book club questions.

1. Becca doubts herself as she is hustling to launch her new business. Has there been a time in your life you doubted yourself? What happened? What did you learn? Would you do it all over again?

2. The friction between Becca and Jason is palpable. Has there ever been anyone in your life you changed your mind about? What happened? Was there a specific moment that changed things, or an ongoing shift?

3. Jason and Becca are incredibly protective of each other. What are you protective of? How does that impact the decisions you make? What does that look like on a day-to-day basis?

4. Becca looks up to Lillian in the story. Who have been the mentors in your life? What happened? When have you been the mentor? Explain.

5. Jason has an unsettled relationship with his deceased father. What advice would you give him? Is there anyone in your life, living or passed, you wish you had a more settled relationship with? What advice would you give yourself?

6. Rose was able to connect with Tucker after his traumatic incident. Why do you think it was easier for him to connect with a stranger after an unsettling event? Has a stranger ever helped you?

7. Meredith felt unsafe at home and acted on it. What resources do you think made it easier, or more possible, for her to do so? What would have made it more difficult?

8. Christopher is caught off guard by the direct, yet compassionate, way he is treated by Doctor Williams. Has there been a time in your life you were treated unexpectedly, good or bad? What happened?

9. What common ground did Jason and Becca find within each other? Has there been a time in your life you made a connection with another that surprised you? What happened?

10. Becca filled her house with very specific mementos. What do you fill your house with? Why? What is the feeling your home evokes within you? What do you want it to evoke?

11. Becca and Jason shared several unexpected meals with each other that sparked growing intimacy. Do you think food can feed our connections with others? Have you ever shared a meal with another that changed your relationship? What happened?

12. Becca built a physical house in the landscape she loved in the hopes of finding home. Has there been a time in your life you didn't know where home was? Where is home to you? What makes it so?

13. Though he has never met them, Tanner feels protective of his siblings, yet Bruce feels no paternal instincts to keep them safe. What is the difference? In your own life, has blood proven thicker than water, or vice versa?

14. When Jason and Becca realized they cared for each other, their point of reference changed, changing their perspectives, including previously held beliefs. Has there been a time in your life you changed your mind after coming to care for another? What happened?